TRACKERS

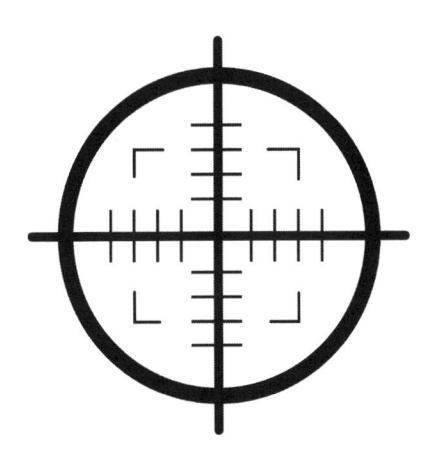

USA TODAY BESTSELLING AUTHOR

NICHOLAS SANSBURY SMITH

Trackers

Copyright July 2016 by Nicholas Sansbury Smith
All Rights Reserved

Cover Design by Elizabeth Mackey
Edited by Erin Elizabeth Long

This book is a work of fiction. Names, characters, places, and incidents are either products of the author's imagination or used fictitiously. Any resemblance to actual events, locales or persons, living or dead, is purely coincidental. All rights reserved. No part of this publication can be reproduced or transmitted in any form or by any means, without permission in writing from the author.

BOOKS BY NICHOLAS SANSBURY SMITH

The Extinction Cycle Series (Offered by Orbit)
Extinction Horizon
Extinction Edge
Extinction Age
Extinction Evolution
Extinction End
Extinction Aftermath
Extinction Lost (A Team Ghost Short Story)
Extinction War (Coming Fall 2017)

Trackers: A Post-Apocalyptic EMP Series
Trackers 1
Trackers 2: The Hunted
Trackers 3: The Storm (Coming Fall 2018)

The Hell Divers Trilogy (Offered by Blackstone Publishing)
Hell Divers 1
Hell Divers 2: Ghosts
Hell Divers 3: Deliverance (Coming Summer 2018)

The Orbs Series (Offered by Simon451/Simon and Schuster)
Solar Storms (An Orbs Prequel)
White Sands (An Orbs Prequel)
Red Sands (An Orbs Prequel)
Orbs
Orbs II: Stranded
Orbs III: Redemption

ACKNOWLEDGEMENTS

Many people have a hand in the creation of this story. I'm grateful for all their help, criticism, and time. I'd like to start with the people that I wrote this book for—the readers. You are the reason I always try to write something fresh, and the reason I strive to always make each story better than—and different from—its predecessors. For those of you waiting on my other books, I thank you for your patience, and hope you enjoy *Trackers*.

Before you dive in, here's a little background on how this story came to be. In 2016 I was finishing up book five of the Extinction Cycle, and at that time, I thought *Extinction End* would be the "end" of the series. I decided to write a new type of story—a story without monsters, zombies, or aliens—about a different type of threat to our national security.

Rewind ten years. I'm sitting at my desk as a planner with the State of Iowa. It was there that I learned a good deal about a terrifying weapon known as an electromagnetic pulse (EMP). During a meeting with several agencies, I was shocked to learn there wasn't much being done to harden our utilities and critical facilities to protect against such a threat.

A few years later, I started working for Iowa Homeland Security and Emergency Management. I had several duties as a project officer, but my primary focus was on protecting infrastructure and working on the state hazard mitigation plan. During my tenure, I helped multiple communities apply for grants to build safe rooms in their schools or municipal buildings to protect from tornadoes. A few years later, I started working on grants that strengthened and hardened power lines in rural communities.

After several years of working in the disaster mitigation field, I learned of countless threats from natural disasters to manmade weapons, but the EMP, in my opinion, is the greatest of them all.

That brings us to today. We're living in tumultuous times, and our enemies are constantly looking for ways to harm us, both domestically and abroad. We already know that cyber security is a major concern for the United States. North Korea, China, and Russia have all been caught hacking into our systems. We also know other countries are experimenting with technology that can shut down portions of our grid. But imagine a weapon that could shut down our entire grid. The perfectly strategized EMP attack gives our enemies an opportunity to do just that.

Before you start reading, I would like to take time to thank everyone who helped make this book a reality, starting with the Estes Park Police Department.

In the spring of 2016, my fiancée and I spent a week in Estes Park, Colorado, a place I had visited many times growing up. I wanted to show her this gorgeous tourist town that borders Rocky Mountain National Park, and I decided it would also make a good setting for a portion of *Trackers*.

The police department very graciously allowed me to tour their facilities and ride along with Officer Corey Richards. Department officers and staff explained police procedure for tracking lost people, and their operations and response to natural disasters. Captain Eric Rose, who is in charge of the Emergency Operations Center, described what they went through in the flood of 2013, when Estes Park was quite literally cut off from surrounding communities.

I've spent time with many law enforcement departments over my career in government, and I can tell you Estes Park has one of the finest and most professional staffs I've ever had the pleasure of meeting. Thank you to every officer for serving Estes Park and assisting with *Trackers*. I hope you find I did your community justice.

I'd also like to thank my literary agent, David Fugate, who has provided valuable feedback on each of my novels. The version you are reading today is much different than the manuscript I submitted, partly because of David's excellent feedback.

Next up is my editor, Erin Elizabeth Long. She has had a hand in every book I've written thus far. I won't lie—*Trackers* was a challenge for both of us, and Erin really encouraged me to continue pushing until I got the story right. Thanks, E. I appreciate you more than you know.

I also had a great group of beta readers that helped bring this story to life. You all know who you are. Thanks again for your assistance.

Trackers is more than just a post-apocalyptic thriller about the aftermath of an attack on American soil. It's meant to be a mystery as much as it is a thriller. There are a lot of EMP stories out there, but I wanted to write one that included new themes and incorporated elements of Cherokee and Sioux folk stories, which I encountered when obtaining a degree in American Indian Studies.

This story, like many works of fiction, will require some suspension of belief, but hopefully not as much as my other science fiction stories. Any errors in this book rest solely with me, as the author is always the gatekeeper of the work.

In an interview several years ago, I was asked why I write. My response was that while my stories are meant to entertain, they are also meant to be a warning. *Trackers* could be a true story, and I hope our government continues to prepare and protect us from such a threat.

Captain Eric Rose of the Estes Park Police Department told me that he wasn't sure he was ready for a post-apocalyptic Estes Park. I'm not either. Let's all hope this story remains fiction.

With that said, I hope you enjoy the read, and as always, feel free to reach out to me on social media if you have questions or comments.

Best wishes,
Nicholas Sansbury Smith

FOREWORD

Dr. Arthur Bradley

Author of *Disaster Preparedness for EMP Attacks and Solar Storms* and *The Survivalist.*

When used conventionally, a nuclear warhead could destroy a city and cover the surrounding region in deadly radiation. Horrible to be sure, but at least it would be localized. When detonated in the atmosphere at the right altitude, however, that same warhead could generate an electromagnetic pulse (EMP) that would cause almost unimaginable harm to our nation.

The most significant effect of such an attack would be damage to the nation's electrical grid. Due to the interdependency of systems, the loss of electricity would result in a cascade of failures promulgating through every major infrastructure, including telecommunications, financial, petroleum and natural gas, transportation, food, water, emergency services, space operations, and government. Businesses, including banks, grocery stores, restaurants, and gas stations, would all close. Critical services such as the distribution of water, fuel, and food would fail. Emergency services, including hospitals, police, and fire departments, would perhaps remain operable a little longer using generators and backup systems, but they too would collapse due to limited fuel distribution, as well as the loss of key personnel abandoning their posts.

In addition to the collapse of national infrastructures, an EMP could cause widespread damage to transportation systems, such as aircraft, automobiles, trucks, and boats, as well as supervisory control and data acquisition hardware used in telecommunications, fuel processing, and water purification systems. Such an attack could also damage in-space satellites and significantly hamper the government's ability to provide a unified emergency response or even maintain civil order. Finally, many personal electronics could also be damaged, including our beloved computers and cell phones, as well as important health monitoring devices.

With the collapse of infrastructures, loss of commerce, and widespread damage to property, an EMP attack would introduce terrible financial ruin on the nation. Consider that it is estimated that even a modest 1-2 megaton warhead detonated over the Eastern Seaboard could cause in excess of a trillion ($1,000,000,000,000) dollars in damage.

Testing done in the 1960s, such as Starfish Prime and the Soviet's Test 184, provided some idea of the potential damage, but weapons have become even more powerful and our world more technologically susceptible. No one really knows with certainty the extent of the damage that would be felt, but expert predictions range from catastrophic to apocalyptic. What is universally agreed upon is that the EMP attack allows for an almost unimaginable amount of damage to be done with nothing more than a single nuclear warhead and a missile capable of deploying it to the right altitude. Given that there are more than 128,000 such warheads and 10,000 such missiles in existence, it seems prudent to better understand and prepare for this very real and present danger.

What many do not know is that the U.S. has been openly threatened with an EMP strike by Russia, Iran, and North Korea. Leaderships of these countries have come to appreciate the truly asymmetric nature of such an attack. Consider that an EMP strike would be largely independent of weather, result in long-lasting infrastructure damage, and inflict a damage-to-cost ratio far greater than any conventional weapon, including a nuclear "dirty bomb." Worse yet is that our enemies would not limit themselves to a single EMP strike. Rather, they would detonate several warheads, carefully timed and positioned across the nation to achieve maximum damage.

Author Nicholas Sansbury Smith understands how an attack could cripple the United States. I first spoke with him when he was working for Iowa Homeland Security and Emergency Management in the disaster preparedness field. He reached out when he was writing a science fiction story about solar storms with some questions about my book, *Disaster Preparedness for EMP Attacks and Solar Storms*. Since then, Nicholas has also spent a great deal of time researching EMPs.

Trackers is a work of fiction, but many of the places in the story are real. Utilizing his background in emergency management and disaster mitigation, Nicholas has done an excellent job of describing a realistic geopolitical crisis that sets the stage for an EMP attack. The following story is a terrifying scenario in which brave men and women must adapt to a challenging new world—a world that we could see ourselves being thrust into. Part of me wishes Nicholas had continued writing purely science fiction stories about aliens and government designed bio-weapons because *Trackers* is a novel that could become non-fiction.

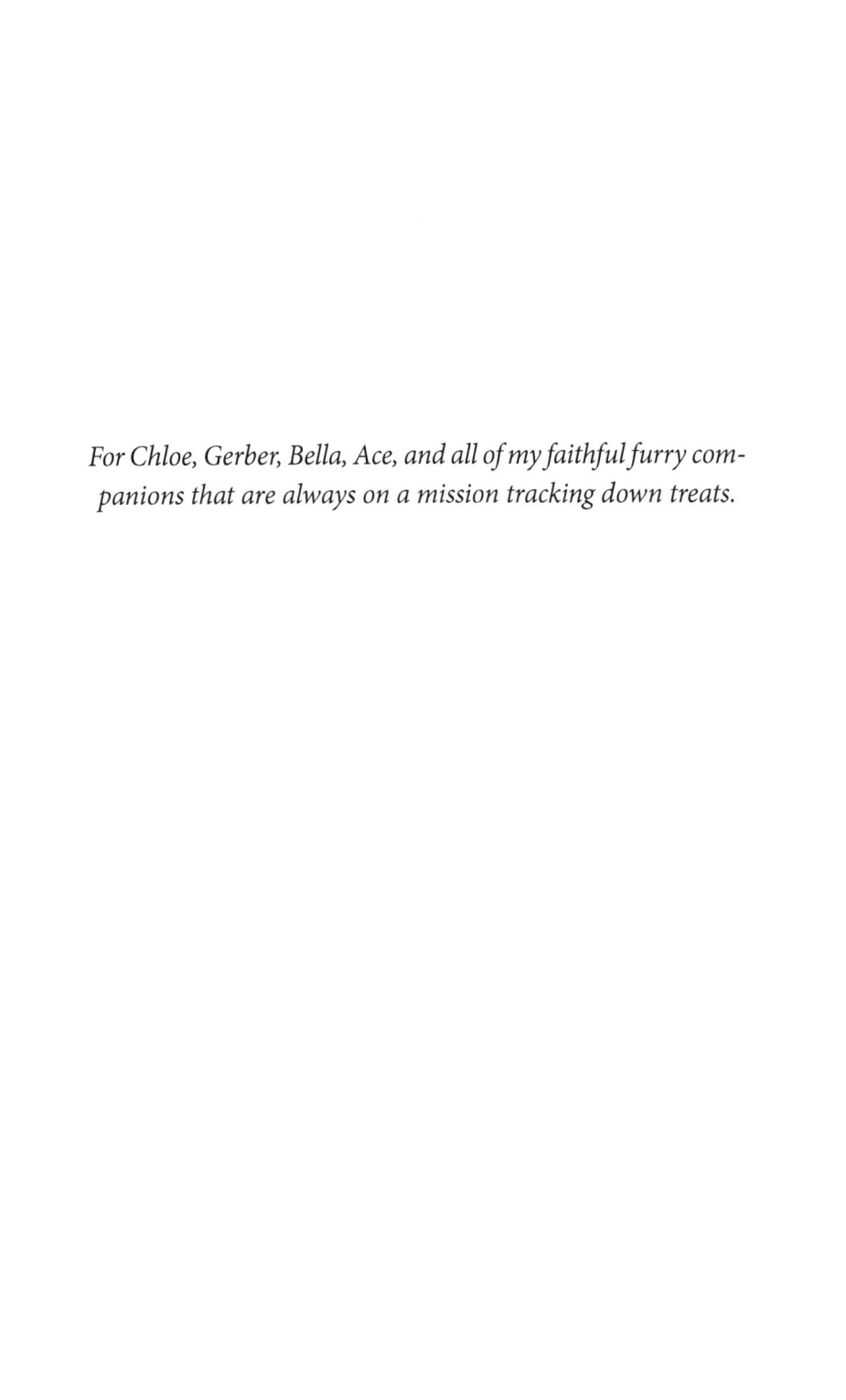

For Chloe, Gerber, Bella, Ace, and all of my faithful furry companions that are always on a mission tracking down treats.

There is no hunting like the hunting of man, and those who have hunted armed men long enough and liked it, never care for anything else thereafter.

—Ernest Hemingway

PROLOGUE

A SIX-MAN MARINE FORCE RECON TEAM BOARDED THE Sikorsky UH-60 Black Hawk just after midnight. Staff Sergeant Sam "Raven" Spears sat inside the belly of the bird, smearing camouflage paint across his tan skin. After a ten-year career with the Marines, he was accustomed to slipping his combat gear over his muscular frame for missions at the ass-crack of dawn, but he wasn't used to the Predators receiving orders directly from the President of the United States.

Raven turned to look out the window as the Black Hawk flew away from base under the cover of darkness. The pilots swooped low over flat fields on approach to the North Korean border.

His current enlistment with the Marines was over in a few weeks. He had hoped to buy land, start a business, and make a home in Estes Park, Colorado after over a decade of war, but the sight of the mine-studded fields and the presence of the Korean civilian in the troop hold made him question if that would happen now.

The Black Hawk was closing in on the demilitarized zone, and Raven could see why it was known as the most dangerous border in the world. To the north was one of the most oppressive and violent regimes on the planet. Barbed wire fences, landmines, and guard posts seemed like flimsy defenses against the totalitarian nation. Troops were stationed on both sides of the border, so close they could practically hit each other with hand grenades. The whole area was a tinderbox—and the Predators were being dropped right into the middle of it.

Shit was about to get very real, very fast.

The Marines with Raven all specialized in deep reconnaissance and were trained in search, seizure, and raid missions. He had a feeling the thin Korean man dressed in black sitting across the troop hold was going to help them track a target. Sad eyes framed by crow's feet met his gaze for a moment before Raven looked away to the members of his team.

The men were all dressed in black-clad armor, fatigues, and helmets mounted with "four eyes" night vision optics. They carried suppressed M4s as well as M9s. Gunnery Sergeant Rodney Black, the middle-aged team lead, had been studying a map as the rotors thumped nearly silently overhead. He folded it and met the eyes of each man in turn with the cold gaze of a Marine that had seen the horrors of war for too long. He had a hard-on for rules and respect, which made Raven the least popular Marine on Team Predator.

"All right. Listen up, everyone, because we don't have much time," Black said in a firm, authoritative voice. "Our orders come from the Commander in Chief himself."

He reached into his vest and pulled out two pictures. The first showed a dark-haired young woman in a party dress smiling happily at the camera.

"This is Hannah Sarcone, or Lima 1," Black said. He passed the photo around for the men to look at. As the picture circulated, Black held up the other photo of a redhead wearing a peace sign t-shirt.

"This is Sarah Baker, or Lima 2. Both girls are being held at a small prison camp near the border. The best map we have of the area is shit, which is why Mr. Lee is here."

The photos reached Raven, and he studied the faces of the young women. They looked…nice. Sweet. How the hell had two pretty girls ended up in a North Korean prison?

Black pointed at the Korean man across from Raven. "Lee here used to work at the prison before he defected to South Korea."

Every helmeted head turned to Lee. Raven wasn't one to judge; his own past wasn't all roses and daffodils. But he could tell the rest of his team was unhappy about having a traitor in their midst, regardless of who he'd betrayed.

"What's so special about these girls?" asked Staff Sergeant Billy Franks.

Black scowled, even though the question was a good one. "They're American citizens and college students who went to Seoul for some human rights protest. They must've taken a wrong turn at the border, because Miss Baker and Miss Sarcone are now being held in a North Korea detention facility."

"Hang on just a sec, Gunny," Franks said. "*Sarcone?* Not any relation to Senator Mack Sarcone, is she?"

Black's hesitation was answer enough, but he admitted, "She's Senator Sarcone's granddaughter."

Raven could guess how the rest of the story went. Sarcone had pulled some strings, and now President Brandon Drake had authorized the Predators to drop in behind enemy lines to bring Sarcone's granddaughter home.

There was a skeptical snort from the other end of the troop hold, and Black held up a gloved hand to silence his men.

"I know what you're all thinking. But we're Marines, and our job isn't to question orders. Our job—our *duty*—is to extract our targets and bring them safely back to base. Got it?"

The Predators answered "Yes, Gunny!" in one voice.

Black held up the map he'd been studying earlier. "We believe Lima 1 and 2 are both being held here," he said, stabbing the laminated paper. "There are three buildings in the compound, but our intel points to this one."

"If we storm the wrong building, Senator Sarcone's going to be really pissed," Billy whispered.

Raven shook his head. He didn't have many friends in the Marines besides Billy. The young man had a sense of humor and could do a killer impersonation of Sergeant Black that consistently earned him and Raven both extra laps and push-ups.

"Lee has given us a rundown of the defenses. He numbers

hostiles at least two dozen soldiers armed with RPGs, .50 cals, and whatever else they've been able to get their hands on. We'll take out the guard towers first with the M240 to clear a path. Then we split up and head in."

Black pointed at Raven. "Staff Sergeants Spears and Franks, you're with me on Alpha Team. Lee will guide us. Everyone else, you're on Bravo Team with Staff Sergeant Nixon as lead."

A few seats down, Nixon acknowledged the order with a nod of his large head. He looked ready to crush some North Korean skulls in his massive hands. Raven caught Billy's nervous gaze and tried to give him a reassuring smile. The kid had been on plenty of missions with the Predators, but nothing like this. Hell, none of them had ever done something this crazy.

Maybe I shoulda stayed on the Rez, Raven thought. At least back on the Rosebud Reservation, the biggest threat had been whatever damn fool his sister was dating.

"We don't believe the North Koreans know who Lima 1 is yet, otherwise they would have already moved the girls to a more secure facility. We've only got one shot at this. If we fail, these young women will be dead or locked up in some Pyongyang rat hole, which could escalate this situation into an all-out shit storm. President Drake wants this done ASAP, which means speed is more important than stealth. Understood?"

Mr. Lee, who had not yet said a word during the briefing, ran a finger across his throat as Black looked at his men individually.

"They kill us all if we get caught," Lee said in halting English.

"Our Korean friend is right," Black said. "He'll lead us inside. The plan is to get the girls and get out as quickly as possible. Bravo team has the C4, and Nixon will be responsible for planting it."

"They have my brother," Lee said. "Put him in prison when I leave. We will get him and American girls."

Command must have promised the former prison guard that they'd rescue his brother. Raven didn't have the heart to tell him that his brother was at the bottom of their to-do list.

"Gunny," Franks said, "just curious, but what happens when the Supreme Leader finds out the US was responsible for this raid?"

Black knitted his brows and very firmly said, "He won't. 'Cause there won't be any evidence."

Staff Sergeant Nixon nodded at that and patted the satchel holding the plastic explosives.

"Prepare for radio silence," said one of the pilots over the comms. "We're approaching the demilitarized zone."

"Any questions?" Black asked.

Franks raised a hand tentatively, but he lowered it when Black looked away.

"That was one of those rhetorical-type questions," Raven said with a chuckle. "Just stay close to me, rookie. I got your back."

Final gear and weapons checks sounded as the Crew Chief, a corporal named Hendrickson, worked his way to the door. The dim light in the cargo bay was switched off, shrouding the team in complete darkness.

Raven listened to the rush of wind and low whoosh of rotors, waiting to flip his optics into position. In the pitch black of the early morning, he could only see outlines of the rolling mountains in the distance. There was a single light somewhere to the west. He had seen satellites images of the Korean Peninsula at night, and the whole country was almost completely dark north of the DMZ. It didn't look much different as he gazed out from the Black Hawk.

He flipped his optics into position as Corporal Hendrickson grabbed the M240. A green-hued view of the North Korean countryside stretched across Raven's field of vision. In the distance, nestled at the base of the mountains, was their target. Four guard towers flanked the trio of buildings, and a skirt of barbed wire fences surrounded the prison. For a North Korean facility, it was on the small side. Raven hoped that meant fewer armed guards.

The pilots dipped lower on approach, the rush of cold wind filling the belly of the Black Hawk. Raven had enough experience under his belt to know this mission was risky in the worst way. They didn't have backup just blocks away like he'd had in Fallujah or Baghdad. It was just the Predators against a small army of North Koreans that could call in MiG fighter jets at any moment.

Raven desperately wanted a cigarette to calm his nerves. Fortunately he didn't have much longer to contemplate the odds they were facing. The pilots began their approach, and Hendrickson angled the M240 toward the buildings.

Black gave the order with a quick flash of his hand, and the chief opened fire on the first guard tower. The bark of the 7.62mm rounds reverberated through the troop hold. Tracer rounds lanced into the cinder blocks as the pilots circled. An explosion burst from the tower, blowing it to rubble, and the chief quickly roved the big gun toward the next tower.

The next North Korean guard got off a single shot before the 7.62mm rounds punched through his body. He tumbled over the side and plummeted to the ground.

"Clear!" the chief said.

Within seconds, the pilots were lowering the bird to the ground just inside the barbed wire fences. Even before Black signaled them, the Marines were lined up and ready to jump out. Raven scanned the terrain as he waited for his turn. The closest building was two stories of brick with multiple windows on the second floor. The other two structures were just single-story concrete blocks. About two hundred feet separated each building. Barrels, crates, and several vehicles provided blind spots for enemy contacts to hide behind. A single hostile came bursting out of the middle building, pulling his pants up as he stumbled out into the cold night.

Staff Sergeant Nixon, the first Marine out of the troop hold, took a knee and fired a burst from his suppressed M4 directly into the surprised guard's chest. The man slammed into the building, leaving a streak of blood as he slumped to the ground.

"Get movin', Spears!" Black said.

Raven jumped out and focused on the structure where the girls were being held. The second his boots hit the dirt, he was running toward it at a hunch. Franks kept low to the left with Black and Lee following right behind them. To the right, the men of Bravo team fanned out. The Black Hawk rose back into the air, and Hendrickson opened up on the other two guard towers across the compound.

Raven shouldered his M4 and flitted the muzzle over his fire zone. His view transformed into two-dimensional canvas as he moved. Scanning it systematically, he looked for hostiles. A North Korean flag whipped from a pole nearby. Raven moved to the next section of the grid. To his left were several trenches dug along the fence.

"Contacts," Franks said. Lee dropped to his belly as Black took a knee ahead of them and fired on two North Korean guards that had come running out of the front door of the first building. Both soldiers dropped, crying out as the lethal shots tore through their bodies.

The crack of automatic gunfire sounded from the left. Raven hit the dirt as rounds split the air he had been occupying seconds before. A cool breeze that reeked of animal manure drifted over him in the respite. The moment of calm before the tempest was shattered by another flurry of gunfire that seemed to come from all directions.

Raven crawled to a boulder for cover, more bullets forming a neat halo around his body. Somehow he made it to the rock without taking a round.

The shots had come from the trenches. Stupid to look away before he cleared the area. That was the kind of mistake that would get him killed, and he was *not* going to be one of those ironic cautionary tales other Marines told each other.

He could almost hear his squad telling the story to the guy who would take Raven's place: *Poor bastard was two weeks away from going home.*

He waited a few moments for the gunfire to stop. Behind him, most of Alpha and Bravo teams advanced toward the third building, while two Marines held security to fire at contacts outside. The Black Hawk was circling, Hendrickson training his M240 on enemy hostiles out of view from the ground. Across the compound, the other two guard towers were silent.

Raven rolled away from the rock and propped his rifle up with an arm, aiming in the direction of the shots. He flipped up his optics with his other hand to scan the area with naked eyes.

Where the hell had the shooter disappeared to?

Shots erupted from behind him, and the sound of suppressed fire answered.

"Hostile down," reported Black.

The target Raven was tracking fired again, and a bullet kicked up the dirt to his side. He rolled to the left as more shots pecked at the ground.

There was a brief reprieve, and Raven scanned the area where he had seen the muzzle flashes. He squeezed off a quick three-round burst, followed by another, trying to draw them out. Someone yelled in Korean, and another soldier replied with a shout.

A beat later, an explosion bloomed from the trench, and a scream rang out. Raven flipped his optics back into position and covered his helmet as dirt rained down on him. When he looked up, Billy was running over to him. He knelt and put a hand on Raven's back.

"I just saved your ass, brother," he panted, reaching under Raven's arms to help him up. "Hope those Korean sons of bitches enjoyed the gift I sent them."

"Thanks," Raven said, managing a nod. He looked over his friend's shoulder at the two-story building when he saw a flicker of motion in a window on the second floor. Down below, a North Korean guard missing an arm crawled out, still screaming. While Raven was momentarily distracted, the window on the second floor shattered. Billy's smirk was erased by a bullet through his chin. Hot blood splattered Raven's face.

More rounds rocked Billy's body before he even hit the dirt. Raven felt one whizz by his helmet as he crawled back to the rock for cover.

"Billy!" Raven shouted. He gritted his teeth, shock turning to anger. Grabbing his M4, he popped his helmet up to look for the bastard that had killed his friend. A muzzle flash came from the window, and a split-second later a round slammed into the rock, forcing Raven back down.

"Spears, what the hell is happening back there?" Black said over the channel.

"They got Billy and I'm pinned down! There's a sniper at—"

Another shot pushed him to the dirt. He lay on his back, staring up at the sky. Green tracers danced across the night as Raven waited for his opportunity. His no-good father hadn't given him much, but the old man had taught Raven to push his emotions deep down, where the enemy couldn't use them against him. He was calm now, patiently waiting for his moment to strike back.

"I'm heading in," Black said over the comms. He ordered Bravo to follow him into the building. The unspoken message was this: Raven and Billy were expendable. The mission was to extract two high-value targets; grunts like them were just collateral damage.

Raven jumped to his feet and fired off several shots at the building. Then he sprinted toward a barrel for cover and a better vantage. He was fast, but not fast enough.

The sniper popped back up at the window and fired a round that hit Raven in his chest, jerking him backward with such force that he crashed to the ground a few feet from the safety of the barrel. His rifle hit the dirt to his left.

Despite the pain, he reached out, and then pulled his hand back as rounds slammed into the dirt. He abandoned the gun and crawled over to the barrel. There was no pain, and Raven didn't feel any blood when he felt for the wound. His vest had taken the brunt of the impact, but he couldn't seem to get enough air.

Gasping, Raven looked back at Billy's ruined body. A shot pinged off the top of the barrel as he pulled his M9. He took in a long breath, and then pushed himself up, squeezing off two shots at the North Korean sniper. There was a shout over the comms about an RPG, but Raven continued firing. He found his target on the fourth squeeze.

Just as the sniper slumped out of the window, a projectile streaked overhead and slammed into the building. The shockwave from the blast hit Raven like a tsunami, lifting him off his feet. He landed hard, the little air remaining in his lungs pushed out from the sucker punch of the blast.

Pain rushed through his body and stars burst before his vision. He could feel the rush of blood singing in his ears. Everything hurt. Even his eyeballs seemed to be on fire.

His vision faded, red rolling in like a bloody tide.

Voices called out in the distance.

"Spears! Where the hell are you, Spears?"

Head pounding, Raven tried to blink away the pain. A tremor rumbled under his body, another explosion rocking the prison compound. He managed to bring his pistol up as he squinted at several figures making their way toward him.

He lowered the gun when he saw it was Sergeant Black and Staff Sergeant Nixon. The men were shielding two girls, both of them bruised, dirty, and wide-eyed with terror. Lima 1 stumbled and fell, and Nixon picked her up. He helped guide the girls to the Black Hawk that was hovering a few hundred feet away while Black remained behind. He pointed at Billy's body and yelled orders to the other two members of Bravo team. The men rushed over to grab the corpse.

A shout came across the prison yard. "Wait!" Lee shouted. "My brother!"

He ran over and grabbed Black's arm, tugging on it and trying to drag him back to the prison block. The Gunny pulled his M9 in a slow, mechanical motion, and calmly fired a bullet in Lee's skull. The man fell to his knees and then slumped on his side like a pretzel.

Raven sucked in another gasp of air as Black ran over to him, half expecting a bullet in his own skull next.

"Why?" Raven gasped. "Why did you—"

He flinched as Black reached down, but the big man was only trying to help Raven to his feet.

"Why?" Raven repeated as he limped toward the bird with the Gunny's assistance. Black raised his pistol and fired at a burning North Korean soldier who was running toward them. His flaming body hit the dirt, smoke rising into the night sky.

"Orders, Spears," Black growled. "Someone had to take the blame for this, and it couldn't be Uncle Sam. We don't want to start a war."

1

18 Months Later

Police Chief Marcus Colton knew the girl was probably dead.

Standing at the trailhead to Mount Ypsilon and Lawn Lake, navy blue police coat zipped up to his chin, Colton took off his aviator sunglasses to scrutinize the Rocky Mountains. His instincts told him the girl he was looking for was somewhere out there, inside the vast sea of shifting green and brown subalpine forests. But the dull ache in his gut also told him she was no longer alive.

Above the spruce-fir tree line, the peaks of Ypsilon, Fairchild, and the rest of the Mummy Range appeared to have been airbrushed with snow. A crimson sunset illuminated the interior of the gray clouds drifting over the jagged summits. If it weren't for the motion of the clouds, he might have thought he was looking at a painting.

It was a Friday in early September, but Rocky Mountain National Park was experiencing lower than normal temperatures. Colton had lived in the quaint tourist town of Estes Park, Colorado, his entire life. He was used to the cold, so when he shivered, he knew it wasn't from the wind.

Little Melissa Stone. The six-year-old daughter of his friend Rex Stone had been missing for three days now. Each second it became more likely that she was dead. Especially now, with the temperatures plummeting.

Melissa had last been seen when the school bus dropped her off on Prospect Avenue. A half dozen of his officers and a pack of volunteers one hundred strong were combing the foothills around Prospect Mountain.

Colton's cell phone vibrated in his pocket. It had been ringing all night. He was expecting to see a call from one of his officers or Mayor Andrews, but it was his wife, Kelly. She was waiting at home with their seven-year-old daughter, Risa. After taking in a breath tinged with the clean scent of cedar, Colton swiped the screen and brought it to his ear.

"Hey, honey."

"I haven't heard from you for hours," Kelly said.

"I'm at the Ypsilon trailhead waiting for Raven. Weather looks like it's about to take a turn for the worse. How are you? How is Risa?"

"I'm fine. Risa is okay, but she keeps asking when you're going to find Melissa. I'm about to put her to bed. We had some soup, and we miss you. When will you be home?"

"It could be a while. Raven is an hour late."

There was a pause, and Colton knew what it meant. His wife was his best friend and biggest supporter. He could read her like a book after twenty years of marriage.

"What are you thinking?" he asked.

"Do you really trust Raven? I mean, you've arrested him twice."

"He's just a troubled young man. You know he's had a hard time since he got back from service overseas. That's why I agreed to drop the DUI charge if he helped me find Sarah Kirkland earlier this year."

"But this isn't just some case where a kid wandered off, is it?"

Colton sighed. His wife was smart. Much smarter than him. "I'm afraid not. I got a tip that brought me up the mountain tonight, but that's all I can say."

"People forget how dangerous it can be living out here."

"Ain't that the truth? Just last week I got a call from the ranger station because a tourist was letting his toddler pet an elk. The guy thought it was some kind of horse."

"Idiot," Kelly said.

There was a brief silence, and in that moment he was back at home with his wife and daughter. But he was more than a loving husband and father; he was a soldier and a lawman. Someone had to be out here to protect the sheep from the wolves.

"Raven's the best tracker in these parts," Colton said. "He found Sarah before it was too late. Hopefully he can help me find Melissa, too."

"He just better get his butt out there soon. I don't want you on the mountain by yourself."

"I can take care of myself; you know that better than anyone. Now go give Risa a kiss for me. I'll be home as soon as I can."

"Okay, I love you, Marcus. Be safe."

"I love you." Colton paused to look at the rainclouds. Normally he didn't talk to his wife about work, but this felt different. "Kelly, you lock the doors, okay? And sleep with your Glock tonight."

"It's that bad?"

"I hope not, but better safe than sorry."

Colton tucked his aviator glasses in his pocket and considered promising that he would bring the girl home, but after two tours in Afghanistan and ten years of service as police chief, he knew things didn't always end up okay.

He put the cell phone back in his pocket. What he hadn't told his wife was that he had called Sam "Raven" Spears out of desperation. Raven had developed some bad habits and made some very poor choices since coming home from the Marines, but the man was the best hunter and guide in the area. It was his tracking skills that Colton needed. Raven was Colton's last hope to find Melissa in these woods.

On the horizon, the fiery glow of the sunset retreated, and the mountains swallowed the final rays of light. Wind gusted through the blanket of pine trees, swaying their branches. The cacophony of whispering ponderosas, spruce, and Douglas firs rose into a noise that sounded like the rapids of the Fall River. A passenger plane flew around the no-fly zone of Rocky Mountain National Park, heading southwest toward Denver. He didn't see many of those out here. The lights blinked as it crossed over the mountains.

The growl of an engine shattered the peace. Headlights cut across the road below. A mid-seventies model Jeep Cherokee raced up the path, a trail of dust and exhaust kicking up into the air.

Colton looked at his watch and snorted. It was almost six o'clock. He grabbed his Colt AR-15 with an ACOG scope and, leaning against his truck, waited for Raven to park.

A raindrop pelted Colton on the shoulder. The storm was rolling in from the west. He cursed their luck and opened the truck door to retrieve his poncho. It was going to be a long, cold, wet night.

Raven pulled into the lot. The Jeep was over forty years old, but even in the faint light he could see there wasn't a spot of rust in the gunmetal paint. He'd outfitted the truck with oversized off-road tires and a front grill guard with a winch.

"Chief," Raven said, opening his door and stepping onto the asphalt. He walked to the passenger door and let out his dog, Creek. The Akita jumped out and looked up at Colton with dark amber eyes surrounded by white fur. Then he ran to the side of the road and lifted up a leg.

"Nice Jeep," Colton said, making an effort to sound friendly.

Raven grinned and patted the hood. "A Cherokee for a Cherokee."

"Thought you were Sioux."

"Half and half," Raven said with a shrug.

Colton grunted. That was enough small talk. "Wasted a good hour of sunlight," he said. "Now we're going to be out here in the rain."

"An hour wouldn't have changed that," Raven said. He swung a pack around his shoulders.

"You do realize why I called you out here, right?"

Raven rummaged in the back of the Jeep for more gear. "The missing girl," he said without turning around.

"Her name is Melissa," Colton said. "The faster we get moving, the faster we find her."

Raven tightened his backpack over his shoulders and then put his long hair into a ponytail. He flashed the dimpled grin that had half the girls in town swooning. Unlike Colton, Raven had managed to serve without picking up any major scars on his face, and he looked nearly a decade younger than his thirty-three years.

"I have some questions," Raven said. "First off, isn't this outside your jurisdiction? Where is that guy that helped us with the Kirkland case? Ranger Fry?"

"Ranger Field," Colton replied. "He's checking leads farther up Trail Ridge Road."

"All right. So what else can you tell me, Chief?" Raven lit a cigarette, took a drag, and exhaled through his nostrils. "I had to cancel a date with a sweet little tourist to be here."

"Melissa was last seen getting off the school bus at her stop on Prospect Avenue, but a local named Bill Catcher thinks he spotted her riding in a blue F-150 pickup truck with a South Dakota license plate up Curry Road near Prospect Mountain. He described the driver as a middle-aged man with tan skin and a shaved head. Bill's a paranoid guy, but he has a good memory."

"Son of a bitch," Raven said. "That sounds like the same truck my sister Sandra saw speed away from her house a few weeks back. My niece, Allie, said some guy was trying to talk to her from the truck."

Colton clenched his jaw. "What? Why didn't Sandra report it?"

"I don't know," he said defensively. "Guess we don't trust cops."

Colton ignored the dig and pressed on with his questions. "What did this guy say to Allie?"

"She was too shaken to even tell Sandra what the dude looked like. Why, do you think it could be the same person?"

"I'd be willing to bet on it."

Raven took another long drag to consider the situation.

"Some campers came out early two nights ago due to the rain. They saw a blue F-150 with a South Dakota license plate parked here at midnight. When my officers interviewed them, they said they remembered seeing a man and a girl about Melissa's age heading up the trail. It could be nothin' or it could be somethin'."

"Well, shit, let's get going, then." Raven whistled at Creek, and the dog trotted over.

"When you finish that coffin nail, we'll get moving," Colton said. Raven wasn't the only tracker out here tonight. Colton knew a thing or two about hunting people, and smoking was a rookie mistake that would tell anyone out there they were coming.

"I was going to put it out. Stop worrying, Chief." Raven flicked the cigarette on the ground and kicked dirt over it. "Now that I think about it, I got a few more questions. What else do you know about our chase? You think he's armed?"

"I'd bet on him being armed and dangerous."

"So you don't mind if I bring my crossbow and hatchets?"

Colton shook his head and cradled his AR-15 across his chest. Raven hurried back to his gear. He picked up a leather belt in the shape of an X that held two sheathed hatchets. He slung it over his back and buckled the clasp across his chest. Then he retrieved his crossbow with mounted scope.

"That truck still around?" Raven clicked on his flashlight and angled it at the parking lot.

"No, I already looked."

Raven clicked the light off and placed it in a pocket. "You got a piece of Melissa's clothing?"

Colton threw on his poncho and then reached into his backpack. Digging through the contents, he found the plastic evidence bag containing the pink mitten Rex Stone had given him.

Raven took it and crouched down in front of Creek, letting the Akita get the scent, while Colton explained the plan. They would head up Mount Ypsilon trail to Lawn Lake, where the campers had reported seeing their chase.

"You think he might have backtracked along the falls?" Raven asked. "Maybe we should split up, cover more ground."

Colton clamped down on the inside of his cheek. If Raven was going to second-guess every decision, they'd never make it out of the parking lot.

"We're going to Lawn Lake, Raven."

"All right then, Chief," Raven said with a cocky grin. "Let's get to work."

Major Nathan "Gambler" Sardetti felt a smile coming on as the gates to Buckley Air Force Base opened. An MP threw up a salute as Nathan drove out onto the open road.

"Finally," he said. He cracked open a Red Bull and took a long swig as he sped away. After months of training and working six days a week, he was completely exhausted. He was going to need an entire pack of energy drinks to keep him awake during the drive to Empire, Colorado. His nephew, Ty, was at the Easterseals camp there, and Nathan had planned a surprise trip to visit the boy.

As soon as Nathan pulled onto the highway, he clicked the phone symbol on his steering wheel.

"Call Charlize Montgomery," he said.

The ringtone chimed from the speakers. Nathan downed half the can of Red Bull as he waited for his sister to pick up. In a few hours he was going to be in the mountains, breathing in the cedar air while pushing Ty's wheelchair down the path around the crystal clear lake. He couldn't think of a better way to enjoy his few precious days off.

A firm yet feminine voice emerged from the speakers. "Good evening, Major."

Nathan smiled. "Good evening, Senator. How's D.C.?"

"Gridlocked, per usual. How's my favorite little brother?"

"I'm your only little brother," Nathan said, chuckling at their familiar banter. "And I'm looking forward to spending some time with Ty. Thought I would call and ask if you had any special requests."

Her voice grew serious. "Just one: Don't tire him out too much. He slept an entire day after last time you visited him."

Nathan nodded as if she was here to see him. "I promise.

And for the record, last time I just took him to the beach. He had his life jacket on the whole time. You know I would never let anything happen to him."

There was a pause in the conversation, and Nathan knew they were both thinking the same thing. That when it had really counted, neither of them had been able to protect Ty. He'd lost the use of his legs from the car wreck that had killed his father, Richard. Charlize had never forgiven herself for not being able to save them, no matter how many times Nathan tried to convince his sister it wasn't her fault.

"Hey, I promise not to get him over-excited this time," Nathan said. "No candy, no soda, and no wild off-road wheelchair races. Cross my heart."

Charlize laughed. "He's going to be so surprised when he sees you."

It had been a long time since Nathan had heard his sister laugh. His smile widened as he eyed the box on the passenger seat.

"I've got a little something for him."

"Oh?" Charlize said. "I sure hope it's not fireworks again."

"You worry too much, Senator."

There was another pause, longer than the first.

"That's all I've been doing lately," she said. All trace of jocularity had vanished from her voice. "Things aren't good here, Nathan. We've got major problems domestically, but honestly my biggest fear is with North Korea. President Drake has taken a hardnosed approach against Pyongyang. There is a lot of tension at the demilitarized zone, especially after news of a top secret raid leaked."

"Raid? I haven't heard anything."

"That's why they call it 'top secret,' Nathan," she said quietly.

He knew better than to ask questions. "I have a few buddies stationed at the border. I heard they're being told to prepare for a potential attack."

A sigh came from the other end of the line. "If Pyongyang decides to invade the south, the twenty-eight thousand troops we have stationed there would be nothing more than a speed bump to the million-strong North Korean army."

Nathan shook his head. "Elections are just a few years away. Maybe what we need right now is President Charlize Montgomery."

"No way. President Drake will definitely run for a second term, and when mine is up, I'm coming back to Denver. It's time for me to be a full-time mother again. Besides, I'll be closer to you and can live vicariously through your missions. I sure do miss being up there."

"I wish you'd reconsider running again for your Senate seat. Ty needs you—but so does our country."

"Thanks. It means a lot, but I also miss..." Her words trailed off, but Nathan knew what she was about to say.

"I know. Richard was a great guy. But you're the best mom who also happens to be a fighter pilot and the most superb Senator that I've ever met."

"I'm probably the *only* one of those you've ever met. Since we're throwing out compliments, did you know you're a great uncle, and that you're shaping up to be a damn good pilot yourself? Might even break some of my records."

"You set the bar pretty high."

The sound of rustling came from the other line. "Hold on a second," she said.

Nathan took another slug of Red Bull as he waited. Before he could swallow, Charlize came back online.

"I'm sorry Nathan, but I have to cut this short. My chief of staff is buzzing in. I'll touch base with you tomorrow, okay?"

"Roger that. Love you, Sis."

"Love you, too, and thanks again for doing this. Means a lot to me and Ty."

"You bet. Stay safe and talk to you soon." He hung up and downed the rest of the can. It was good to chat with his sister, something that seemed to happen less and less now since she had been elected to Congress and he had been promoted. At thirty-one he was young for a major, but he had earned it.

He turned on the radio to the local NPR station just in time for the news.

"Good evening," came a deep, smooth voice of a rehearsed orator. "Tonight we bring you a fresh report from the Korean peninsula. Pyongyang has released a statement vowing that if more US warships approach they will consider it an act of war."

"Jesus," Nathan said. Charlize was right; things were crazy over in Korea. He went to switch the station when his Bluetooth buzzed. His heart hammered when he saw it was Colonel Howard. Clicking the call button, he prepared for bad news and said, "This is Major Sardetti."

"Major, I hope you haven't gone far because I need you to return to base."

Nathan closed his eyes for a single second and cursed in his mind. "No, sir. I'm just a few miles out."

"Good. Get your ass back here. We need you and Mutt in the sky. The governor has ordered a few fighters for a CAP." Howard paused, then added, "It's just a precautionary CAP, I'm sure, but I'd like you up there."

"Understood, sir. I'm on my way back." He punched the off button on his steering wheel again and cursed. Why couldn't he just get one weekend? The 120th was always ready, and Nathan was proud to be part of the squadron. He just hoped Colonel Howard was right and this was nothing more than a precautionary combat air patrol.

Nathan checked his rearview mirror and waited for a truck to pass him on the left. Then he turned on his blinker and made a sharp U-turn through the median. The Jeep jerked up and down over the rocky ground, and the box containing the model F-16 he'd bought for Ty crashed onto the passenger floor with a rattle of broken pieces.

"Damn," Nathan whispered. His weekend was not getting off to a good start—and the sight of the destroyed plane didn't exactly inspire confidence.

2

Raven Spears liked Chief Colton about as much as he liked his old Gunnery Sergeant Rodney Black. Both men had a strong prejudice against anyone who challenged the rules. Funny enough, neither of them seemed to like Raven much, either.

Guess that's why your best friend is a dog, he thought. Creek was always loyal and never talked shit. He was bolting up the trail ahead, navigating the rocky terrain with grace. He stopped only to check for a scent. Raven didn't bother whistling after him. He enjoyed giving the dog his freedom, especially since Colton was keeping him on such a tight leash.

Raven drew in a long breath and reminded himself that although things weren't great, he was lucky to be alive at all. It seemed like a lifetime ago that he had escaped the Rez by joining the Marines, and after ten years of fighting wars in foreign lands, he'd come to quiet Estes Park to rebuild his life and forget the things he had seen and done abroad. Using his meager savings and a loan from a full-blooded Sioux named Nile Redford that everyone called Mr. Redford, Raven had adopted Creek and purchased property to start a hunting and fishing business. It was amazing how much tourists would pay to hunt with an authentic Native American guide.

The man trekking through the forest in front of Raven had helped bring his dream of a normal life to a crashing halt by arresting Raven for poaching. His business was shut down, and the court costs and fines had eaten up his remaining savings. Now Raven was behind on his payments to Mr. Redford. He was the type of loan shark that charged blood instead of interest, and he was starting to get impatient. That's when the drinking got worse, and when the nightmares of the things he had tried to forget started coming back every night.

The musical rush of water pulled him back to the trail. To the west was the Roaring River, which originated at Crystal Lake. From there it flowed through Lawn Lake and down the valley to where it met Fall River. This trail was one of Raven's favorite spots in the park.

Fifteen minutes into the trek, he spotted the brown, rocky embankments framing the river. A fence of aspen trees grew out of the steep inclines. He stopped at the edge of a dirt path, cautiously making his way to the side to angle his flashlight over the edge. Fifty feet below, the clear water rushed around and over boulders, polishing them smooth.

Thirty-four years ago, the dam at Lawn Lake had broken

and emptied thirty million cubic feet of water into the valley and Estes Park. It had resulted in three deaths. Since then, the walls had continued to erode, pulling more of the montane forest into the valley.

Raven moved away from the ledge and continued up the trail, stepping over fallen trees and around rocks covered in moss and orange growths that reminded him of whale barnacles. The loose dirt and rocks were already slippery from the rain, and the canopy of ponderosa, spruce, and Douglas firs provided little protection. He directed his light back to the ridgeline above the Roaring River, keeping it in sight.

Colton trekked ahead with his AR-15 lowered toward the ground. Tonight he was acting like Raven's buddy, but they weren't friends and that wasn't going to change. He was here to collect a paycheck and hopefully find the kidnapped girl. If it was the same man that had scared his niece, then all the better. Raven had an arrow with the bastard's name on it.

He tightened his grip on his custom TenPoint Venom crossbow. Holding the weapon was reassuring. Not as reassuring as his old automatic M4, but the Marines didn't let him bring that gun home. He preferred his crossbow to a semi-automatic rifle on a hunt; not because it was more powerful, but because it was quiet.

The grumble of thunder broke in the distance, reminding Raven he had other problems beyond Mr. Redford and their chase. A dozen people died from lightning strikes out here every year, and a strong wind could also kill whatever scent Creek had picked up. The dog had reappeared on the trail ahead, his muzzle wet and covered with flecks of leaves.

"You got something, boy?" Raven asked. The dog sat on

his hind legs, and Raven bent down next to him, cradling his crossbow in his arms.

Creek looked up and snorted. That was Creek speak for *Yeah, dummy*. The dog knew over one hundred commands and was far smarter than any bomb-sniffing dog Raven had worked with. He could do everything but speak—which was good, because sometimes he felt like even the dog was judging him.

"Storm's getting worse," Colton said. He stopped on the side of the trail and looked skyward. Lightning webbed over the mountain peaks. Clapping thunder came a few seconds later, punctuating his words.

The radio on Colton's hip crackled, and he plucked it off his belt. "Colton here. Go ahead."

"Chief, it's Don reporting in. Trail's cold out here. Dogs don't have anything. You havin' any luck on Ypsilon?"

Colton exchanged a glance with Raven.

"Creek's picked up a scent," Raven said. "Too early to tell what it's from."

Colton brought the radio to his lips. "Maybe, Don. I'll report back later. Stand by."

"Copy that. Good luck."

Another torrent of electricity snaked across the horizon. Colton went to put the radio back on his hip but hesitated. His lips moved as if he was counting.

The next boom of thunder shook the marrow in Raven's bones. The storm was definitely getting worse.

Colton brought the radio receiver back to his lips. "Don, send everyone home for the night. Weather's getting too bad to risk it."

Raven pulled his Seattle Mariners hat from his bag and pulled it over his hair as the sky opened up. Sheets of rain hit the army of ponderosas at an angle, the patter echoing all around.

"Copy that, Chief," Don replied. "See you back at the station."

Colton attached the radio back on his belt.

"Keep away from the trees," Colton said. "The lightning—"

"I *know*," Raven interrupted. "You want to turn back?"

Colton frowned and then said, "No. I can't look Rex Stone in the eye if I didn't do everything I could to find his daughter."

Raven nodded and then patted his dog. "Show us. Find her."

Creek took off running through the woods. His nose was remarkable. Even in the rain, Creek was working a scent, following what Raven hoped was Melissa's trail. They continued along the path for another thirty minutes, jogging to keep up with the Akita. Colton didn't say much, and Raven was fine with that. He'd grown up in a household that was almost completely silent. On the rare occasion when his parents had spoken to him, his sister, or each other, it had usually been with raised voices.

He should have known the quiet was too good to last.

"You did good work on the Kirkland case," Colton said.

"It was either find the girl or go to jail," Raven said.

That effectively killed the conversation.

Creek reemerged on the trail ahead. He jumped over a fallen log, wagged his tail, and took off again. By the time

Raven angled his flashlight into the forest, the Akita's white tail was vanishing through a cluster of ash trees.

Raven pointed and signaled. Colton was already on the move. The men hurried over the terrain, careful not to slip on the wet bed of pine needles and loose dirt. Rain tore through the canopy overhead. Raven's coat and pants were waterproof, but his gloves weren't. They were already drenched, and his fingers were freezing. He never went into the wilderness without the proper gear. This goddamn debt had him on edge.

Light as a feather. You're light as a feather, he thought. It was the motto that always grounded Raven. He put every worry out of his mind and focused on the tracking. They were still a good three miles from Lawn Lake.

The forest became a two-dimensional canvas, and Raven divided the terrain horizontally into thirds like he had learned in the Marines. His eyes were accustomed to systematically scanning the canvas from left to right, right to left. If he detected any movement, he would stop to search.

Tonight the canvas was almost pitch black. The beam from his flashlight illuminated a narrow path through the dense woods. He ran and ran, needle-covered branches reaching out to grab him. A bird called out in the distance, a sign that Creek was too close to its nest.

Lightning streaked overhead and thunder clapped a few seconds later, echoing over and over through the valley. The chatter of raccoons followed as the forest came alive around Raven. He was completely in tune with his surroundings, at one with nature. He sniffed the air, checking it for signs of campers or their chase. There was no scent of cooking or smoke, only the fresh smell of rain and evergreens.

The canvas transformed the farther up they moved. A massive storm, far worse than this one, had blown through the forest a few weeks prior. The straight-line winds had taken down thousands of young or unhealthy trees. Beams from their flashlights danced over the debris still scattered across the path like a battlefield. The trees that had perished would take months to rot and return to the earth.

Creek reappeared on the trail and then turned and bolted into the woods. Colton flashed an advance signal after the dog. Normally Raven would have marked where they left the trail, but he didn't have time.

Crossbow dangling from the strap on his chest, he put his flashlight in his mouth and grabbed a tree branch to pull himself up a small embankment. Colton was already a hundred feet ahead and moving at a good clip.

Raven jogged after him, branches from fallen trees reaching up and cutting his legs. He was careful to keep his light low. A beam into the sky would warn the chase that they were being hunted. He ran until his lungs felt like they were going to pop. A Marine never stopped to rest, but Raven wasn't in the same shape he had been eighteen months ago. Of course, he also hadn't smoked half a pack a day—or drunk a six-pack every night—back then, either.

Colton stopped ahead, scanning the forest with his AR-15 and flashlight. Despite his labored breathing, Raven was moving a minute later. He did his best to whistle to Creek, but it came out as more of a hiss.

The dog suddenly appeared in a clearing with something

hanging from his mouth. Raven nearly tripped over a log as he directed his light on Creek. The beam fell on a wall of Douglas firs that opened to a meadow beyond. Boulders, glossy from the rain, and knee-high shrubs speckled the landscape. Before Raven could see what was in Creek's mouth, the dog took off running toward the maze of mossy rocks, zigzagging to follow the scent on the wind.

Colton shouldered his rifle and approached cautiously while Raven raked his light over the ground. He held the light on what looked like a footprint. He quickly raised a hand at Colton to tell the story. The lawman nodded and hunched down.

Raven leaned down to get a closer look at the track that was partially filled with water. It was male, about a size ten or eleven. This was too far off the trail to be the random track of a camper, and if Creek had picked up a scent here, they couldn't be far from their chase.

They were close. But his tracker's sense told him they weren't the only people on the mountain tonight. Raven couldn't shake the feeling that someone was nearby—waiting, watching. *Hunting.*

Nathan Sardetti kept his hand on the side-mounted control stick as his F-16 Viper tore over the Denver skyline.

His wingman, 1st Lieutenant Mark "Mutt" Blake, flanked him on the right. They were heading west over Denver to patrol the surrounding areas. The rumble of their single-engine fighters was likely to draw some attention as the Vipers provided a combat air patrol. Restaurants and bars would be hopping below, with patrons anxious to de-stress after a long week. The sound of fighter jets was going to freak out a lot of civilians.

Nathan scanned the city. He had spent his fair share of Friday nights down there, drinking whiskey and watching the Colorado Rockies get their asses kicked. Part of him missed those wilder days. He'd earned his call sign, "Gambler," for his legendary all-night poker parties as well as his risky moves in his F-16. His older sister had left the skies to settle down with a family and a career in Washington. They were both driven, hardworking, and loved flying, but unlike his sister, Nathan had never married or had children. He wasn't sure he'd ever be happy with a desk job, but lately the idea of settling down with a nice girl had started to appeal to him.

Blake's voice broke over the comms. "Gambler, you got any idea why we were called out for a CAP? I have a hard time believing we're up here to sightsee."

"Negative, Mutt, but I think it's supposed to make the governor feel better while he sleeps tonight."

"Holy shit, what a waste of tax dollars."

Nathan chuckled. "Did you hear how much the new helmets cost for the F-35s? Four hundred k, brother."

"Damn! That can't be right."

"Believe it."

"I guess I don't feel so bad about burning some fumes, but Kiley's mad that I'm not home for the weekend."

"She'll forgive you," Nathan said with a smile. "I was supposed to go see Ty. Good thing he didn't know I was coming, or he would have been disappointed."

"Maybe you can still drive up tonight."

"Hopefully," Nathan said. They pulled away from the city, heading northwest. The vibrant lights of Denver vanished behind them as the two F-16s raced toward the Rockies. Nathan blinked several times in an effort to keep his tired eyes open. Shit, he was exhausted.

He opened up a line to the other two fighters from the 120th. 1st Lieutenant Kyle "Rabbit" Swanson and Captain Tim "Bullseye" Negan were patrolling the southern part of Colorado.

"Bullseye, this is Gambler. How's it looking to the south?"

"Mostly clear skies out here, Gambler. We're passing over Lamar."

"Copy that," Nathan said.

In the distance, the jagged white peaks of the mountains came into focus, a long jaw of teeth that never seemed to end. Lightning streaked across the dark sky, illuminating a fort of clouds with brilliant flashes as they approached a storm.

For the next thirty minutes, Nathan and Blake cruised the angry skies. Below, hubs of light glowed from the small cities nestled in the mountains. While citizens prepared for sleep, Nathan and his wingman watched over them.

All traces of civilization vanished below as Nathan passed over Rocky Mountain National Park. The no-fly zone was off limits to civilian aircraft, and there weren't any communities in the park.

A voice came over the channel. "Viper 3, this is Strobe. You have traffic at nine o'clock. Chinese ARJ21, 100 miles, angels 35, heading 120 toward Wichita. Check."

Nathan was wide awake now. The last thing he was expecting tonight were orders from an E-3 Airborne Warning and Control System (AWACS) specialist out of Tinker Air Force Base in Oklahoma. He checked the radar for a Chinese commercial airliner heading east at thirty-five thousand feet.

"Copy that, Strobe. Viper 3 is radar contact, tally-ho."

Nathan watched the radar blips for Viper 3 and 4 change direction to intercept the Chinese plane. A bead of sweat dripped from his short-cropped hair.

He glanced at Blake's jet and opened a private line. "Mutt, keep sharp. Something's off."

Nathan shifted his gaze from the controls to the view. Flying a fighter jet was all about multi-tasking, and he was damn good at it.

Another message came over the channel. "Viper 3, Strobe. That ARJ21 is now angel 38, heading 135. Pilots are unresponsive."

"Copy that, Strobe. We're on it. I'll let you know when we have visual," replied Negan.

Nathan tried to wrap his mind around what the radio chatter meant. Could there be a technical problem aboard the Chinese craft? If so, why the hell would the pilots be ascending? And why had they changed course? If they kept this heading, they would be above Denver within thirty minutes.

"Gambler, I got a bad feeling about this," Blake said.

"Agreed. Stay on me."

Nathan twisted his side-mounted control stick and tore through the clouds. They were north of Rocky Mountain National Park now. Nathan surrendered to the forces lashing his body as he increased his velocity to twelve hundred miles an hour.

There had to be a rational explanation for the rogue plane's behavior. Sometimes pilots lost contact with the ground and changed course due to technical issues, but that was rare. Maybe this wasn't a bullshit mission; maybe the governor had known something when he sent the 120th up here tonight.

Nathan opened a line to Viper 3. "Bullseye, Gambler. Do you have a visual?"

"Negative, Gambler."

Nathan studied the radar. The air traffic controller came back online, but this time his voice was panicked. "Viper 3, ARJ21 is still unresponsive. Angels is now 46."

The update made Nathan scrunch his brows. The F-16s had a max ceiling of fifty thousand feet. Swanson and Negan wouldn't be able to pursue much past that.

"Strobe, Viper 3, I have a limited visual," Negan said. There was a pause, and then, "You said that was an ARJ21, right?"

"Copy that, Viper 3."

"Stand by for confirmation," Negan said.

Nathan's F-16 rattled as he shot through a pocket of turbulence. He held steady and waited for Negan to relay a visual.

"Strobe, Viper 3, this is *not* an ARJ21. I'm looking at what appears to be a Soviet-built…"

Static broke over the line.

"Viper 3, Strobe. Come again, I didn't get your last."

Nathan held in a breath.

"Holy shit! It's an Ilyushin Il-28," Negan shouted over the comms.

Nathan swallowed hard. That couldn't be right. The only country still actively using the big gray Soviet Union birds were the North Koreans. They were supposed to have a max service ceiling of around forty thousand feet, but this one was still in a climb, pushing its advertised limits. He had only seen pictures of the old planes, but he knew their purpose, and he knew they would likely be stripped down to hold as much jet fuel and as many bombs as possible. If that was the case, then they were facing the North Korean version of the American Doolittle Raid into Tokyo during WWII.

"Weapons hot, Mutt," Nathan said. "On me!"

They came together in a fighting formation and ripped south over Rocky Mountain National Park, punching toward Mach 2 as the Ilyushin continued ascending. The plane was now at fifty thousand feet.

Questions ping-ponged in Nathan's mind, but one kept coming to the surface: How could the North Koreans have made it into US airspace disguised as a Chinese ARJ21? They would have had to spoof multiple transponder codes.

"Strobe, Viper 3. I am weapons hot. Do I have permission to engage?"

"Copy that, Viper 3. Take that plane down and—"

The transmission suddenly cut out in a wave of static, the connection severed.

Nathan dipped his helmet to check the radar, but the contact was gone.

"Bandit just faded," Blake said. "Where the hell did it go?"

Nathan checked the radar again to see Viper 3 and 4 vanish. An instant later, a brilliant flash lit up the sky to the south.

"Evasive maneuvers!" he yelled. "Get out of there, Mutt!"

Blake was already turning. "Is that a bomb? What the—"

The comms crackled off. All at once, warning sensors chirped in Nathan's cockpit. The electronics were going haywire—and he was seconds away from losing control of his bird over the jagged peaks of the Rocky Mountains.

3

The rifle crack of thunder rattled Raven's bones. It sounded like a bomb going off in the heavens. The ground shook as he switched off his flashlight and got down on his belly next to the track.

To the south, a brilliant flash of lightning seemed to illuminate the entire skyline. It lingered for several moments before fading away. The blaze of the lighting strike faded, and darkness clamped around him like he had been pulled into a wet, black hole. It took him several seconds for his eyes to adjust. Clouds blocked out the moon, making it difficult to see much besides outlines and shapes. The cold mud coated his exposed skin, and his fingers were frozen, but he didn't dare move.

Another flash of lightning backlit the meadow. He spotted Colton, and while Raven couldn't see Creek, he knew his buddy was out there. They waited for several minutes, motionless. Lightning webbed across the sky that was pouring rain.

Raven glimpsed Creek's brown and white coat in the grass near a boulder in the next flash. The dog was sitting calmly with something still in his mouth.

Scanning the meadow a third time, Raven got to his feet and signaled Colton toward Creek. At a hunch, they slowly worked their way across the field.

"I think someone's out here, Chief," Raven whispered.

Colton glanced over his shoulder but kept moving. Creek came trotting over, whatever he had found hanging from his maw.

The men slowed as they approached. An uncharacteristic wave of anxiety rushed through Raven, and it wasn't from the sensation of being watched. He'd seen plenty of death in Iraq, and he thought he had been prepared to find the little girl dead, but when he rounded the boulder and saw her corpse, his heart slammed against his rib cage like a blacksmith hammering the blade of a sword.

Colton motioned for Raven to hold security and then bowed his head and dropped to his knees. Melissa lay curled up in a fetal position, still dressed in a coat and jeans.

Raven brought the scope to his eye and scanned the trees. He had replaced the custom scope with one of his own for hunts like this one. Tree limbs shifted across the illumination. There was no sign of their chase, but he was definitely out there, watching.

"Fuck," Colton whispered. He put on a pair of rubber gloves and put a finger to her ghostly pale skin to check for a pulse.

Raven looked away to scan the meadow for any sign of movement. Whoever was out there was well hidden. Creek dropped one of her shoes and sniffed the air.

A flash of lightning arced into the trees to the north, sparks raining onto the forest floor. The clap of thunder that followed rumbled for several moments, like nature herself was screaming at the injustice of Melissa's death. The pointless death of this little girl disturbed the balance of the world.

"I'm sorry," Raven said.

Colton didn't reply. He slowly rolled the girl onto her back, exposing the gash across her neck. Raven shook his head and forced himself to look away.

"What kind of animal does this to a little girl?" Colton said. He let out a long sigh and stared before finally reaching down to close her eyes.

Raven caught a drift of what smelled like burned flesh. He raised his bow into the darkness, finger hovering over the trigger. He still felt eyes on them.

"What is it?" Colton whispered. "You think the guy that did this is still out there?" He slowly rose to stand next to Raven. "I'll kill the bastard with my bare hands."

Frozen like a statue, Raven scrutinized the terrain, waiting for lightning to illuminate the meadow. Whoever had done this was playing some sort of a sick game, and Raven and Colton were just pawns. If the guy wanted them dead, they would already be bleeding out next to Melissa. Chances were, he was observing from a safe distance and taking pleasure in the terrible thing he had done.

"Jesus," Colton muttered. He had bent back down and was brushing the leaves and dirt off Melissa's legs. Then the barbeque smell made sense—both of her legs were burned to the knee.

Raven's guts ached at the sight, a memory surfacing from the dark place where he kept the evil he had witnessed in Iraq. This wasn't the first child he had seen burned. But Melissa's injuries weren't from an explosion. Someone had done this to her deliberately.

Something about the way her feet and lower legs had been burned reminded him of something that he couldn't quite place. This memory was older than the war, something from his childhood. Growing up on the Rez, he'd been raised on Cherokee folktales, and in one of those stories, demons known as Water Cannibals would kidnap victims and roast them, feet first, over their bonfires.

Raven shuddered. He'd hated that story when he was a kid, but surely this was just a terrible coincidence. The Water Cannibals weren't real—and from his experience, humans were much crueler and more brutal than any monster.

Colton's voice pulled Raven back to the mountains.

"You with me, man?" he asked.

Raven nodded, keeping the story to himself. Only Cherokees would have known of the story, and there weren't many of them around in these parts besides him and his sister. No way in hell was he about to give Colton a reason to arrest him again.

Colton began whispering something under his breath that might have been a prayer. They waited there for several moments before Raven gave the all clear. The sensation of being watched had finally passed.

Colton pulled his radio from his belt and said, "Don, you copy? Over."

Thunder rolled in the distance. The storm was moving to the east, but the rumble drowned out the crackle of static from the radio in Colton's hand.

Don came online a moment later. "Roger that, sir. Just arrived at the station. You on your way back?"

Lips trembling, Colton said, "We found Melissa." He paused, sucked in a breath, exhaled. "She's gone. Call the medical examiner and get 'em up to the Ypsilon and Lawn Lake trailhead ASAP."

White noise broke over the channel. The growl of thunder sounded again. Raven glanced at the sky. Odd. He heard the thunder, but where was the lightning? The weather in the Rocky Mountains could be strange, but something about this storm seemed off.

"Don, did you get my last, over?" Colton said.

Raven looked down at the radio. The screen was blank, and when Colton turned the knob, nothing happened.

"Shit," Colton said, smacking the side of the radio. "Batteries were fine when I checked this morning."

Raven went back to staring at the sky, zoning everything else out, his brown eyes searching for the source of the rising thunder. The edge of the storm had rolled to the east and the rain was letting up, but the roar continued to reverberate off the mountain peaks.

"What are you looking at?" Colton asked.

"I—I'm not sure."

Just then a pair of F-16s raced over the distant peaks and roared southwest over the valley below. He lowered his crossbow to watch the silhouetted jets tear through the cloud cover under the moonlight. The pair suddenly broke away from one another, peeling off in different directions.

One of the aircraft roared toward Estes Park. At least, that's the direction he thought it was headed, but when he looked, the glow of artificial light was gone. Was he disoriented, or was the town dark?

"Chief …," Raven began to say.

Colton pushed himself up to stand next to Raven. The jets appeared to be slowing as they swooped toward the valley. The lead aircraft's nose dipped so low it looked like the pilot was attempting a dive.

"Something's not right," Colton said.

Creek bared his teeth, growling in a low tone. Raven was kneeling down to calm the dog when one of the jets veered in their direction. The pilot jerked to the right, trying to avoid the peaks, but it was like he had no control over the plane. The fighter tore overhead, the roar so loud it hurt Raven's ears. The air current bent the tips of the ponderosas and ripped the baseball cap from his head, sending it rolling across the meadow.

Raven ducked down as the current slammed into him and Colton bent over Melissa's body like he was trying to protect her.

The jet smashed into the summit of Mummy Mountain, a fiery blast blooming across the snowy peak. Raven shielded his eyes from the explosion. The second fighter impacted with a cliff in the distance a few seconds later.

"My God," Colton said quietly.

They stood over Melissa's body and stared in shock at

the fires. Neither of them said a word until Raven broke the silence.

"Did you see anyone eject?"

Colton shook his head.

"Must have had some sort of malfunction, right Chief?"

"Both of them?" Colton shook his head again.

"What the hell were they doing out here, though?"

Colton bent down to pick up Melissa and Raven crouched to help.

"I've got her," the police chief insisted.

Raven held up his hands and turned back to the valley. Estes Park had gone dark. The only lights out there now were the fires from the downed jets. The scene transported him back to the rescue mission at the North Korean prison eighteen months ago. In his mind's eye, he pictured the Black Hawk pulling away from the compound as Staff Sergeant Nixon detonated the C4. The scene had looked a lot like this as they'd flown over the dark terrain in the pitch black of night with only the fires flickering in the distance.

Raven had never expected to see such utter darkness here at home.

➤——

Sandra Spears sat patiently in her Toyota Corolla, listening to the light rain as it beat down on the roof. The warmth from the seat heaters was slowly fading, and she was cold in her scrubs. If she couldn't get the car started soon, she'd be late for her shift at the medical center. The prospect of walking in the cold rain wasn't appealing, but it seemed like she might not have a choice.

Twenty minutes earlier, the car had lost power, and it had coasted to the side of Highway 34 about two miles from town. Hers wasn't the only stranded vehicle. For the hour, traffic was heavy. Tourists had been returning from Rocky Mountain National Park, their vacations spoiled by the storm. The vague outlines of other stalled cars were littered down the highway.

One moment she had been thinking about her nightly routine at the hospital—what the staffing ratio would be, and if Doctor Newton had written broad enough orders to cover the multitude of issues they usually dealt with on a Friday night. The next she was in a dream-like state, unable to comprehend the events unfolding around her as fighter jets fell from the sky and her faithful Corolla died.

She reached for her phone to call her brother again, but there still wasn't a signal. It was like someone had flipped a switch and everything, including her damn car, had stopped working.

Even in the rain, the fires from the wreckage continued to burn in the distance. She tilted her head for a better view, catching her reflection in the rearview mirror. Even in the dim light she looked exhausted. Her long black hair was trying to escape from its braid, and purple bags hung under her brown eyes.

Sandra had been under a lot of stress at work and at home lately, but it was the note she had found on her car earlier that day that had left her feeling rattled. She'd decided to drive through Rocky Mountain National Park before her shift to clear her mind.

At least Allie was safe. Well, relatively safe. Her daughter was staying with her father at his new home in Loveland, Colorado. Mark was an addict, and even though he had been clean for a year, it wasn't until just recently Sandra had agreed to overnight visits once a week.

Ever since Allie told her about the man outside their house, Sandra had been paranoid about letting the girl out of her sight. Mark had laughed off her worries, telling her she was overreacting as usual. Now that her car wasn't working, she felt helpless, like she was a world away from Allie even though it was only thirty miles to Loveland.

Sandra opened her purse and pulled out the cryptic note she had found and read it again. It still didn't make any sense to her, and she didn't recognize the bold, almost childlike printing.

THE STORM IS COMING.

"Hey!" someone shouted. She flinched and dropped the paper on her lap.

A man dressed in jeans, cowboy boots, and a sweatshirt was slowly making his way from car to car. She cracked her door open to listen, trying not to let in any rain.

"Does anyone know what's going on?" he asked as he passed other cars. The man was soaked to the bone, but he didn't seem to notice. Sandra didn't recognize him, and instantly labeled the man as a tourist.

He straightened a baseball cap as he approached her car. His sweatshirt read *Colorado Springs Auto Clinic*. If anyone knew what was going on with the cars, he should.

As he drew closer, however, Sandra reconsidered asking the man for help. His eyes were roving and seemed unfocused, and his hands were shaking. Her trained nurse's eye picked up on the signs immediately—the signs that she'd ignored in Mark for far too long. She would never forget the crazed look in her ex-husband's eyes when he was using. It was a look she should have known. The same one her father had shown when he drank heavily, and it was near identical to the gaze of her ex-boyfriend Mike Tankala back on the Rez after he used peyote. For her entire life she had ignored the signs. But those days were over.

Sandra closed her door as discreetly as possible and locked it.

The patter of rain slowed to single drops, then to nothing. Sandra closed her eyes, breathing softly in the sudden quiet. That's all she needed. Just a few moments of quiet to figure out what she should do. The sound of knuckles rapping on the window snapped her eyes open. She looked up to see the man with the baseball cap flash a nervous smile and bend down toward her door. She met his eyes and saw that the guy wasn't strung out—he was just scared.

Not every man is an asshole or an addict, she reminded herself.

"Ma'am, excuse me, do you have any idea what's going on?"

Sandra unlocked the door and cracked it open warily. "I'm not sure," she said. "Figured you might know about the cars. Are you a mechanic or something?"

The man raised his eyebrows. "No, why? Oh," he said looking down at his shirt. "No, I just sell the cars."

A crowd had gathered at the edge of the road to stare at the fires dotting the mountains. The man pointed at them.

"It doesn't make any sense. How could they have all gone down like that? How is that possible?" Panic was rising in his voice.

Shaking her head, Sandra said, "I have no idea."

The man continued to the next car, and Sandra made her decision. Help wasn't coming. Her North Face jacket would keep her warm enough for the long walk, and she had bottled water in her bag. Raven had insisted she keep a knife in the glove compartment after she'd refused to buy a gun, and had shown her how to use it. She tucked the sheath into her waistband, and locked her car door manually when the automatic lock button didn't work.

Once she reached the hospital and figured out what was going on, she would find a way to contact Mark and get to Allie. She tried not to worry as she slung her backpack over her shoulders.

One thing at a time, Sandra, she thought. *Allie is safe for now, and it's not that far into town. You can do this.*

After taking in a deep breath, she broke into a trot, her tennis shoes pounding the wet concrete. If she jogged most of the way, she would reach civilization again in thirty minutes.

The distant glow of Estes Park was gone on the horizon, but she knew this road. The turnoff for the Alluvial Fan and Lawn Lake was about a quarter mile behind her. That meant she was pretty close to the park entrance.

"Where you going?" Mr. Colorado Springs shouted after her.

"To get help," Sandra replied. "Just stay here and stay calm, okay?"

She opted for the rocky dirt path along Fall River to avoid more questions and other stranded drivers. The water babbled to her right, cascading over rocks. A natural fence of bushes and trees ran along the side of the river, wind tickling the tips of the branches. She loved it up here. The aroma of the ponderosas, the jagged snowy peaks, the collage of colors, the wildlife—and, most of all, the constant murmur of running water. It all helped take her mind off whatever lousy thing was happening in her life.

The first time she had visited Raven here eighteen months ago, it was supposed to have just been a vacation, but these mountains had quickly become her home. The Rez had sucked the life out of her. Rocky Mountain National Park had breathed it back in.

But Sandra always felt like she was running from someone. First her father, then Mike Tankala, and finally her ex-husband. Now that Mark had moved to Loveland she was finally free of those men, but she still felt like someone was chasing her.

Ten minutes into the run, her foot hit a root, snapping her alert just in time to brace herself as she tripped and fell.

"Stupid, stupid," Sandra hissed. She got to her knees and wiped the mud from her hands onto the grass. As she did, she caught a glimpse of something hanging from a tree across the river. It looked like a plastic sheet draped over the top of the pine tree.

Never in her life had she seen trash out here. The rangers and volunteers kept the park immaculate, and most visitors obeyed the littering laws.

Curious, she worked her way carefully down to the

water's edge. The green tarp was hard to see at first, almost camouflaged. Her breath caught in her chest when she realized it was a parachute.

"Ma'am?" came a voice.

Sandra whirled in a defensive position with her fists up, just like Raven had taught her, as a man wearing a flight suit and holding a helmet limped out of the underbrush. He held up his free hand.

"Whoa, it's okay, ma'am. I'm not going to hurt you."

She slowly lowered her fists as he stepped forward, the moonlight revealing the handsome, chiseled face of a man in his mid-thirties with a full head of brown hair and sharp green eyes.

"I sprained my ankle pretty bad and need to get to the nearest town as quickly as possible," he said. "Can you point me in the right direction?"

Sandra gave him the elevator eyes treatment. His olive drab flight suit was soaked up to his waist, and his boots were covered in mud. He limped a step closer, grimacing as he looked up at the road above.

"I'm a nurse," Sandra said without thinking.

The pilot's eyes flitted back to hers in the moonlight. "Then I'd be grateful if you took a look at my ankle real quick."

Sandra hesitated and then pulled off her backpack and set it on the ground. She carried a medical kit with her everywhere.

"Take a seat on that rock," Sandra said, pointing toward a boulder.

"Thanks," he said, limping over to take a seat. "My name's Nathan, by the way. Major Nathan Sardetti."

She smiled thinly at him. "Sandra. Nice to meet you."

"How far are we from the nearest town? Did you see the other pilot eject?"

Sandra opened her med kit, talking as she worked. "Two miles or so from Estes Park, maybe less. I didn't see anyone else. Can't you call them on your radio?"

When Nathan didn't reply, Sandra asked, "What happened to your plane?" She carefully cut through his flight suit and started wrapping the sprain.

"I'm not authorized to say, ma'am." He craned his neck at the road. "Please hurry. I need to get to that town."

Sandra tightened the wrapping and narrowed her eyes. "Major, I may be just a nurse, but I know fighter jets don't drop out of the air like that. So are you going to tell me what's going on or what?"

Nathan cleared his throat as if he was considering his next words carefully.

"The United States has just been attacked."

4

Colton carefully carried Melissa's body, wrapped in his coat, down the trailhead. The rain had let up, but his heart was still racing. He had faced a hard decision: leave her there and hope the coyotes didn't get to her before they could return with the medical examiner, or bring her body home to her parents.

Protocol would have been to leave her so the crime scene could be preserved and documented accurately, but things had changed when those jets crashed. He'd done what any father would have done. Rex and Lilly didn't deserve to wait any longer to get their little girl back.

Colton's arms burned as he carried Melissa over the slick terrain. Dead bodies were always heavier than live ones. He'd learned that the hard way in Afghanistan. Since returning from his last tour, he'd managed the anger just like the doc had told him to. Counting to ten, meditating, even getting in a goddamn downward-facing dog position. He'd already tried the first of the two, but nothing was working. And he wasn't about to do yoga on the trail, not in the rain and definitely not in the company of Raven Spears.

"You sure you don't want me to carry her?" Raven asked.

"No, I'm fine. I told you to watch my damn back."

A drop of rain plummeted into Colton's eye. He paused to wipe it away and stare at the fires in the distance, his mind racing with possible scenarios, each one worse than the last.

What he did know was those flames wouldn't be going out anytime soon. Jet fuel was extremely flammable. When Osama bin Laden couldn't launch missiles at America's infrastructure, he had picked the next best thing—jumbo planes full of jet fuel.

"Chief, do you have any idea what happened to those F-16s?" Raven asked. He stood at the side of the trail, crossbow draped across his chest, and his mud-caked Seattle Mariners baseball cap tilted back so he could look at Colton. Creek sat on his hind legs, fur soaked and matted.

"Enough with the questions," Colton said. "You'll tell our chase exactly where we are."

"He's long gone, and if he wanted us dead he would have killed us back in that meadow when he had the drop on us. Now why don't you let me carry the girl for a while?"

"I said I'm fine," Colton said, glaring at Raven.

Raven muttered something that sounded a lot like "hard-ass" and turned away, clearly not believing his lie. Colton wasn't fine at all. Melissa was dead, there was a killer on the loose, and with the radio down, he had no way to contact his officers to see what was going on in Estes Park. Something had happened to those jets at the same moment his radio went dead. It might be a coincidence, or it might be a pattern. Until they reached civilization, there was no way to know for sure and no point in talking to Raven about theories.

The trio continued down the path, rain pattering off their clothing, questions swirling through Colton's mind. He was doing his best to keep it together, but it was hard not to think the worst. It didn't help that he could feel Raven's eyes on him.

"What?" Colton asked. "You got something else to say?"

"Nope," Raven said.

Colton hoisted Melissa's body up against his chest. Pain lanced up his arm and neck. He gritted his teeth and pushed on. The military had taught him how to manage pain. Now if he could just learn to manage his anger the same way...

"Want me to carry her for a while now?"

"Goddammit, Raven, I told you to watch our backs."

Raven stopped mid-stride and straightened his baseball hat. "You trusted me enough to help you look for her, but you don't trust when I tell you we're the only two people on this mountain right now?"

"You're right, I don't trust you," Colton said.

Raven halted and pursed his lips like he wanted to say something else, but he didn't reply.

Colton continued down the trail, leaving him behind. The veins in his muscular forearms bulged as he tightened his grip on the dead girl. How was he going to tell Risa that her little friend would never be coming over for another playdate or a sleepover?

The wind whistled through the treetops, and pine needles cartwheeled to the ground. Something trickled down Colton's face. It had been a long time since he shed a tear, but he was too busy staring through the canopy of trees to wipe it away. Overhead, a single rogue cloud rolled across the horizon, leaving behind a jeweled sky. He stepped carefully over a downed branch but kept his gaze on the cloud.

"You're not even going to tell me a theory about what happened to those jets?" Raven asked. When Colton only grunted in response, he continued, "I have a few. My people, the Sioux and the Cherokee, have many stories about the end of the world."

Colton wanted to snap but he knew it wouldn't do any good. Raven wasn't going to shut his mouth.

"End of the world?" Colton asked. "See, that's the type of path I don't want to go down right now."

Raven pressed on. "Some stories say that the Star People, our ancestors, will return. The signs will be clear. Flooding, fire, earthquakes…"

"Christians have been saying the same thing for millennia."

Raven tipped the bill of his hat toward a towering ponderosa silhouetted in the moonlight. "I'd say the signs are pretty clear, Chief. That flood a few years back, and now the fires from these jets. I'm just saying."

"Raven, you're really starting to piss me off. Whatever happened has nothing to do with your Sky People, or Jesus, or whatever." Colton lifted Melissa's body up higher. "A man did this."

The words finally seemed to silence Raven. He whistled for

his dog and hurried along the trail. As they walked, Colton kept his gaze on the dazzling sky. Out here it was vast and serene, undisturbed by the glow of human engineering. When he was a kid, while his friends had been watching TV, he had been lying with his back to his parents' deck, studying the stars. Centuries ago, Raven's ancestors would have done the same thing.

The sky *was* their TV.

But something seemed off about the sky tonight—something was missing. "Raven, hold up."

He stopped and followed Colton's gaze upward. "You see another plane or something, Chief?"

Colton scrutinized the sky for several seconds. The weight of Melissa's body was making his arms tremble, but he hardly noticed anymore.

"No," Colton finally replied. "That's just it. I don't see any aircraft at all."

The scent of charred flesh lingered in Brown Feather's nose as he waited near the house where his woman lived. He had brought her a present from his kill, a warning. Anger rose like a tide through his gut as he waited, but he pushed it back down. He'd waited years to see her again and tracked her across state lines. No matter where she tried to hide, he would find her. They were meant to be together. She had promised.

He couldn't wait much longer.

With his truck not working, he'd had to abandon his original plan, which was to throw her in the back and drive until he found a place where they could be alone. She was supposed to be happy to see him. She was supposed to have waited for him. Instead, she had proven herself to be a faithless liar.

She was going to pay for her deceit.

On the day his long hunt for her had finally ended, when he'd tracked her down to this shithole in the middle of nowhere, he'd seen she had started a family with another man. The little girl was a display of her betrayal in the flesh.

The demons had always said she would betray him, but he hadn't wanted to believe them. They had been right. They were always right. He understood that now.

After so many years with only the demons for company, he should have learned to trust them. They were wise, but they were also merciless. He needed to learn to be more like them. They were strong and fast, and they did not waste time waiting for what they wanted.

No, they simply took it.

The girl he killed had been a spur of the moment decision. After he had realized the depth of his woman's betrayal, he'd driven back up the mountain with rage in his heart. Then he'd seen her, another dark-haired girl dressed all in pink and white, skipping away from the bus stop like a lost rabbit kit. He'd lured her into the truck and taken her into the woods with him, thinking that maybe if he had a daughter of his own, his woman would see what a good father he was and return to him.

That had been a foolish thought. He could see that now.

Instead of being grateful to be chosen, the little brat had kicked and bit him—as if any of this was his fault—and screamed and screamed until he had finally cut her throat. It had taken her less than ninety seconds to bleed out, and as he watched her feebly kicking like a toad with its legs broken, he had decided that there was only one way this could end. He had begun building up the campfire with extra logs until the flames were nearly as tall as a man.

The demons did not waste time, and they did not waste meat.

When the time had come, he hadn't tasted her after all. He wasn't worthy yet to call himself a Water Cannibal. But he would be soon.

Still half asleep, Senator Charlize Montgomery scanned a dark room and tried to remember where she was. Reality fought with her nightmares for control. Something had woken her, a strange sound that wasn't part of her dream.

It was an odd thing, knowing when you're sleeping but not being able to wake. This sensation wasn't new to her; the nightmare was a reoccurring memory of the worst day of her life. The pain from losing Richard, and the constant struggle of raising a child, had had a long-lasting effect on her mind and body.

She felt like she should have been able to handle the stress. Before her career in politics, Charlize was one of the first female pilots to fly combat missions from the cockpit of an F-15 Strike Eagle over Iraq and Afghanistan. She had been feared in the air and feared on the campaign trail when she had unseated an incumbent Senator in Colorado.

But Charlize was no longer that woman. She felt broken, and sometimes she wasn't sure how much longer she could hold the pieces together.

She pulled the covers up to her chin, shivering as if she could still feel the freezing wind of that day in Denver when she'd gotten the call about the car wreck that killed her husband Richard and put her son Ty in a wheelchair. The next breath was cold enough to sting her lungs. The room was cold. Too cold.

Sitting up, she rubbed her eyes and scanned the bedroom of her D.C. apartment, just a few blocks from Capitol Hill.

Usually, she would be able to hear the sporadic honking of cars and the blare of emergency sirens, no matter how late or early the nightmare woke her. Tonight, there was only silence.

Something was wrong.

The bedside alarm clock was dark. She grabbed the remote and pointed it at the TV to check the news, but nothing happened.

She plucked her cell phone from the nightstand and clicked the home button. The screen was blank.

She tried a second time.

Nothing.

The building must have lost power, and her phone, which had been nearly dead when she went to bed, had died on the charger. She crossed the room to the window and pulled back the curtain. Rain slid down the glass. Past the blur of water, she gazed out over the nation's capital.

The city was shrouded in darkness.

She flinched at a rap on her apartment door, but she didn't turn away from the view. Four stories below, she could see the silhouettes of cars on the street. None of the vehicles were moving. It was if they had all just run out of gas.

An arc of lightning webbed across the skyline, providing a momentary glimpse of the city. The outlines of the US Capitol, the White House, and the National Mall emerged for a single moment before the light receded.

She focused on the flickering glow of what could have been a fire. It was miles away, far enough that she couldn't see what had caused it.

Another knock sounded on the apartment door, harder this time.

"Hold on," Charlize said as she threw on slacks and a t-shirt.

She opened the door to see the trusted face of her chief of staff, Clint Johnson. The forty-five-year-old staffer was drenched to the bone. He was panting and his hair was mussed.

"Why are you out of breath?" Charlize stepped to the side and gestured for Clint to come in.

"I ran here," Clint gasped. He took in another long breath and added, "From the Capitol."

"Sit down and get a hold of yourself," Charlize said. "Tell me why you're here."

Clint nodded and pulled off his coat and draped it over the back of a chair. Then he took a seat at the dining room table. "Ma'am, there's a situation."

Charlize looked back at the bedroom window. "Some sort of wide-scale power failure?"

"Not exactly," Clint said. He allowed himself another breath and scratched at his perpetual five o'clock shadow like he was trying to buy himself time to find the right words.

Her mind was racing like it did back in the days when she flew an F-15 into battle. "Clint, tell me what the hell is going on."

"I got a call from General Lexton a couple hours ago. He tried calling you first, but you didn't pick up."

"My phone's dead," Charlize said. Brett Lexton was an old friend now serving as Chief of Staff of the Air Force. They went back twenty years, but this was the first time he had ever called her at night. "I'm supposed to meet with him tomorrow at the Pentagon."

"This wasn't about your meeting, Charlize. He had new intel on the situation on the Korean Peninsula."

Charlize narrowed her green eyes. The last time Clint had called her by her first name was four years ago, the night of the wreck that changed her life.

"What kind of intel?"

"He wouldn't say; he just told me to tell you to call him. Could the power outage be from an attack on the grid?"

She moved into the other room to look out the window again. The tensions were at an all-time high between the United States and North Korea. They couldn't prove the Americans had been behind the raid that had saved Senator Sarcone's granddaughter eighteen months prior, but between that and President Drake's aggressive maneuvers with the Navy, the North Koreans had been on edge. Other than the usual saber rattling, however, they hadn't threatened any specific actions against America.

"It's crazy down there," Clint said. "Every car I saw is dead."

As she watched, a police officer approached one of the growing groups with his hands raised in a placating gesture. She guessed the mob was bombarding him with questions.

Clint continued talking, but Charlize wasn't listening. Her eyes were locked on the faint glow to the north. As she scanned the horizon, she saw more fires burning at the outskirts of the city.

Something terrible had happened out there tonight. As her mind reeled, she clung to one urgent thought: *I have to get to my son.*

"Is your phone working? Ty is at the Easterseals camp in Empire, Colorado. I need to make sure he is safe."

"I don't have a signal," Clint said, holding up his phone. He slipped it back in his pocket. "I'll find someone that does and have Ty picked up."

"How, if the power and phones are out?"

"They can't be out *everywhere*, right?"

Charlize shook her head, uncertain. "The Capitol and the White House will have backup power."

A horrible suspicion entered her mind as she studied the darkened city. In the wake of Nine-Eleven, the government and the military had begun toughening their defenses and planning for every possible type of terrorist attack. She'd been briefed about the possibility of a coordinated electromagnetic pulse attack. The United States was far more vulnerable than the average citizen realized, and it wouldn't take much to completely disrupt life in the country. Such an attack could knock out the power grid, disable all electronic devices, and even cause planes to fall from the sky.

"So what do we do, ma'am?" Clint asked.

Half of Charlize's focus was in Colorado. Nathan was probably already in Empire. He would look after Ty. But what if he hadn't made it there? If he'd been recalled to duty, and if the power outage was the result of an EMP, then... no, she couldn't even think about that. After everything she'd been through, she couldn't lose her little brother, too.

She pivoted from the window to face her chief of staff.

"What do we do? We prepare, Clint. We prepare and head to the Capitol."

She stalked to her closet, recalling something she had learned when she flew missions over Iraq and Afghanistan. Watching the government crumble there had taught her that when the infrastructure of a country collapsed, it didn't take long for civilized society to break down. If the grid was down from an EMP attack, it wouldn't take long for chaos to reign over the United States.

Opening her closet, she bent down and reached for the lockbox at the bottom.

"Go get my car keys from the kitchen table," she said. He returned a minute later and handed her the key ring.

Charlize inserted the smallest key into the lockbox to reveal her M9 and four extra magazines.

"Ma'am, with all due respect...."

Charlize silenced him by palming one of the magazines into the pistol with a click. She tucked it into her waistband. Then she put the other magazines into her bugout bag and threw it over her shoulder.

"Do you trust me?" she asked.

There wasn't a single second of hesitation in his voice. "Yes, Senator."

"Good, because I have a feeling that whatever happened may have just changed the world."

5

"WHAT DO YOU MEAN THE COUNTRY HAS BEEN ATTACKED?" Sandra asked the wounded pilot.

"I can't tell you anything more than that because I simply don't know." Nathan limped down the dirt path, leaning on a stick he'd found.

"So you can tell me we've been attacked, but not by who, or why, or…"

"That's exactly what I'm saying. I'm a pilot, not a politician, but you've heard the news. I'm sure we can both guess who was behind this."

"North Korea?"

Nathan didn't reply. He was moving at a good clip, faster than Sandra could comfortably walk. She increased her pace to a jog.

"Listen, I'm not going to tell anyone," Sandra said. "But

I have a daughter in Loveland. If she's in danger, I deserve to know what's going on."

"I'm sorry, ma'am—"

"*Stop* calling me that. My name is Sandra Spears, and I am not an old lady."

Nathan halted and turned around so fast she almost ran into him. They were close enough she could smell his breath. It was odd being this close to a man and not catching the scent of alcohol.

"Ms. Spears, I also have family out there. My nephew is at a camp not too far from here. I appreciate you wrapping my ankle, and I understand your concern. But I can't tell you anything beyond what I've already said. If I learn otherwise, I will gladly share this information. But for now, my mission is to get to the nearest town and find a way to communicate with command."

Sandra sidestepped around the pilot and kept walking down the hill leading back to Highway 34. He followed in silence, descending carefully down the steep trail. Yellow and purple wildflowers with bell-like petals grew along the path. The bottom of the trail opened into a meadow carved in half by the Fall River, which cut through the green pasture and wrapped back up to the highway.

"Keep low," Nathan said, watching the cars and stranded motorists on the road above as if he wanted to avoid civilians.

Sandra considered asking why, but she'd had the same idea to avoid other people. For a fleeting moment, the observation terrified her. If Nathan wanted to avoid contact with anyone else then something was really wrong.

The country had been at war for as long as she could remember. But that was overseas. Had he meant there was an attack on American soil?

Of course that's what he meant.

Sandra paused in her tracks, her heart beating so hard she could feel it throbbing in her neck.

"Major, should I be worried about my daughter's safety?"

Nathan had opened his mouth to reply when a shout echoed from the road.

"Hey! Hey, *you*. Down there!"

Sandra and Nathan looked up to the road. A crowd of stranded drivers had gathered along the railing by the side of the highway. In the front of the group stood a barrel-chested man wearing a tight flannel shirt. He wedged a cigarette between his lips, took a drag, and then shouted, "You one of them pilots?"

Sandra took a step back when she saw the shotgun the man was carrying.

"Stay by your vehicles, help is coming," Nathan yelled back.

The man flicked the cigarette onto the ground, crushed it with his cowboy boot, and hocked spit over the railing. "Like hell. I want to know what killed our cars."

"Keep walking," Nathan whispered. He started moving back to the trail, and Sandra trotted after him.

"Hey!" the man yelled. "I asked you a *goddamn* question. Don't you turn your back on a soldier."

Nathan stopped and pivoted back to the road. "I don't know what happened, sir, but help will be coming soon. Just stay where you are or walk into town."

The other people muttered and began to disperse, but not the soldier. He climbed over the railing and slid down the embankment. "Get back here and tell me what the hell is going on."

"Is this guy serious?" Sandra muttered.

Nathan turned his back on the irate man. "We don't have time for this."

Sandra eyed the shotgun one more time, then took off running after Nathan. He moved fast enough that she had trouble keeping up, and when she told him to slow down or risk doing more serious damage to his ankle, the pilot only sped up.

"If you hurt yourself, I'm not carrying you through the woods into town," she said. "And since I'm the only one of us who actually knows how to get there, maybe you could slow down and let me lead."

That made him pause. He looked back at her and then stepped to one side to let Sandra walk ahead of him. She would have laughed at the surprised expression on the major's face, but she was too worried to enjoy the moment.

Only an hour had passed since the planes had dropped from the sky, but some people were already panicking. It wouldn't take long for others to follow. Fear was, in Sandra's opinion, the most powerful emotion in the world. It was fear, not love, that had trapped her in a series of bad relationships with addicts who vented their rage on her. Fear turned normal, law-abiding citizens into panicked mobs—and drove paranoid soldiers to chase strangers through the woods with a shotgun.

Sandra flinched at the crack of a gunshot nearby. The

blast echoed through the valley, framed on both sides by raging fires, and she began to run.

>>——

"Did you hear that?" Raven asked.

He helped Colton lay Melissa's limp body in the back seat of the Chief's Ford Explorer. They draped a blanket over her.

"Sounded like a gunshot." Raven pulled off his baseball cap and looked toward Highway 34. "My ears are still ringing from those explosions. I must be hearing things."

"Must be, 'cause I didn't hear anything," Colton said. He carefully shut the door to the truck. "You heading back to town?"

Raven shrugged and looked toward Estes Park, trying to find its familiar glow in the distance.

"You can follow me to the station, and I'll have Margaret cut you a check."

Raven put his soaked cap back on and attempted to straighten the bent bill. "Sounds good." He turned to his Jeep Cherokee but hesitated. "You sure you don't want to tell me any of your theories about those jets?"

Colton climbed into the driver's seat and inserted the key into the ignition. "I thought you were already convinced it was the end of the…"

He trailed off as he turned the key and nothing happened. "What the hell?" Colton muttered. He cranked the key again, but there was nothing. No click, no whining sound. Nothing at all. Glancing up, he checked the overhead lights, then turned to look in the back seat.

"Won't turn on? I have a pair of cables," Raven said. He stepped closer to the truck, eyeing the dark taillights. That was odd. Not a single light had turned on. They hadn't been gone that long. No way the truck would lose all of its juice so quickly.

Colton stepped back out onto the parking lot, rocks crunching under the weight of his boots. Raven lit a cigarette. Drawing in a long drag, he watched warily as the Chief began eyeing his Jeep.

Colton held out his hand. "Give me your keys."

Raven took in another drag and raised a brow. After exhaling a cloud of smoke, he said, "Keys to what?"

"I don't have time to play games right now. Just give me your keys."

Raven fished in his pocket and pulled out a keyring with a coyote's foot on the end. He wasn't sure what the hell was going on, but he was too cold and downright scared to argue with Colton. Instead of tossing the keys over, however, he slid behind the wheel of his Jeep and cranked it. The engine rumbled to life. He turned it off again and looked at Colton.

"Looks like it's just your ride," he said.

"How old's your Jeep?"

"1974. This baby's older than me."

"Shit," Colton muttered. "This ain't good."

"Chief, you want to tell me what the hell is going on? You're really starting to screw with my head."

"You want to know my theory? Well here it goes, Raven. I don't think this was an accident. I think an EMP did this."

"EMP? Isn't that a band from the 70s?" Raven asked.

"Electromagnetic pulse," Colton explained, shaking his

head. "Could be caused by a nuclear weapon being detonated in the upper atmosphere."

"A nuke? You got to be fucking kidding me. You think someone nuked the United States?"

Creek sat on his hind legs beside Raven and whined, pawing the man's leg. Raven bent down and stroked the Akita's fur.

"You been listening to the news, man?" Colton said, "The situation with North Korea is really bad. One of my old service buddies told me there's a rumor that a senator's kid got herself caught on the wrong side of the border, and a whole platoon of Marines had to blow up a prison compound to get her out."

Raven scratched nervously at his nose and considered setting the record straight. He tried not to think about his final mission too often, and he'd been sworn to secrecy about what he'd witnessed in North Korea. In the year and a half since leaving the Corps, Raven had tried to drown those memories in a bottle, but he could still see Billy's shattered face and the look of betrayal in Lee's eyes in the split second before Gunnery Sergeant Black blew his brains out. But surely that mission had nothing to do with whatever had happened here tonight?

The Chief was doing what cops always did—looking for somebody to blame. He didn't know the North Koreans were behind this, and he certainly didn't know that Raven had been part of the team who rescued Sarcone's granddaughter.

"You remember that flash we saw up in the meadow that was followed by what sounded like an explosion? That could have been from a bomb," Colton was saying.

"Hold on, Chief," Raven said, holding up his hands. "If that was a nuke, it would have been much louder than thunder and we would have seen more than a flash."

"Not if it was set off really high in the atmosphere. That would let the electromagnetic pulse cast a very large umbrella. Think of it like a massive lightning bolt that hits every house, car, and electrical device in a region. It would fry everything with microcircuits. That's why my car won't turn on and why my radio is dead. My cell signal is gone, too."

Colton jerked his chin toward the fires in the distance. "Your Jeep was built before the fancy computers were installed in cars."

Raven patted the hood of his Jeep and forced a smile, something he had practiced many times, but deep down he felt sick to his stomach. *This has nothing to do with you,* he told himself. *It's not your fault.*

"Must have been a really powerful EMP to drop those jets out of the air," Colton continued. "It could have also knocked out the grid in multiple states. I'm pretty sure those jets were from Buckley AFB. They don't fly training missions this way. I had a buddy that worked with the 120th a few years back."

"You don't know what really happened," Raven said, choosing to ignore the fact that he'd been the one asking the Chief to theorize in the first place.

Colton nodded curtly. "You're right. And I won't know until I get back to town."

"And I'm guessing you need a ride."

"If it's not too much trouble," Colton said. "Otherwise, I could just commandeer your vehicle."

"Okay, but hurry it up. I want to check on my sister."

With another nod, Colton marched over to his truck and struggled to lift Melissa's body. Raven hadn't realized his Jeep would be serving as both taxi and hearse tonight, but he hurried over to help the Chief anyway.

Together, they carried her body out of the Explorer and put her in the back of the Jeep. Raven had added a second row of seats in the old vehicle, and the cargo space was cramped.

The blanket covering Melissa's face slipped down as Colton set her carefully inside. He pulled it back up to cover her with deliberate care. Then he walked back to his own vehicle and started pulling out heavy duffel bags, a shotgun, and his AR-15, stacking it all neatly in the back of the Jeep.

"What is all this stuff?" Raven asked.

"My war bag and my primary bug-out bag," Colton replied. "Plus my work gear. You tellin' me you don't carry a bug-out bag?"

Raven raised a brow. "I have some survival gear at home."

"That's the point. It's at home, not here when you need it."

Shrugging, Raven whistled at Creek, who jumped into the passenger seat of the Jeep. Raven shook his head and pointed at the back, and the dog reluctantly climbed into the second row.

"Thanks," Colton said.

"For what?" Raven asked.

Instead of answering him, Colton piled into the Jeep and tried his radio again. With Creek, Melissa, and Colton's gear safely inside, Raven climbed into the driver's side and fired up the Jeep again. It purred to life, the forty-three-year-old engine settling into a steady rhythm. Part of him still wanted to believe that Colton was wrong, that everything they'd witnessed tonight was just a series of unfortunate coincidences.

Colton suddenly looked up, an expression of dawning horror on his face. "Oh my God," he whispered.

"What?" Raven asked.

"I just realized something."

Raven remained silent, afraid to ask.

"Fallout," Colton said quietly. "If that was a nuke, then the radiation could kill us all."

6

Sandra panted heavily as she ran through the underbrush. Chokecherries and junipers scraped against her legs, tearing holes in her scrubs. She stepped in a pile of elk shit and cursed as she wiped it off in the dirt.

"Keep moving," Nathan whispered.

Moonlight guided them deeper into the forest. The steep ground was slick and studded with sharp, moss-covered rocks. She was worried about Nathan's ankle. One wrong move, and he could end up making it worse.

He stopped and gestured for Sandra to get down. She knelt next to him behind a maple tree and scanned the meadow they had left behind. Her breaths came out in icy puffs. She was wet, cold, and now she was bleeding from dozens of scratches.

"I don't think he followed us," Nathan said after a few moments of silence. "How far are we from town?"

"Half a mile from the first of the resorts, maybe a bit farther."

Nathan looked over Sandra's shoulder, squinting as if he was trying to focus. She turned and froze, heart punching her ribs when she saw a huge silhouette moving through the trees. As the creature moved up the embankment, she saw it wasn't the soldier but an elk. After a moment, a second, smaller silhouette moved into the light.

They watched the majestic animals walk across the meadow, stopping to graze every few seconds. The male suddenly looked in their direction, mouth still chewing. Ears perking, the creature halted. A moment passed and it bent back down to eat, clearly deciding that the humans weren't a threat.

Sandra envied the animals. They were protected by law in the park, so they didn't have to worry about much. Most of them weren't scared of humans anymore, and other predators were rare. Sandra still hadn't forgiven Raven for letting a couple of rich assholes kill a beautiful bull elk for money.

The babble of the Fall River, unseen beside the trail, did little to calm her nerves as she walked. She waded through the forest, pulling back limbs and stepping over fallen trees. The hardest part was feeling out the uneven ground. Rocks of all sizes peppered the forest floor, camouflaged with yellow moss and orange lichen.

For fifteen minutes they trekked deeper into the woods. Sandra checked behind them every few steps to see if the soldier was following, but she couldn't see much in the darkness. With only the glimmer of the half-hidden moon to guide them, she was having a hard time seeing ten feet in front of her.

But every time she stumbled, it only strengthened her resolve. She had to get back to civilization and figure out what was going on. Allie would be in bed by now, so that gave Sandra at least eight hours to find a ride to Loveland to pick her daughter up. She barely trusted Mark to watch Allie overnight, let alone in a crisis.

At last, they reached a grassy slope leading back up to Highway 34. The rooftops of a resort crested the pines down the road.

"Do you know where we are?" Nathan asked.

"We're past the park entrance and back in the city limits." Sandra looked to the east. "I don't think we can go much farther without returning to the road. It's too dark out here."

Nathan didn't hesitate. He continued up the hill, grimacing with each step. Sandra hurried after him. She wasn't used to being around men like this. Her brother was a strong man, but he never seemed to have much direction, especially after he left the Marines. He wouldn't tell her what had happened to him on his last tour of duty, but he had come back changed. Not so much that anyone other than his closest family would notice, but his smile had seemed more brittle, his behavior more reckless. The worst part was that he wouldn't tell her what was wrong.

Nathan grabbed the side of a tree and started working his way up the steep hill. She continued after him, feet sliding on pine needles. She reached out to grab a rock, skinning her palm.

"Ouch," she muttered.

"You okay?" He was leaning against a Douglas fir at the edge of the highway. There was a car a quarter mile away, but she couldn't see any passengers, and there was no movement at the first of the cabins along the road.

"I'm fine," she said.

"Let's keep moving then," Nathan ordered. He stood and waved her into the street as another voice echoed down the road.

"There you are!" The soldier with the shotgun stumbled out of the bushes.

"Dammit," Nathan growled. He held up a hand. "Listen, sir, I don't want any trouble. I'm just trying to get to town."

"Should we run?" she whispered.

Nathan shook his head.

"I told you to wait up," the soldier said, exhaling a cloud of cigarette smoke. He reached for the strap of his gun. "Is this some sort of terrorist attack? I need to know. I need to *prepare*."

Nathan didn't reply, and the man continued to walk toward them.

"You hard of hearing or what?" He flicked his cigarette onto the trail.

"Hey," Sandra said. "Pick that up."

The man looked down and then back at her like he didn't understand what the problem was.

"I'm not talking to you, lady," he said. Headlight beams swept across the road as the soldier hefted his shotgun. "Well I'll be damned, looks like the cars are back on!" he shouted.

Nathan grabbed Sandra by the wrist and pulled her back.

"Let's go," he said. She shook off his grip and started walking, but she could still feel the warmth of his fingers on her skin.

They made it a few feet before the soldier shouted after them. "Hey, who said you could leave!"

There was a clicking sound as the man pumped a shell into his shotgun.

"Just what I needed," Nathan whispered. He reached for his gun again, but this time she was the one to grab his wrist.

"Don't, please."

The source of the headlights came around a bend in the road. It was an old Jeep Cherokee.

Sandra smiled for the first time since her car had died.

"Raven," she said, letting go of Nathan.

"You know the driver?"

Sandra smiled. "He's my brother."

The Jeep stopped a few feet from the soldier. Two men stepped onto the road. It was Raven—and the person she least expected to see him with, Estes Park Police Chief Marcus Colton.

"Evenin', Chief," the soldier said.

Colton grabbed a rifle and then shut the car door. He kept the muzzle toward the ground.

"Dale," he replied. "Want to tell me why you got that shotgun out?"

Raven continued around the back of the truck to let Creek out while Colton approached Dale.

"Reckon we're under attack. Just trying to get some answers," Dale replied.

"These people aren't a threat to you," Colton said. "Why don't you lower your gun?"

"Sandra, is that you?" Raven asked.

She ran toward her brother, moving in a wide arc around Dale. Raven reached out and folded her in a hug. Creek ran up and nudged Sandra's leg.

"What the hell are you doing out here?" Raven asked.

"It's a really long story," she said. "Why are *you* here?"

Raven shook his head. "I'll tell you later."

Colton was approaching the irate soldier with his hand out. "I'm not going to tell you again to lower that shotgun."

"You got your gun out," Dale said as he raised the barrel of his shotgun from the ground. The muzzle swept past Sandra, and Raven pulled her out of the way, shielding her body with his.

"Watch it, asshole," Raven snapped. Creek bared his teeth, reading his handler's body movements.

"I'm just protecting myself," Dale said. He turned to look at Nathan but found himself staring directly into the barrel of a pistol.

"I'd listen very carefully," Nathan said in a firm voice. "This police officer asked you to drop your gun."

Dale's nostrils flared, and his eyes widened as he focused on the barrel.

"Drop the shotgun," Colton repeated in a low voice.

Sandra wrapped her arms across her chest, shivering from more than the cold.

"Last chance," Colton said.

"I'm a retired Army Ranger. Not a fucking terrorist," Dale said. "You're going to have to pry my gun out my cold…"

Colton directed the muzzle of his rifle at Dale's head,

pushing it against his skull. "I do not have time for this right now." He looked to Raven and said, "Take his shotgun."

Raven didn't hesitate. He pried the gun away from the soldier with little resistance.

"You're going to regret that, Injun," Dale said. Sandra scowled at him, struggling to hold back the torrent of insults she longed to shout at the racist prick.

Nathan backed away and holstered his pistol like nothing had happened. "I need a ride into town. Will that be a problem?"

"Nope," Colton said as he took Dale's gun from Raven and slung it over his back.

Raven was still glaring at Dale. "This guy is not getting in my Jeep."

Dale spat on the ground. Sandra pulled on her brother's hand, but he jerked it away, advancing on the soldier.

"Stop, Raven. Just walk away," she said.

"Listen to your Injun girlfriend," Dale said.

This time Sandra nearly hit the man.

"Dale, you just don't know when to shut your mouth," Colton said, stepping between them. "Back up toward the edge of the road, or I'm going to have to place you under arrest."

That seemed to get through to Dale. He walked a few paces to the side of the highway. Colton nudged Raven, and Sandra pulled on his arm. He stood there, breathing heavily. Creek was at his feet, waiting for orders.

"You're going to regret this, Marcus," Dale said.

"It's a long walk into town," Colton said. "Use it to cool off."

Dale spat on the pavement a second time. His face twisted into a scowl. "You're going to leave me out here barehanded to fend off the wolves?"

"There are no predators up here, dummy," Raven said. "Just you. What kind of man raises a gun toward a woman?" He shook his head and stomped away, muttering to himself.

When they got to the truck, Colton offered his hand to Nathan. "Chief of Police Marcus Colton."

"Major Nathan Sardetti."

They shook and Colton looked back at the mountains. "What happened up there?"

Nathan clenched his jaw and ignored the question. "You didn't see my wingman eject, did you?"

"Afraid not, but I didn't see you eject either, so he could have made it out." Colton looked toward the back of the Jeep. "This is going to sound crazy, but we're transporting the body of a young girl back to town. It's going to be a little crowded in the Jeep."

"You found Melissa?" Sandra asked. She avoided looking in the back window. Her Allie was about the same age, and she couldn't imagine the horror Melissa's parents were going through. She didn't *want* to imagine it.

"Let's get going," Colton said. He opened the front passenger door, put the seat down, and helped Sandra into the second row of seats. Then he scooted next to her. Raven opened the back lift for Creek. He jumped in and sat on his haunches.

Sandra twisted around to pet the dog on the head. A blanket covered Melissa's body, but it did little to stifle the smell. Ten years as a nurse had taught Sandra about all sorts of foul odors, but this one didn't make sense. It smelled like burned flesh, not decay. She held her breath and rolled down the window.

Raven fired up the Jeep and steered it away from Dale, who was standing in the middle of the road, hands on his hips. Colton pumped the shotgun shells out of Dale's gun and dropped it onto the pavement as they sped away.

Charlize cursed a blue streak the moment she reached the lobby of her apartment. A few residents were downstairs in their pajamas, some with flashlights, all asking what was going on. Candles burned on a centrally-located wooden table, the glow dancing off the walls and illuminating the exhausted faces of her neighbors.

She tried to avoid their curious gazes. She rarely talked to anyone here, but she did recognize some faces. The last thing she wanted right now was to field their questions.

An elderly woman with a cane shuffled over towards Charlize. "Senator, do you..."

Clint met her halfway and redirected the question to himself.

"Do you know why the lights are out, sir? It's cold in my apartment. When are they going to turn the heat back on?"

Charlize didn't stick around to listen to the conversation. She heaved her backpack higher on her shoulders and continued across the lobby. The digital clock on the wall had stopped at 9:45 p.m. It had to be after midnight now, but the streets were filled with people.

The double glass doors swung open, and Albert Randall rushed inside wearing his usual navy blue suit with a pair of tennis shoes instead of his polished dress shoes. He ducked his shaved head to clear the door and searched the room with the beam of a heavy flashlight, stopping when he saw Charlize.

"Damn, it's good to see you," Charlize said. Her eyes flitted to his shoes. On any other occasion, she would have cracked a joke.

Albert wiped his forehead. "It's getting wild out there."

"Is your family okay?"

"My wife Jane is taking our daughters Kylie and Abigail to her mom's farmhouse first thing in the morning. It's about a day's walk out of the city. My brother Fred is going with them."

"That's probably a good idea," Charlize said. She reached up to put a hand on Albert's shoulder. "I appreciate you sticking with me, Big Al. I know you'd rather be with them."

"Not abandoning you now, ma'am." His southern drawl was strong and reassuring. Charlize was glad to have him by her side. The six-foot-six former football player had been on her security detail for five years, and he'd seen her through some hard times. She was more grateful than he knew for both his strength and his kindness.

"Good. I'm heading out," she said. "I need to get to Capitol Hill."

"Are you sure that's a good idea? Maybe we should stay put for now," Clint said, joining them.

"We trained for this, sir," Albert said. "Remember Eagle Horizon?"

Clint nodded. "We're supposed to be making a mad dash

to the Capitol, I know. But the more I think about it, the more that sounds like a terrible idea."

"We're not going to fix anything by hiding here," Charlize said. "Let's go."

Albert opened the door and waved them onto the sidewalk. He kept out in front, walking slowly, one hand inside his suit jacket, the other directing a flashlight on every civilian as if they might be a threat.

As they left the glow of the lobby, the darkness of the massive city closed in. The suffocating atmosphere made everything seem distorted, like Charlize was a lone fish exploring a coral reef.

"Stay close, ma'am," Albert said. He centered his flashlight on the sidewalk, pointing out hazards for Clint and Charlize to avoid. They worked their way down 12th Street, keeping away from people as best they could. Candles flickered in the windows of apartment buildings. On one stoop, residents were huddled around an oil lamp, talking in low, worried voices. Stranded drivers stood beside their cars, unsure whether to abandon them. Everyone was asking the same question: "Why are the lights off?"

Albert motioned for Charlize and Clint to cross the street as they approached a Walgreens. A throng of people had gathered outside the shuttered store. There were a few stragglers outside the nearby Radio Shack, peering into the window. If the power didn't come back on soon, she feared there would be looting or riots.

Charlize's gaze flitted to the sky. Where there should have been a steady stream of jets taking off from Reagan and Dulles, there were only clouds drifting aimlessly across the horizon.

"A couple thousand planes were probably airborne when the power went off," she said. "The only reason we're not seeing wreckage here is because of the no-fly zone over D.C."

"Yeah, and think about all of the fighter jets we probably scrambled," Clint said. "I'm guessing we lost…" His words trailed off when he saw Charlize's face.

Dear God, please let Nathan be okay. Please let my son be okay.

Over the years, Charlize had prayed less and less often. Most of the time it didn't seem like anyone was listening, especially after the accident. But deep down she still had faith, and she called on it now to steady her. Falling apart wouldn't help Ty or Nathan. She would have to trust God to keep them safe until she could reach them.

Charlize looked away from the vacant sky. Ahead, a group of people had surrounded a police cruiser. Two officers were trying to reassure the crowd.

"What do you mean, you don't know what's going on?" a woman asked in a raised voice. "My car won't turn on, my phone won't work, and I don't see a single light in the entire city."

"I bet it was those Russians I read about on the internet!" a man cried.

"Idiot," snapped another woman. "Haven't you been listening to the news? If we were attacked, it was by ISIS."

"Please, people, calm down," one of the officers said.

No one was saying what she was thinking—that the

North Koreans had hit D.C. with an EMP. She certainly wasn't going to volunteer her opinion.

Charlize shook her head as more rumors began to fly from the crowd. Rumors would make things worse, escalating the fear and unease into outright panic. She recalled Hurricane Katrina, when New Orleans collapsed into pure anarchy. Without power, communication, and emergency services, things would fall apart here, too.

It was all the more reason they needed to get to the Capitol. The first objective was to get to her office and figure out what was going on. From there she would work with her colleagues to determine a plan, and finally, she would communicate that plan as far and wide as she could. With the plan complete, she would find a ride to Empire, Colorado, and pick up her son.

"We should cut across the Mall," Albert said. "Fewer civilians."

He walked out into the intersection of 12th and Pennsylvania. The block was mostly void of people, but a few teenagers were hanging out outside the Washington Wine and Liquor shop, eyeing the windows. Big Al walked past them, giving his best glower, and the teens thought better of looting the liquor store.

As she walked, Charlize went over scenarios in her mind, but the more she thought about it, the more it didn't make sense. Why would North Korea launch a preemptive EMP attack? Mutually assured destruction had stopped America and the Soviets from firing nukes during the Cold War, and it had prevented India and Pakistan from blowing each other to hell. So what had driven the supreme leader of North

Korea to plan an attack against the US when he knew it would result in the death of his people?

Madness, Charlize thought. She had heard the intelligence reports on the North Korean leader. It was no secret the bastard was insane, but she didn't know he was *this* insane.

"Wouldn't go that way if I were you!" one of the teenage boys shouted. "Some dude got stabbed before the lights went out. You can see his guts!"

The teenagers were standing on the corner of the sidewalk now. They pointed toward an ambulance halfway down the street. Several people were lingering around the paramedics, who were working on a patient.

"Go home," Albert ordered.

"Whatever," said the teenager. The kids laughed and took off on their skateboards.

Charlize could see the wheels turning in Albert's mind, but he only hesitated for a moment. With a wave of his flashlight, he directed them onward. They kept to the side of the street opposite from the paramedics. As they passed, one of them stood and pulled off gloves dripping with blood.

"Call it," she said.

Charlize was focused on the scene and didn't notice the blur of motion coming around the corner until it was too late. The front window of the CVS on their right shattered, sending shards of broken glass to the pavement.

"Grab the hard shit!" someone shouted as two black-clad figures rushed the pharmacy.

"Get back," Albert said, waving Charlize behind him.

A woman screamed as the two hooded men used bricks

to punch out the jagged glass. They dropped the bricks and climbed inside.

Albert held out a tree trunk of an arm and ushered her away from the broken windows. "Ma'am, let's go."

More people were watching now, including the two paramedics.

"Ma'am!" Albert repeated when Charlize didn't move. He turned to look at her, his eyes widening as he saw the gun in her hands. "Where the hell did you get that?"

Pulling the M9 was almost a reflex. She was trained to protect herself, senator or not. The smooth handle of the gun felt reassuring in her hands.

The clatter of falling shelves and breaking glass came from the store, and a moment later the two men re-emerged cradling boxes of prescription drugs. Their faces were covered with skulls masks, but Charlize could see their wild eyes.

"Hey, you!" shouted a voice.

Two figures were approaching—police officers with shotguns shouldered.

"Agent Randall, Capitol Police!" Albert shouted back. He held out his badge, but both officers were already directing their guns toward the looters.

"Hands on your head!" one of them shouted.

Both of the men stepped forward, glass crunching under their shoes. The bigger of the pair dropped the boxes and turned to run.

"Don't move!" the other officer yelled.

The looters took off in separate directions, prescription drug boxes tumbling across the concrete. The officers gave chase, and Charlize finally lowered her gun. She stuck it back into her waistband as the police vanished around the next corner.

"Ma'am," Albert began to say.

"I know. Let's go."

The paramedics retreated to their ambulance and the crowd moved on, the chatter of the shocked citizens echoing down the streets.

Albert kept his gun out as he crossed into Pennsylvania Avenue. The dome of the Capitol looked eerie in the moonlight, like something out of a dream—familiar, and at the same time, utterly strange.

They turned down 12th Street, heading for the Mall. Albert guided them around the dead vehicles, some of them still guarded by their owners, all waiting to be rescued or told what to do.

Charlize, Albert, and Clint didn't stop to answer their questions. The nighttime trek through the nation's capital reaffirmed her worst suspicions. Americans, in most cases, were not ready for a catastrophe. Most of these city dwellers wouldn't survive the month without cell phones and take-out dinners.

Pop, pop, pop.

Gunshots sounded nearby, and Charlize's hand went for her gun. There was no way to know if the officers were firing on the looters, or if the looters had been armed, or if it had anything to do with the robbery she'd just witnessed.

Waving with the beam of his flashlight, Albert said, "Come on, ma'am, we're almost there."

The familiar shapes of the Smithsonian Institution

emerged in the darkness. Charlize kept pace with Albert as they neared the National Mall. They had made it to Constitutional Avenue when another sound rang out. It started off as a guttural booming not unlike a rocket blasting off, and it quickly rose into a thundering *vroom*.

Charlize halted in the middle of the empty street. Far beyond the edges of the dark city, something was rising into the sky above the ocean, leaving a trail of fiery exhaust. She followed the trail up, recognizing the nuclear-tipped ballistic missile. *Mutually assured destruction,* she thought. Intellectually, she had already accepted this could be the end of the world, or at least the world she knew. But actually seeing the launch of the retaliatory strike was different. She felt the shock like a physical blow, not unlike the times her F-15 Strike Eagle was shot at in Afghanistan.

The missile, joined by several others in the distance, streaked into the clouds as they curved away from an American submarine lurking somewhere under the chilly surface of the Atlantic Ocean. She had little doubt they were headed to turn North Korea into a smoking crater.

"My God," Clint said.

"God has nothing to do with this," Charlize whispered. "This is mutually assured…" Her words trailed off, unable to finish her sentence. Somewhere inside of her she had held onto hope that things weren't as bad as they seemed, but that, she knew, was a lie.

Albert lowered his gun and flashlight like a soldier surrendering to the enemy. "Were those nukes?"

Charlize nodded and said, "Fire from the clouds," the

motto of the 33rd Fighter Wing—a motto she never thought she'd use again.

She watched the final missile disappear into the sky, and then she took off running toward Capitol Hill.

7

Raven slowed as his headlights washed over a snaking line of people on the road. Hundreds of people from Estes Park had been out looking for Melissa Stone when the F-16s fell from the sky. Those that weren't with the largest group searching at Prospect Mountain were returning from a sweep of the foothills outside the park.

Raven was still attempting to process everything that had happened in the past four hours, and Major Sardetti wasn't helping matters.

"This is all confidential," Nathan was saying. "What I'm telling you should not be relayed to the public. It will only incite panic; that's why I was reluctant to tell you anything, Ms. Spears."

"Understood," Colton said. "But as police chief, I need to know what's going on."

"First Lieutenant Blake and I were sent on a combat air patrol earlier this evening at the governor's request. It seemed like a routine CAP. Thirty minutes in, the air traffic control from Tinker Air Force Base in Oklahoma contacted the two other pilots from the 120th to check out a Chinese commercial airliner heading toward Wichita over the Rockies. A few minutes after that, the Chinese pilots became unresponsive. The airliner changed course toward Denver and started climbing."

"Chinese?" Raven asked. "So this wasn't North Korea?"

"Let the major finish," Colton said. "I'm guessing there's more to the story."

Nathan nodded. "It wasn't a Chinese plane; it was a North Korean Ilyushin II-28 that was carrying a nuclear weapon. Best way I can figure it is the North Koreans used fake transponder codes to look like a Chinese plane. Those bastards are damn good at hacking. Blake and I turned around for support when the plane went off radar. By the time we saw the blast, it was too late. The EMP fried our systems, and I lost all control of my Viper."

Raven wanted to pound the steering wheel but gripped it tighter instead. His jaw clenched as if he was trying to bite back the confession of what his team had done in North Korea eighteen months earlier. He already felt like the guilt was going to smash him flatter than roadkill.

Sandra caught his gaze in the rearview mirror. She had a hand over her mouth, and her eyes were shining with unshed tears.

"I have to find a working radio to contact Buckley AFB," Nathan said. "Do you have any ham radios at the station?"

Colton shook his head. "Afraid not. Everything went to digital."

"Great," Nathan said. "My nephew is near Empire, so if I can't find a radio here, my next priority is to reach him. How far is it from Estes Park?"

"A couple hours south of here by car," Colton said. "But on foot…"

Raven steered the Jeep around an abandoned car and continued toward the town, passing the cabins and resorts nestled along Fall River.

"Major, what about the nuke?" Colton said. "How much of the grid would it have knocked out?"

"Hard to say. Depends on how powerful the weapon was."

"Guess," Raven said.

Nathan scratched his chin. "From what I know about nuclear attacks, experts say it would only take one very powerful weapon set off at eighty thousand feet or so over Missouri or another central location to knock out our entire grid."

"How far up was that plane?" Raven asked.

"Over fifty thousand feet," Nathan replied. "My guess is that all of Colorado is dark."

Sandra gasped from the back seat. "The entire state?"

"What about radiation?" Colton asked. "Should we be worried?"

Nathan focused his green eyes on Colton. "It depends on the winds, and again, on the power of the weapon."

"I'll ask my officers to find the battery-operated Geiger counters as soon as I get back to the station."

"I have another question," Raven said.

Nathan looked over.

"Is it possible there were more nukes set off across the country?"

"I'm praying that's not the case," Nathan said. "But I think we should all prepare for the worst."

A hard silence filled the vehicle. Raven wished he could turn on some tunes to lighten the mood, but none of the regular channels were broadcasting anymore. More than anything, he wished he could drown himself in a bottle of liquor. But if the country was at war, he would need his senses sharp.

He eased off the gas as they approached a group of people waving from the center of Highway 34 just outside of town.

"Keep driving," Colton ordered.

No one spoke for several moments. Sandra broke the silence with a whimper. She cupped her head with her hands. "This day just keeps getting worse. First that note, then..."

"What note?" Raven asked.

Sandra looked up and shook her head. "It's nothing. I just want to get Allie back."

"Don't worry, Sis. We'll get her after we drop them off at the station."

"Okay," she said, sucking in another breath. "Okay."

"Honestly, if I were you, I'd stay put," Nathan said.

Raven twisted to look him in the eye. "Why's that?"

"Aside from the threat of radiation? Look ahead."

Clicking the high beams back on, Raven steered down the final stretch of the highway before they hit town. The lights hit more figures trekking along the roadway, but he didn't see anything out of the ordinary. If there was one thing he hated more than being told what to do, it was being patronized.

"What, Major? Why don't you tell me what you see, 'cause I just see more people walking."

"That's the point," Nathan said. "There isn't a single other working car on the road right now. When people realize their cars aren't going to turn back on, they are going to be looking at this one with very envious eyes."

Raven reached for a cigarette and wedged it between his lips with shaky fingers. He didn't like Nathan's attitude, but the major was right. People were already stopping to look at his Jeep. If Nathan's theory was correct, then those curious stares were going to turn into something much worse in the coming days.

When they reached town, Raven turned onto the main street, a stretch of restaurants, jewelry and t-shirt shops, ice cream parlors, and hiking stores that was usually alive with tourists. Now it was empty save for a few pedestrians. One of them pointed at his vehicle, and Raven hit the gas.

The parking lot beside the town hall was mostly vacant, and the immaculate green grass of Bond Park was untouched by the usual couples and families. Raven pulled into the lot and put the Jeep in park. He tucked the unlit cigarette under the side of his baseball cap. If the world really was ending, then he'd need to ration his smokes.

"I'll help you with Melissa, then we're out of here," Raven said.

"You don't want to stick around to see what the Geiger counters say?" Colton got out of the truck and threw the strap of his AR-15 over his back.

Raven checked with his sister, but she shook her head. "I have to get to Allie."

"We're sure, Chief," he said.

"Suit yourself."

"Thanks for wrapping my ankle, Sandra," Nathan said, holding out his hand to her. Raven did not like the way the stuck-up major was looking at his sister. "Best of luck getting to your daughter."

Nathan glanced at Raven next. "Be careful out there. The roads are going to get dangerous. You drive to Loveland as fast as you can and don't stop for anything until you get there. That goes double for the trip back."

"Yes sir," Raven replied, barely keeping the sarcasm from his voice. Between Colton and this guy, he felt like he was back in the Marines again, being ordered around by a couple of bullies.

Nathan looked at Sandra one more time and then limped toward town hall. She climbed into the front seat and whistled for Creek to jump up with her.

Colton dropped his gear outside the front doors of town hall, propping one open with a bag. Then he returned for Melissa's body. With Raven's assistance, they hoisted her from the Jeep.

"Thanks for what you did up there. When you get back from Loveland, stop by the station. I'll make sure you get paid, plus a bonus for the extra trouble," Colton said.

Raven had completely forgotten about the check, which

was very unlike him. Hell, he wasn't even sure the bank would be able to cash a check now.

"Thanks, Chief." He paused and then added, "I'm sorry we couldn't save her."

Colton picked Melissa up in both arms and carried the dead girl into the building. Several officers came to help. One of them was Don Aragon, who gave Raven a stern look. If it were up to the patrol sergeant, Raven would be sitting behind bars in the Larimer County Jail. Raven tipped his hat to him with a wry grin as he walked away.

"You know where those Geiger counters are, Don?" Colton asked.

Raven didn't stick around to listen to the conversation. He shut the lift gate after retrieving his crossbow and his Remington 700 rifle. He didn't want to use them, but he was glad they were armed. Shit was about to get chaotic out here, and he had his family to protect.

Jumping in the truck, he handed Sandra the rifle. "Remember how to use this?"

Sandra stared at the rifle like it was some sort of alien artifact. He checked his sister's dark brown eyes. They were wide and frightened, but not panicked. After a moment, she rested the stock against her shoulder and angled the muzzle toward the open window.

"Yeah, I remember," she said.

"Good, because you're riding shotgun tonight, little sister. Let's go get Allie."

Charlize wished she could climb inside a fighter jet and tear through the sky, dropping bombs on the North Korean bastards that had sent the United States back to the stone age in the blink of an eye.

She could still hear the rumble of the rockets in the distance, but by the time the nukes reached Pyongyang, most of the government leaders and their families would already be underground. Satellite images had showed the massive bunkers the North Koreans had built to shield the elite from nuclear attacks. There were entire cities built below ground.

The twenty-eight thousand American troops on the border, along with the innocent North Korean and South Korean civilians, would likely die from the blast while the madman who had ordered the strike against the United States sheltered in luxury. She closed her eyes, hoping that the soldiers and civilians had gotten evacuation orders in time.

"You okay?" Clint asked.

Charlize lied to her Chief of Staff with a nod and continued down Madison Drive NW toward the Capitol. There were only two cars on the entire road, and Charlize didn't see a single person inside the dead vehicles. The soothing trickle of rain and the breeze whispering through the branches were the only sounds. The silence of the usually vibrant city gave her the chills. It was like being in outer space.

Albert jogged down the road, gun still drawn but the muzzle pointed at the ground. He checked their six every few feet and scanned the park for any signs of civilians, but the National Mall was deserted. Nothing stirred in the shadows.

It took them ten minutes to move down Madison Drive. They passed the National Gallery of Art, where Richard had liked to take Charlize on dates when she had first been elected to Congress. That seemed like so long ago. How long would it be before power and normalcy was restored to Washington? She had the terrible feeling that nobody would be enjoying lattes at the museum café for a long time—maybe never again.

"Ma'am," Albert said, keeping his voice low. He pointed at the intersection of 3rd Street, and Charlize ran to catch up. Clint panted a few paces behind her.

"I told you to quit smoking," Charlize said.

Clint forced a smile between breaths. "Working for you is stressful, ma'am. I have to relax somehow."

When they reached the corner of Pennsylvania, Albert clicked off his flashlight and halted. A cloud swallowed the moon, and blinding darkness spread across the city like a blanket had been pulled over it.

"Why are we stopping?" Clint whispered.

Charlize strained to see through the wall of darkness. It closed in, suffocating, pressing on her in the silence.

"Stay back," Albert said. "Senator, get behind me."

Charlize made out shapes moving across Pennsylvania Avenue. Combat experience taught her that the eyes could play tricks on you in the dark. The shapes might have been hostiles, or they might have just been shadows.

She reached for her M9, but she didn't yet pull it from her waistband. She kept an eye on the moving shapes, waiting for the next break in the clouds.

"Big Al, can we get some light back here?" Clint asked.

Albert didn't reply, and Charlize slowly pulled her M9. Something had the big guy spooked. The sound of footfalls on the concrete sent a spike of adrenaline through her veins, the tingle prickling up her arms. The noise seemed to be coming from every direction, but that was impossible. Charlize hadn't seen anyone behind them.

"Ma'am, Clint, put your hands above your heads," Albert said, his voice calm but firm.

A sliver of the moon suddenly emerged, and its glow fell over two dozen police officers surrounding them. They came from all directions, assault rifles and shotguns shouldered. Most of them were dressed in SWAT gear except for a squad of men moving up Pennsylvania wearing black suits and ties. The leader, a middle-aged man with a crew cut and solid jawline, shouldered a Knight's SR-16 CQB assault rifle.

"Drop your guns!" he shouted.

Albert quickly placed his pistol on the ground and said, "Albert Randall, Capitol Police. Badge number…"

An officer in SWAT gear kicked the pistol away from Albert and put his hands behind his back.

"Hands above your heads!" someone shouted at Charlize and Clint.

They both did as ordered.

"I'm Senator Charlize Montgomery, and I'm trying to get to my office," Charlize said.

The leader lowered his assault rifle as the SWAT officers patted Charlize and Clint down. One of the men yanked Charlize's M9 away. A flashlight shone in her face. She squinted at the bright light but didn't raise a hand to shield her eyes.

The man with the assault rifle kept the flashlight on Charlize. "I'm Special Agent Timothy Redline with the Secret Service. What's your security number, Senator?"

"1984Whiskey2001," Charlize quickly replied.

Agent Redline directed the light to a pad of paper and then glanced back up.

"My apologies, ma'am, but we've been moved to DEFCON 1 so I have to check everyone. My team will escort you to the Capitol."

Charlize wanted to ask a hundred questions, but there was just one that mattered right now. "How widespread is the power outage?"

Redline was looking over her shoulder, distracted.

"Agent?"

"Sorry, Senator, but I'm not sure. Things are chaotic and communication is slow," Redline said. "We need to keep moving. You will receive a full briefing once you get to safety. COOP has been implemented. We will be evacuating somewhere safe as soon as we have transportation. For now, we're heading to the Capitol."

"COOP, as in the Continuity of Operations Plan?" Clint asked, glancing at Charlize.

"Correct," she said.

"So that means…" Clint began to say.

Charlize finished his thought. "We're being moved out of D.C."

The news wasn't surprising, considering the nuclear missiles, but she had hoped this was a localized attack. Now she was starting to wonder. Could the entire grid be down nationwide?

"My gun, please," she said and reached out for her M9.

The officer who had taken the weapon handed it to her. Across the street, another team wearing SWAT gear was setting up a perimeter to cover the south streets. There were other checkpoints already set up to the west and east.

Redline motioned for three of his team members as the rest of the guards fanned out across the National Mall. Albert dipped his chin, signaling it was okay for Charlize and Clint to follow. They continued down the street after Redline and his men, the moonlit dome of the Capitol rising in the distance. Dozens of Secret Service officers and Capitol Police with assault rifles patrolled the grounds as if they were preparing for an imminent attack.

Charlize was a combat pilot before she was a politician; she knew no one could guarantee her safety. But now she wondered if the Secret Service was aware of other threats from North Korea. Could the EMP have been an overture to something worse?

8

There were bad nights on the job, and then there were terrible nights. This one was shaping up to be one of the worst in Colton's years of law enforcement. He palmed the table and waited for the chatter and the questions to die down.

He had a hundred things he needed to do, and his mind was racing. His first order had been to activate the emergency operations center. Captain Jake Englewood, his right-hand man, had already handled that. He stood next to Colton in the conference room, his burly form and bright red beard making him appear too big for the small space. Jake had coordinated the response and recovery to the floods that had knocked out much of the town's water and power in 2013, and Colton trusted him to help with this disaster.

"Hold your questions and stay calm," Jake said in his

authoritative voice. He rolled up his sleeves like he was preparing for a fistfight, revealing several tattoos—his way of telling everyone to shut the hell up. His size, his ink, and his booming voice had earned him the nickname "The Viking," but most people were too scared of Jake to say it to his face.

Officers Tom Matthew and Rick Nelson filed into the room. Both men were young, and Rick had a newborn at home. Colton had seen their frightened looks before on the faces of green soldiers in Afghanistan. He'd never thought he would see that kind of fear back at home. He nodded and gestured for them both to take a seat next to Margaret, the station's administrative assistant and dispatcher.

Next up was getting the battery-powered Geiger counters out to make sure they weren't about to all die of radiation poisoning. Once he figured out what they were dealing with, he would be better able to plan a response. After that he could handle the rest of his unpleasant to-do list, like contacting Rex and his wife to tell them their daughter was dead. Finally, he needed to get home to his own family and start making preparations. His wife and daughter were probably worried sick.

"Has anyone been able to get ahold of Mayor Andrews?" Colton asked.

"You don't really want her here right now, do you, sir?" Detective Lindsey Plymouth answered from across the table. Colton had recruited the feisty redhead from Denver as the newest member of his team, but sometimes he wondered if he'd made a mistake.

Colton acted like he hadn't heard Lindsey, but she was right. Mayor Gail Andrews was a micromanager, and she was constantly getting involved with police business. He scratched at the space between his upper lip and nose and then exhaled.

"All right, everyone, listen up. It's going to be a very long night. Here's the situation. Raven Spears and I found Melissa Stone about two hours ago on Ypsilon. She...she didn't make it. While we were up there, a pair of F-16s fell from the sky after a nuclear weapon was detonated at fifty two thousand feet."

The gathered officers gasped, and Lindsey shouted "Bullshit!" Colton couldn't give them a chance to digest the information. He continued before anyone could ask questions.

"Major Nathan Sardetti was able to eject from his F-16 before it crashed," Colton explained. "He's trying to get our radio to work and contact his base. The EMP knocked out every electronic in the city."

Detective Tim Ryburn ran a hand through his hair. "A nuke? Are you sure?"

"I bet that's what my wife and I heard at our ranch," Matthew said. "Sounded like a massive explosion, but we just thought it was the storm."

Lindsey was still shaking her head. "You're absolutely sure, Chief?"

"Hold your questions until I'm done."

She settled back into her seat and folded her arms.

"Most of you were here for the 2013 floods," Colton continued. "We were cut off then, and it looks like we're cut off now. But this is different. We may be at risk from fallout, and there's a murderer on the loose."

He scanned his officers. Several of the men and women in this room were rookies. Most of them had come here to avoid major crime in cities like Denver or Chicago. Estes Park was a quaint tourist town; the last murder had been years ago. But these were all good officers and he had to trust them.

"I've put Jake in charge of the EOC, but things are going to work differently than last time. For one, we probably aren't going to have access to the Red Cross, National Guard, or other agencies. I'm hoping we can make contact with Sheriff Gerrard at the Larimer County Office, but he's going to have his hands full."

The officers began muttering anxiously again, and Jake stepped in to settle them down. "We're lucky this happened off season. There are probably only around ten thousand people in town tonight, if you include all of the tourists."

Colton nodded. "Jake, I want you to work with Lindsey and Margaret on an inventory of every resource in town. From food and water to vehicles that still work. If it could possibly be useful, I want it on the list."

"Roger that, sir, I'll start first thing in the morning."

Colton shook his head. "Not in the morning. Right after this meeting."

"Do we *have* a single working vehicle?" Lindsey asked.

No one replied. Colton thought of Raven's Jeep and cursed himself for letting him take it to Loveland. He should have commandeered it when he had the chance.

"How about that guy on Moraine Avenue with the old Volkswagens for sale?" Ryburn asked. "I bet those will work. Maybe our H1 will start, too."

"Someone check it out after this," Colton said.

"I haven't started up my 1952 Chevy pickup in a while," Jake said. "I'll try it when I get home."

"Sounds good. Can someone check on Major Sardetti's progress with the radio?" Colton asked.

"I'll go," Margaret said.

"What about refugees?" Jake asked. "If there's fallout, then people are going to start leaving the cities. I'd be willing to bet some of them will make their way up here."

Colton shared a meaningful look with Jake. They had served together overseas on two tours. Their first time out, they'd been National Guardsmen stationed in Kabul, Afghanistan. The United States and her allies had softened up the city with bombing raids. When ground troops had finally infiltrated the capital, it had been in complete chaos. That was just one of multiple examples he could think of, from Syria to Lebanon to the Gaza Strip. When basic services like power were cut off, the refugees fled.

"We're going to have to set up shelters," Colton said. "What about the Stanley?"

"I'll talk to Jim," Matthew said.

Colton and the manager of the iconic hotel had been friends for a long time. The place had become famous after *Dumb and Dumber* and *The Shining* miniseries had been filmed there, and the old buildings were large enough to house thousands. It was a start.

"Refugees and stranded tourists aren't our only concern," Colton said. "Once people figure out what's going on, they are going to raid every supermarket, pharmacy, and hardware store."

"Most of the perishable stuff is gonna be spoiled in a day," Ryburn said. "Might as well eat it now."

Colton stood up straighter and, using his most commanding voice, said, "The first thing I'm officially doing as Chief of Police is declaring a state of emergency. I want an officer stationed at every building we deem a critical facility, starting with food, water, and medicine."

The order drew a few uncertain gazes, but he continued with his speech. "We are in a unique situation, folks. We have a constant water supply from the mountains, and we have a decent stock of food, but if that nuke knocked out power in several states, then we can't expect help anytime soon."

Several voices broke out around the table.

"What do you mean? Do you think there was more than one nuke?" Lindsey asked.

"Could there be more attacks?" asked Matthew.

"Chief, my wife and I have a baby at home," Nelson said. "If there's a killer on the loose, then…"

Colton sighed. "Everyone, please calm down."

The questions kept coming until Jake finally pounded on the table. "Chief Colton said to calm down!" he boomed.

The room quieted like the President of the United States had suddenly walked in.

Rustling came from the hallway, and then the door opened. Don, his uniform drenched, stepped into the room holding a large plastic crate. He placed it on the table. Panting, he announced, "I found them!"

Lindsey scooted over to make room. "What are those for?"

"They detect radiation," Colton said. He pulled out one of the Geiger counters and held up the probe. It had been years since he'd used one, and it took him a second to re-familiarize himself with the control panel. He found the audio switch. A clicking sound came from the device as he walked into the hallway and out of the building.

His staff followed him outside. Several flashlights flicked on, spreading beams over the parking lot. It was eerily quiet, and a soft drizzle fell from the sky. Jake and Don flanked Colton as he stepped out into the street. Holding up the probe to the sky, Colton watched the needle. The machine hissed static as he waved the probe back and forth.

"That doesn't sound good," Jake said.

Don leaned closer. "What's the reading?"

After making another pass, Colton checked the screen again and turned back to his staff.

"Looks like about .04 millrads per hour right now, which is normal. But the fallout might not have hit us yet. It could take a day or more depending on the winds."

The front doors swung open and Nathan limped out. He eyed the Geiger counter and raised an eyebrow.

"Are you detecting any radiation?" the pilot asked.

"Not yet," Colton said.

Nathan looked to the sky. "I'm not an expert, but I don't think there would be fallout if the fireball from the nuke didn't touch the ground, but that doesn't mean we're in the clear."

"How do you mean?" Colton asked.

"It's possible that a radioactive cloud might still be headed our way," Nathan said. "Again, I'm not sure because I have no form of communication to confirm this. Everything digital is fried. What I really need is a battery-powered analog radio. Doesn't anybody have a ham radio in this town? That's my best shot of contacting Buckley AFB."

"Bill Catcher is a ham radio operator," Jake said. "He also used to be a technician for the power company, way back in the day."

"And he's a spook," Lindsey said. "The guy signs his signature in blood."

"Yeah, he's not a big fan of the government and won't help us willingly if we ask for assistance," Jake said.

Colton lowered the probe and shut off the Geiger counter. "Don't phrase it as a question then. Jake, once you get the EOC set up, why don't you go pay Bill a visit? We're going to need his help whether he likes it or not."

"On it, Chief."

"I'll ride along," Nathan said. "If that's okay with you?"

Colton nodded at the pilot. "Whatever you need, Major. The rest of you head back inside for your assignments."

He lingered outside, gazing up at the moon hanging low over the mountains. It looked peaceful enough, but Colton had a bad feeling about all of this. He turned the Geiger counter back on and held up the probe toward the sky, hoping to God that something worse wasn't heading their way.

Rocky bluffs arced over Highway 34, blocking out much of the moonlight. If it weren't for the Jeep's headlights, Raven wouldn't have been able to see ten feet in front of him. He kept an eye out for stranded tourists or worse, a wandering elk. Hitting one of the beasts would be the end of his Jeep—and likely his and Sandra's lives.

His sister was staring blankly out the passenger window. "I still can't believe Melissa is gone. Could her killer really be the same person that was talking to Allie outside my house a few weeks ago? And what about that weird note I got? Could it be connected?"

"I don't know. According to Colton, the suspect was driving a blue F-150 pickup. That's the same type of truck you saw outside your house, right?"

"Yes," Sandra said. She looked away from the window, her face drawn and haggard. "How could any of this happen?"

Creek let out a low whine and then tucked his head back under her arm. She scratched him behind the ears, and the dog settled.

"What did that note say again?" he asked.

"*The storm is coming.* What is that even supposed to mean?"

"Honestly, I don't think it's connected to what happened to Melissa. One of your crazy neighbors or a lovesick patient you turned down for a date probably wrote it." He twisted the steering wheel to avoid a minivan stalled partway in his lane. The headlights captured a man putting gas into the van with a red canister. He looked toward the Jeep, shielding his eyes with one hand.

Raven glanced at the fuel gauge; the Jeep was down to less than half a tank. It would get him to Loveland, but not all the way home.

"My heart hurts, Raven. I'm truly scared right now."

"It's okay, Sis. We'll get Allie, and I won't let anything happen to either of you." He pulled the cigarette from his hat and placed it between his lips, trying to hide his anxiety. Sandra hated it when he smoked around her and flat-out refused to let him light up around Allie, but he was having a hard time focusing without it.

It was already ten p.m. and it would take another forty-five minutes to get to Loveland, maybe more. He was driving slower than normal on the winding roads. That would put him back in Estes Park around one, as long as everything went smoothly.

"Think Mark is going to let her go willingly?" Raven asked.

Sandra's shoulders tensed, but she didn't reply immediately.

"It's okay," Raven repeated.

The moon cast an eerie blue light over the tips of the trees. It was normally a beautiful drive, with rocky cliffs framing the highway on both sides with forests of ponderosas and aspens climbing up the inclines. The Big Thompson River rushed alongside the road.

Most of the houses out here belonged to preppers and survivalists that wanted to live away from civilization. There were a few million-dollar houses nestled between the shacks powered by solar panels and geothermal energy, but most of the resorts and vacation cabins were clustered on the other side of Estes Park.

The tires thumped over the road as they approached a bridge. The Big Thompson River roared in the distance.

"Bad spirits," Sandra muttered.

Raven took his eyes off the road for a second to look at her. "What?"

"The bad spirits have finally come to reclaim the Middle World. The storms, Melissa, now this attack."

Raven chuckled, but then he saw the serious look on his sister's face. She wasn't kidding.

"Remember what Grandma and Grandpa used to say about the way we treat the earth? They used to talk about the myths from *The Origin of Disease and Medicine.* Remember?"

Raven recalled the stories. The Cherokee viewed the world as having three parts: the Middle World, where plants, animals, and humans lived; the Upper World, where the protective spirits lived; and the Under World, where the bad spirits dwelled.

"Yes," Raven said. "I actually told Colton something similar when we found Melissa. The signs of the apocalypse have been here for a while, but—"

"But nothing. Maybe nature is finally reclaiming what we have destroyed. Maybe the animals and plants have had enough."

"Those are just stories."

Sandra shook her head at him like she used to when they were kids after Raven had said something stupid.

"No, big brother. They aren't. Remember the Water Cannibals?"

Raven sucked on the cigarette hanging from his lips. God, he wanted to light it and take a drag.

"I know you remember," Sandra said. "You used to crawl into my bed when we were little because you were so scared."

He tried to laugh. "Never happened."

Raven had been terrified of those creatures when he was younger, but tonight his fear had become real. He could still smell the little girl's charred flesh lingering in the back of his Jeep. Sandra didn't need to know that particular detail. It had to just be a coincidence. There was no chance that the man who killed Melissa would have known the Cherokee story. He shook the thought away and looked at Creek.

"What do you think?"

Creek glanced up and growled.

"There you have it," Raven said. "Creek agrees with me. Just stories, Sis. Water Cannibals aren't real."

Sandra turned away, stroking the barrel of the rifle with a finger as she stared out the window. They were silent for the next ten minutes. Raven was okay with that. He needed the silence right now.

Every time he saw a stranded vehicle, he put his foot on the brakes, but he didn't stop. Not even for the family walking on the side of the road. A man and his wife were holding the hands of their two kids as they made their way toward Loveland, guided only by a tiny flashlight.

"Maybe we should help them," Sandra said.

"We can't. We need to get to Allie." Raven hated to agree with Major Sardetti about anything, but he was right about one thing. Once people figured out what was going on, his Jeep would be a prime target. They had to pick up his niece and get to safety before the shit hit the fan.

A few minutes later, the beams fell on the jagged bluffs of Big Thompson Canyon. Here the road twisted out of the mountains and into the foothills. They passed several ranches and small shops selling jam and pies. The dense woods thinned and the pines were replaced by shrubs and bushes in the arid landscape.

They were almost to Loveland.

Raven had kept his foot on the gas as they climbed a steep incline, but he eased off the gas when he saw the crimson glow of a fire rise over the foothills. Sandra saw it at the same time. She leaned forward in her seat.

"What is that?" she asked.

"Looks like a pretty big fire to me."

Raven gently pressed down on the gas. They drove for several minutes in silence, both of them looking out the windows for a better view around the twists and turns of the road.

The fiery glow was coming from the east, not too far from Loveland. Tendrils arched away from a fire, licking the sky. The smoke drifted into his open window. He rolled it up almost all the way and wedged his cigarette back under the side of his baseball cap.

"That looks really close to the city," Sandra said.

"Don't worry, it's on the outskirts. Far from where Mark lives."

As they approached it, the fire increased in size until it was a massive, flaming ball.

"I bet it was a plane," he said, taking his eyes off the road to look at Sandra. "The EMP would have knocked them out of the sky. Anything with modern electronics like that…"

"Watch out!" Sandra screamed.

Raven swerved just in time to avoid a motorcycle abandoned in the middle of the lane. The tires squealed as he fought for control. He almost overcorrected, but training from his days driving a Humvee in Iraq kicked in.

"I'm sorry," Raven said, body numb from a shot of adrenaline. "I didn't see it." He checked his sister with a glance. She was gripping her chest as if she was suffering a heart attack. As soon as Raven looked back to the road, he could see why.

They were coming up on the wreckage of a plane just off Highway 34. The pilots appeared to have attempted a landing on the road, but had missed and crashed into a field instead. A wing protruded from the blazing wreck. Whole groves of trees were ablaze, and the fire was spreading.

"Holy shit," Raven said, shaking his head in awe.

There were several people on the shoulder of the road watching the flames, but no one seemed to be approaching it to help. Not that they could have done any good. Even if someone had survived the crash, they would have perished in the inferno.

"Where are the emergency crews?" Sandra asked.

"Probably stranded at their stations." Raven forced his gaze back to the road as they passed the wreck. There still wasn't a single working vehicle in sight.

"I should really get back to the medical center as soon as possible," Sandra said. "They are going to need me."

"It's going to be chaotic, Sis. Think about it. Anyone who was on life support isn't going to last."

Sandra's hand fell away from her breast and she sank in her seat. "Teddy," she whispered.

"Who's Teddy?"

"A five-year-boy who lost his right arm to Necrotizing Fasciitis."

"Necrotizing what now?"

"Flesh-eating bacteria."

Raven bit the inside of his lip. He had seen a Marine with that in Iraq. Poor bastard lost half his leg. It was nasty stuff.

"He's on a ventilator," Sandra said.

"How about I take Allie back to my place while you go to the hospital? I'll come get you after your shift."

Sandra wiped away her tears and put a hand on his arm. "Thank you, Sam. I don't know what I would have done if you hadn't found me. I love you."

"I love you, too."

It felt awkward saying those words after so long, but if there was one good thing that had come out of tonight, it was bonding with his sister. He hadn't always been a great brother, but at least he had the chance to be there for Sandra and Allie when they needed him most.

Raven tossed his unlit cigarette out the window. His urge to smoke was gone. All he could think about now was how he was going to protect his family when the bad spirits from the underworld really did emerge.

It was almost midnight by the time Raven drove through the city limits of Loveland, and the place was wide awake. The plane crash on the edge of town had roused what looked like half the population. People were out on the sidewalks and standing in the streets. Some pointed or waved at Raven's Jeep, but most seemed too preoccupied with the fire.

"I can't believe how many people are outside," Raven muttered. "Don't they have the sense to stay at home?"

Sandra pulled the bolt back in Raven's rifle to check for a round. "Let me do the talking when we get to Mark's," she said.

Raven wasn't sure why, but he smiled. His little sister was a healer at heart, but that didn't mean she wasn't also a fighter. When it came to Allie, she was as fierce as any mother lion. He just wished she cared about herself as much as she did her daughter. Raven had watched her go from one bad boy to another.

"You sure know how to pick 'em," he said.

Sandra grunted. "At least I got Allie out of the deal with Mark. More than I can say for you. Last girl you dated was a stripper, Raven."

He chuckled. "Scarlet was a professional dancer."

"Oh, that's what they call them these days?"

"That's what she said. Who am I to disagree? You wouldn't call a Marine a soldier, would you?"

He slowed as a pair of kids no older than ten darted across the street. They stopped to gawk at Raven's Jeep.

"Where the hell are their parents?" he grumbled.

"Hurry up," Sandra said.

"I'm hurrying, but I don't want to hit anyone."

Sandra stroked Creek's head and leaned forward, as if she could make the car go faster by sheer willpower. They passed the rundown middle school, and Raven turned onto Mark's street.

A pair of headlights shot around the corner as a small car putted down the street from the opposite direction.

Raven eased off the gas and pulled to the side to let an old Volkswagen Beetle by.

"Looks like we're not the only ones on the road after all," Raven said. "Which house am I looking for again?"

"Green one on the corner."

Raven gripped the steering wheel tighter and scanned the street. He had only been here once before, a few months back when Mark needed to be taught a lesson about respecting his baby sister's boundaries after the divorce. He would have killed Mark if he had gotten there before the police. He wasn't happy about leaving his only niece with the bastard, even if Mark wasn't drinking anymore, but that was Sandra's decision. Still, if he harmed Allie, they'd be finding pieces of Mark for weeks.

"That one," Sandra said. She pointed at a large ranch-style house at the next intersection.

"Remember, don't say anything to piss him off, and leave the rifle in the truck," Raven said. "We're just gonna get Allie and haul ass back to the car, okay?"

He turned off the Jeep, stuffed the key in his pocket, and reached under his seat for his Glock. With the gun in hand, he stepped out onto the pavement. Whistling at Creek, Raven checked the street again for any onlookers and stuffed the gun behind his shirt. By the time he had turned back to Sandra, she was already fast walking to the front door.

"Hey, hold on," Raven said, keeping his voice low. "Watch the truck, Creek."

The dog whined but settled onto his hind legs when Raven held his gaze. Creek was as loyal as a dog could be, but sometimes he was a little too anxious to get into trouble.

Kind of like me, Raven thought.

He caught up to Sandra at the front step just as she knocked on the door. It creaked open, and the silhouette of a large man appeared. Mark stepped into the moonlight, his blue eyes flitting from Sandra to Raven. "What the hell are you two doing here?"

Raven faced him, catching a whiff of what smelled like whiskey on his breath. It took everything in Raven's power to not punch Mark in the face right then.

"Evening, Mark," Raven said calmly. "We're here to pick up Allie. I know it's late, but—"

Mark cut him off with a grunt. "Like hell. I have rights, you know. This is my night with her."

He stepped closer, looming over them both. Raven stood his ground, keeping his hands at his sides. Mark was nothing but a drunken coward, the type of man who preferred to push around women because he was too afraid to fight a man—even when he outweighed his opponent by fifty pounds.

"You want to keep those rights?" Sandra asked. "Because I can smell liquor on your breath. You reek of it. You said you were sober, Mark. You *promised* you were sober."

"I am," Mark said. He ran a hand over his thinning hairline. "I haven't had a drink since..." He looked at the fire on the horizon, squinting like he hadn't noticed it before.

"Mommy?" whispered a voice.

Sandra wrenched the screen door open. "Allie! Come here, sweetheart."

Mark stepped in front of the girl, blocking her and holding up a hand to stop Sandra from entering. "Like hell you're taking her in the middle of the night. She's supposed to be in bed right now. And you," he shook a finger at Raven, "No way I'm letting you in my house after what you did. I haven't forgotten."

Raven ignored him and smiled at his niece. "Hey, kiddo. Do you want to go home?"

Allie nodded and clutched her stuffed pony closer to her chest. "I want to go with Mommy. It's dark here, the lights are all out."

"Just a power outage. Now go back up to your room." Mark looked toward the horizon, his eyes unfocused in his drunken haze. "Is something on fire?"

A low growl came from the street, and Raven turned slightly from Mark to see several large men walking down the sidewalk. Creek bared his teeth at them.

Great. Just what I need.

When he turned back to the door, Mark was already closing it. "Come back tomorrow—without your brother."

In a swift motion, Raven stuck his foot in the door, put a shoulder into it, and pushed his way inside. Mark sprawled backward to the floor, letting out a muffled cry.

Reaching for Allie's hand, Raven said, "Time to go."

Allie ran past him and wrapped her arms around Sandra.

Mark was already getting to his feet. Some bastards never learned.

"You're trespassing, you mother—"

Raven dropped Mark a second time with a punch straight to the nose. The crack of breaking cartilage was followed by a thump as Mark crashed back to the floor.

"You never were good enough for my sister," Raven said, rubbing his knuckles.

9

Capitol Hill was a madhouse.

Charlize followed Clint and Albert through hallways lit by emergency lamps. Agent Redline led the way. He hadn't said another word to them, despite being peppered with questions.

Capitol Police, Secret Service, and metro police officers wearing SWAT uniforms stood every ten feet, cradling automatic rifles across body armor. The sight of all that firepower did little to relieve the anxiety she felt. While most of the country slept in blissful ignorance, WWIII was well underway.

Charlize thought of Ty, hoping he was sleeping peacefully in his cabin at camp. She wouldn't be able to focus on anything else until she knew he was safe.

The entourage continued through the busy halls. With

a start, she realized they were only a few doors down from her office.

"Can I make a stop?" she asked. "I just need to grab something."

Redline turned to one of his men.

"Harrison, have you heard anything about the vehicles?"

"ETA about fifteen minutes, sir."

"You got five minutes, Senator," Redline said.

Albert opened the door to the reception area and holstered his pistol. "Ma'am, I'll be right outside if you need me."

"Thanks, Big Al. You did a fine job getting us here."

Clint entered, sweeping his flashlight over the space as Charlize walked to her private office. The room was furnished with two chairs in front of the desk, a larger oval mahogany table behind those, and two white couches facing one another in front of the window across the room. Bookshelves lined the walls. On the top shelf was a model F-15E Strike Eagle.

Charlize sat down at her desk and took a deep breath. Her office smelled like leather and books, and its familiarity comforted her. She'd spent countless hours here, burying herself in her work after Richard had been killed. She let her eyes close, and for a moment she could pretend this was just a normal day.

"We really should hurry," Clint reminded her.

Framed pictures of her family rested on the middle shelf of the bookcase behind the desk. Her favorite was the one taken at the National Mall six years ago when she had first been elected to Congress. Richard, Nathan, and Ty had all been with her that day. In the picture, they had all been sitting on a bench in front of D.C.'s famous cherry blossom trees. Charlize almost didn't recognize herself with short hair and a wide, untroubled smile.

She grabbed the picture and stuffed it into her bag, along with a framed snapshot of her and Richard on their honeymoon in Mexico.

"Okay, I'm all set," she said, joining Clint at the door. They returned to the hallway to find Senator Mack Sarcone waiting for them. He was an old-school politician who had held his seat for three decades. He also happened to be the grandfather of one of the girls taken prisoner in North Korea over eighteen months ago.

"Please tell me this shit isn't true," Sarcone said in his heavy Brooklyn accent. Using his fingers as a comb, he parted his thinning black hair to one side.

"We don't know anything more than you do," Charlize replied.

"This was definitely an attack by the North Koreans," came a voice. Senator Jack League, one of the oldest members of Congress, was walking down the hallway with several of his staffers. Despite the hour, the old Southern Republican looked as if he'd just come from the Senate floor.

"My staff just confirmed it," League said.

Sarcone's fingers slipped down his wrinkled forehead. "Those *were* nukes we launched, weren't they? And they were heading toward North Korea, right?" He didn't give League a chance to reply. "I sure as hell hope they kill every single one of those bastards. After what they did to my..."

Charlize didn't blame Sarcone or his granddaughter for what was happening, but she couldn't help but wonder if that raid had played some role in the events unfolding around her.

"We're at war," League said, stroking his long mustache. "Power is out all along the East Coast, not just here. I'm—"

"Where else?" Charlize interrupted.

League shook his head. "That's all I know right now."

"We have to find out," Charlize said. "Virtually every aspect of American society depends on power. Without it, our cities will descend into chaos."

The hallway quickly filled with more Congressmen and their support staff, party lines forgotten as they scrambled for every scrap of news. Lanterns and flashlights lit up the frightened faces of colleagues Charlize had worked with—and sometimes against—for years.

"It's time to move, Senator Montgomery," Albert said. He had his gun drawn again.

A dozen Capitol Police Officers rushed down the hallway, all of them armed with automatic rifles or shotguns. Flashlight beams danced across the marble pillars and stenciled walls like strobe lights. Halfway down the passage, Special Agent Redline was talking to Senator Jamie Ellen. She stood there in heels, a Coach bag in one hand and a briefcase in the other, her cream-colored suit accented with tasteful gold jewelry. Leave it to her to get dressed up for the end of the world.

"Everyone, please come with us," Redline said. "We're evacuating."

Sarcone grunted. "And going where?"

"Please follow me, sir," Redline said, avoiding the question. Passing through the rotunda, he led the group away from the Senate chambers. Charlize couldn't help but wonder if this was the last time she would ever see the place. Two sentries were standing guard at the back exit, earpieces hanging uselessly from their ears. The man on the left propped the door open, allowing Redline to advance with his assault rifle shouldered. Charlize half expected to hear the whoosh of a Black Hawk as they left the building, but as soon as they were outside, the stillness of the night closed in.

It was raining again, just a drizzle compared to before, but Charlize was already cold and the rain made her shiver. She hurried after the group. She was doing her best not to fear the worst, but all she could think of was Ty's innocent giggle and perfect little smile. He was such a happy kid, despite everything that had happened to him.

Redline waved the group toward a half dozen black Suburbans. Even more officers waited around the vehicles.

"Senators Montgomery and Sarcone, with me," Redline said. He moved to the sixth truck and opened the rear passenger-side door. Clint and Albert tried to follow, but Redline shook his head. "I'm sorry, gentlemen, but this is a priority transport."

Charlize halted and asked, "What do you mean?"

Sarcone elbowed passed her and climbed in, sliding his bulk over the seats.

"We don't have room to evacuate everyone right now," Redline said woodenly. "We will come back for the others."

Charlize watched other ranking senators pile into the vehicles ahead, but when she turned, Ellen and League were still standing with a small group behind the SUVs.

"We need to hurry, ma'am," Redline said. There was an

urgency to his words that scared Charlize. Secret Service Agents rarely lost their nerve. The threat, whatever it was, must be imminent.

"It's okay," Clint said. "You go."

"No," Charlize replied. "I'm not leaving them. There's room for everyone if we squeeze in."

Redline cursed under his breath. At first Charlize thought she was going to have to pull rank, but Redline must have known better than to argue. He jerked his chin at the vehicle.

"Thank you," Charlize said.

"Why are we not being moved?" Ellen asked. "I want to go with them!"

She rushed past Redline, but the convoy was already moving. Several staffers ran after her, and Charlize forced her gaze away.

"Hold on," the driver of her vehicle said. "We're going to be moving pretty fast in a minute."

Officers at the barricades moved back as the SUVs raced away from Capitol Hill.

"Where are we going?" Sarcone asked.

The driver, a middle-aged Secret Service Agent, turned the wheel slightly and pulled out onto Pennsylvania, providing Charlize with the answer. She knew exactly what building was in that direction.

Clint leaned closer to Charlize and said, "I thought we would be leaving D.C."

"I did, too, but there must not be a way to get us out in time," she whispered back.

The convoy picked up speed as they moved down Pennsylvania, weaving around stalled cars, tires squealing.

Charlize didn't bother asking how the Secret Service had procured functional vehicles. They could have been in an underground location, or perhaps they were hardened to begin with. She didn't care, as long as they kept running. Stranded motorists got out of their cars and waved from the side of the road, but the driver didn't slow.

Within minutes, their headlights shot across the White House lawn, capturing Secret Service and Marines running to set up positions. Behind them was Marine 1, a magnificent VH-3D Sea King helicopter, rotors idle.

The trucks rolled to a halt on the southwest side of the building. Albert jumped out and opened the back door, holding out a hand for Charlize. She grabbed her backpack, climbed out of the Suburban, and followed the group toward the dark building. She had the bizarre impulse to run for the chopper, fire it up, and fly all the way to Colorado. Charlize blinked the fantasy away. If the Sea King helicopter still worked, it would already be in the air.

"This way, Senator," Albert said. He directed her toward the heavily guarded back entrance. Inside, the West Wing was lit with lanterns. Flanked by Albert and Clint, she rushed after the group of politicians and staffers who were on the list to be evacuated first. Charlize tried not to think of Senator Ellen running after the convoy, her hair mussed and her Coach bag forgotten. The truth was that some people in Washington were considered more essential than others in an emergency.

They were directed through several vault doors. A Secret Service agent instructed them to wait as he punched biometric access codes into the control systems and swiped his card. The final door opened to an elevator.

"Single file. The elevator can only hold twenty at a time," he said. He gestured toward Charlize, and she quickly stepped into the elevator and hugged the left wall. Sarcone wedged inside and used a handkerchief to wipe his forehead.

"Why is this elevator working when the lights aren't?" he asked.

No one replied to Sarcone's question. There was only the sound of labored breathing and a muffled cough. The doors sealed, and a slight jolt rocked the elevator as it descended. In her mind's eye, Charlize pictured them moving down six stories to the Presidential Emergency Operations Center. It hardly seemed deep enough to survive a direct hit from a nuclear bomb, but that was what it had been designed to withstand.

A few seconds later the doors whispered open, and two guards waved everyone out into a brightly lit hallway. The White House had been hardened after all, or at least the grid connecting to the PEOC had been spared. Either way, there was light underground.

Footfalls echoed down the tile floor as the group continued toward the East Wing. With every step, Charlize felt a seed of hope blooming inside of her. Maybe the government was more prepared for an EMP attack than she had thought. She couldn't wait to see President Brandon Drake. If anyone could lead the country after a catastrophic attack, it was the decorated Vietnam veteran. Drake wasn't just a respected war hero—he was a leader who brought people together from both sides of the aisle. She felt sure their foreign allies would rally to America's aid at his call.

Charlize picked up her pace at the sight of the red blast

doors sealing off the PEOC. The double doors parted, revealing a room she had only seen in pictures.

The walls were lined with large monitors, data scrolling across some, video footage playing on others. In the center of the room was a long table that seated at least thirty people. Senator Ron Diego stood at the head of it. He was the President Pro Tempore of the Senate, and one of the only Senators Charlize didn't get along with, even though they were from the same party. Dressed in a pinstriped suit, he stood with his hands clasped behind his back as he surveyed the newcomers.

Charlize quickly avoided his gaze to search the room for President Drake or his Vice President, Christy Pederson. Neither of them were in the main chamber.

The blast doors clanked shut behind Charlize. She walked toward the table with Sarcone and Clint. There were already a dozen people seated there, including Secretary of State Denise Loyola and Secretary of Defense Carl Smith.

"Welcome to the PEOC," said Diego in the crisp voice that normally made Charlize shudder. She took her baseball cap off and loosened her ponytail, black hair falling around her shoulders. She ran her sleeve across her wet forehead.

"Where's President Drake and Vice President Pederson?" she asked.

Diego lowered his head, and for a moment, everyone in the room stopped what they were doing. The non-response was the only answer Charlize needed. She slowly took a seat in the closest chair, her brief feeling of hope deflating like air from a punctured tire.

"Air Force One went down a few hours ago somewhere

over Nebraska. It was taking President Drake to Offutt after a public event in South Dakota," Diego said. "Vice President Pederson's plane was taking her to Raven Rock Mountain Complex when it disappeared from radar."

There were a dozen other conversations going on in the background, but Charlize blocked them all out. If the EMP had knocked Air Force One out of the sky above Nebraska, then it would have likely hit Colorado, too.

"How?" Senator Sarcone asked. "How were these EMPs set off?"

"We're still trying to piece together the evidence, but it appears the North Koreans used fake transponder codes to get several Ilyushins into our airspace," Diego said. "We managed to take out two of them, but the other three were able to detonate nukes at altitudes ranging from fifty two thousand to sixty five thousand feet at strategic points over the United States."

Charlize balled her hands to keep them from shaking. Nukes? The North Koreans had detonated nuclear weapons?

"Where?" she managed to ask.

"Above Iowa, Virginia, and Colorado."

The last word sent Charlize into a tailspin like she was in a jet that had just been hit by a missile. The faces in the room blurred, and voices became garbled.

She fought her way back to the present moment. She did not have time to fall apart right now. She walked away from the table to the radar stations across the room. Vice Chairman of the Joint Chiefs of Staff, General Jay Pennington glanced at her with crystal blue eyes under thick gray brows.

"Senator Montgomery," he said with a nod.

"I need to know two things. One, where was that bomb set off over Colorado? And two, were any of our fighter jets in the air at the time?"

Pennington relayed her questions to a young female officer named Jennifer, who was monitoring the radars. Charlize waited anxiously as Jennifer filtered through the data. After a moment, Charlize felt a presence to her right. Clint stood beside her, offering his silent support.

Chaos continued throughout the PEOC as staffers and military personnel gathered information. A colonel Charlize didn't recognize motioned for Pennington to join him.

"Excuse me, Senator," Pennington said.

Charlize felt her hands shaking again. She clenched her fists and held in a breath.

Jennifer had her answer another moment later. She pointed to a map on her screen. "Senator, the bomb looks to have detonated at about fifty-three thousand feet over this area."

The air hissed out of Charlize's lungs when she saw the blast wasn't far from Denver.

"The National Guard had four F-16s in the air at the time, and the Air Force had—"

"Which squadron?" Charlize interrupted.

"The 120th, ma'am," Jennifer replied. She looked back at her screen. "Looks like they lost First Lieutenant Swanson, First Lieutenant Blake, Captain Negan, and Major Sardetti."

"Oh my God," Charlize said. She felt a hand on her shoulder.

"Charlize, I'm so, so sorry," Clint said.

"Have we heard from any of the pilots?" Charlize asked.

"No, ma'am, they all went off radar shortly after the blast," Jennifer said.

Charlize felt like her legs were going to give out. Her brother was dead, and her son was perilously close to the blast zone.

Behind her, a shout echoed through the room. It sounded strangely far away, as if she was listening from the other side of a thick pane of glass.

"Attention, everyone!" It was Pennington, and he looked like he had aged a decade in the last five minutes. All eyes centered on him.

"We just got word that Speaker of the House Catherine Hamilton was also in the air during the time of the attacks." Pennington blinked, as if he was considering the full meaning of his own words even as he said them.

"We have to assume that the president, vice president, and speaker are dead or at least missing, until we learn otherwise..." Pennington said. He stepped to the side so everyone could get a good look at the Acting President of the United States, Senator Ron Diego.

10

COLTON FROZE LIKE SOMEONE HAD JUST POINTED A GUN at his head. Rex and Lilly Stone were outside, and they didn't know yet that their daughter was dead. He stood and grabbed the lantern off his desk. Exhausted and unprepared to talk with the Stones, he walked out of his office like a soldier heading home after losing a battle. Jake walked with him, his head bowed.

The anxiety built with every step as Colton made his way through the station. He unlocked the door leading to the lobby beyond their office. Rex stood just beyond the door, holding his wife. Lilly trembled in his arms. Behind them, outside the glass doors, there were people gathering in the streets and in Bond Park, waiting for answers.

"Rex, Lilly," Colton said, slowly walking toward them. "I'm so sorry. We did everything we could, but we were too late."

Lilly burst into tears, burying her face against her husband's swelling chest.

"Where is she?" Rex said, his voice surprisingly strong.

"She's here at the station, but I don't think you should see her like—"

"I want to see my baby girl, Marcus. Don't make me beg."

Colton hesitated, exchanging a glance with Jake. The captain nodded back.

"Follow us," Jake said.

Side by side, the two officers led Rex and Lilly into the office. Colton stopped outside the door to the empty room where they had stored her body. Normally they would have had the medical examiner transport her to the morgue, but with communications down, he'd had no choice.

He didn't ask the Stones if they were sure a second time; he simply inserted the key and opened the door. The glow from the lantern spread through the room, washing over the blanket-draped form on the table.

Rex and Lilly slowly walked into the room. Halfway across, Lilly collapsed to her knees. Rex put his hands under her and helped her stand. They continued to the table.

"Please, you shouldn't see her like this," Colton said.

"My God," Lilly whimpered. "What's that smell?" She looked over her shoulder, eyes pleading with Colton to tell her that it wasn't anything to do with Melissa.

He put a hand on Rex's shoulder. "You shouldn't remember your daughter like this."

Rex pulled from his grip. "What happened to her, Marcus? What the hell happened to our baby?"

Colton set the lantern down on the floor. "Your daughter

was murdered, Rex. I don't know who did it, or why, but I promise you I will do everything in my power to find that person."

Rex pulled the blanket away from Melissa's face, his hand shaking. His expression twisted into a mask of horror in the dim light. There was a moment of silence before the big man broke into tears. Lilly screamed, and the sound seemed to go on and on in the unnaturally quiet night.

It was one in the morning by the time Raven pulled up to the Estes Park Medical Center. Sandra studied the building as they drove into the parking lot.

"You see any lights?" she asked.

Raven shook his head. "The generators must have been knocked out."

Sandra continued running her hand through Allie's hair. Her daughter was sleeping peacefully and Sandra hated to wake her, but her patients needed her now.

"Baby, wake up," Sandra whispered in Allie's ear.

It was amazing how dark it was, even with the moon high in the sky. Sandra could hardly see Allie's face as she blinked around groggily.

"You can go back to sleep in a little bit," Sandra told her. "But I have to go to work for a while."

"I want to come," Allie said.

"You sure you don't want that hand looked at? It looks pretty swollen." Sandra looked at Raven's knuckles, which were indeed swelling from the punch he'd thrown at Mark.

He shook his head, pulled his baseball cap off, and put it on Allie's head.

"You get to stay with me for a bit, *Agaliga*," he said playfully.

The nickname, Cherokee for "sunshine," made Sandra smile. Raven pulled the bill of the hat over Allie's eyes. She giggled and pushed the hat up so she could see.

"Can we go to your house? I want to see the chickens," Allie said.

Raven grinned, his teeth so white they seemed to glow in the faint moonlight. "Yeah, and you can play with Creek as much as you want."

"Okay," Allie said. She pulled the hat off and suddenly looked down. "Daddy said he was going to get me a puppy just like Creek."

Sandra and Raven shared a meaningful look. If she had a dollar for every time Mark had broken a promise, she'd be able to retire tomorrow.

"She'll be safe with me and Creek," Raven said. "What time should I come back to get you?"

"What time is it right now?"

Raven looked at his analog watch. "A quarter after one," he said with a yawn.

"That thing works?"

He shrugged. "I guess so."

"Stop back around noon then."

"Sounds good."

Sandra slid Allie off her chest and buckled her in.

"I really wish you'd get a car seat, Raven," Sandra said.

"Sis," he huffed. "She's fine, and I'm tired. I promise I'll drive safe."

Sandra leaned in and kissed Allie on the forehead. "I love you, sweetie. Be good to Uncle Raven."

Sandra locked eyes with Raven one more time, and he offered a reassuring nod. Holding in the tears, she jogged toward the emergency room. There was a lantern set up in the small lobby. Several people were sleeping in chairs with blankets draped over their bodies. "Sandra, thank God you're here."

A woman with tattoos on her upper chest hurried out from behind the reception desk. It was the nursing supervisor, Kayla Clark. She repositioned a candle on the counter and motioned for Sandra to come through to the small office.

"I'm so sorry," Sandra whispered, keeping her voice low so she didn't wake the sleepers in the lobby. "I was in the park when…" Sandra caught herself from revealing what she knew about the EMP attack. "When my car died. My brother picked me up and took me to Loveland to get Allie."

Kayla, in her usual rapid-fire manner, explained that the generators had never come on after the power outage. There were only two doctors in the ER and one in the skilled nursing facility, and only four of their usual ten nurses had shown up for work.

"We lost two of the patients on life support," Kayla finished, looking at the floor.

Sandra turned toward the doors leading to the ICU and ER. She was afraid to open them. There were only three patients hooked up to life support, and Teddy was one of them.

"None of the key cards work. You'll have to use this," Kayla said. She grabbed an extra key from a ring on the wall and handed it to Sandra. The room beyond was eerily quiet, all of the bright LEDs, beeping machines, and other equipment gone dark.

"Sandra, about time you showed up," Doctor Newton said. There was frustration in his tone, but Sandra couldn't blame him for that. He was sitting next to Teddy's bedside, carefully pumping air by Ambu bag. The boy was still intubated and in a chemically-induced coma. The stump of his right elbow was wrapped to protect it from further infection, but she could see the dressings needed changing.

Sandra put her hand on her heart. She was relieved to see Teddy still alive, but the odds of his survival were grim. It was almost impossible to bag a patient for the long term.

"Do you have news from the outside?" Doctor Duffy chimed in. He was supervising another patient with two nurses across the room in an area cordoned off by curtains. "We heard Chief Colton found Melissa, and there's talk of some sort of attack."

"Are we really at war?" Newton asked.

The truth almost rolled off Sandra's tongue, but she hesitated. No, telling the truth now would only make things worse. She needed to focus on saving lives, not spreading gossip.

"The police are doing everything they can," she said at last.

She crossed the room and pulled up a stool next to Teddy's bedside. His closed eyelids fluttered ever so slightly.

"Let me take over," Sandra said.

Newton and Sandra changed hands, and she immediately began squeezing the bag in a slow, steady rhythm.

"We lost Charles and Monica," Newton said after trying and failing to hold back an exhausted yawn. "I hear things are bad in the nursing wing too. Already lost a patient there that was on a breathing machine. A CNA apparently didn't know how to bag."

Sandra closed her eyes for a brief moment, saying a silent prayer for the people they'd already lost.

"We can't keep this up for long," Newton continued. "Teddy needs more than air. He needs medicine that requires refrigeration. We have everything on ice right now, but I'm not sure how long we can keep it cool."

Sandra looked up and met Newton's gaze. "What are we going to do?"

He heaved a sigh. "Honestly, I have no idea. But if the power doesn't come back on soon, I'm afraid we're going to lose him."

Nathan sat in the operations room of the Estes Park police station, staring at the radio equipment. Everything was destroyed. Even the two-ways didn't work.

He ignored the officers that rushed through the area to gather equipment and gear from their lockers in the other room. Several of them stopped to chat, but Nathan wasn't in the mood to answer any questions.

Never in his life had he felt this defeated. His wingman and friend was dead, his nephew was close to a nuclear blast zone, and his sister was half a country away.

He ran his fingers up and down his scalp and bowed his

head, trying to think. He needed a plan, but what could he do without a radio or a vehicle?

"Sir?" came a soft voice.

He turned to see the female detective with freckles and red hair from the meeting earlier. She held out an ancient-looking radio in a wood box.

"This is a vintage tube radio that I got from my grandma. I had the six vacuum tubes replaced a few years back. The batteries were museum pieces and cost me a small fortune, so use it sparingly." She pushed the box toward Nathan. "Go ahead and try it out, Major."

Nathan tried to remember her name. "Thank you, Detective…?"

"Lindsey Plymouth," she said with a smile. "Here, let me show you how it works."

She set the battery-operated tube radio on the table in front of the oil lantern and leaned over to work the dials. Colton joined them a few minutes later. The police chief's shoulders sagged slightly with defeat and despair.

Nathan had heard the scream a little while earlier, and he could guess Colton had just told that little girl's parents their worst nightmare had come true.

"Any updates on the equipment?" Colton asked.

"I can't get anything to work, but Detective Plymouth brought in this old tube radio. We can't contact anyone with it, but we can listen and see if we can get any news."

Lindsey leaned over the table and continued to scroll through the stations. White noise crackled from the old speakers. She moved the dials with deliberate care until there was a beeping sound.

Colton stepped closer, hovering behind her. She slowly twisted the dial until a voice came over the speaker.

"This message is transmitted at the request of the Federal Emergency Management Agency. At 7:21 p.m. Pacific Standard Time, NORAD detected multiple foreign threats in American airspace moving east over the country. It is believed that these aircraft were carrying weapons of mass destruction."

The message ended and, after a pause, began again.

"Multiple threats?" Lindsey asked.

Nathan caught Colton's gaze. Both soldiers knew what the message meant. The bomb over the Rockies hadn't been the only one.

"Keep this between us three for now," Colton said. "I don't want to raise any more alarm. If there were more bombs, then help might be farther away than we thought. It's that much more vital to maintain the peace."

Nathan nodded curtly, but he wondered how long the police chief expected to keep people from the truth. It had a way of getting out—and when it did, all hell would break loose.

11

CHARLIZE WANTED TO SCREAM AND RUN FOR THE BLAST doors, but instead she forced herself to remain seated at the conference table, the only outward sign of her distress the tapping of her fingertips on the wood. Until she saw otherwise with her own eyes, she had to keep believing that Ty was alive.

Secretary of Defense Smith and Secretary of State Loyola sat down at the table next to her. More staff filed in behind them. Leon Crosby, one of the leading experts on North Korea at the CIA, wedged between Loyola and Charlize.

Last time she had seen Crosby was at an Armed Services Committee hearing about current North Korean nuclear capabilities. He had claimed they were still far from developing weapons that could threaten the continental United States.

Charlize didn't take any pleasure in seeing him proved wrong.

Acting President Diego shut the door and walked to the wall-mounted monitor.

"As I'm sure you're all aware, I launched a nuclear attack against Pyongyang approximately two hours ago," Diego said, his voice brisk and seemingly free of regret. "The duty fell on me when we weren't able to contact President Drake, Vice President Pederson, or Speaker Hamilton. The twenty warheads I authorized were plenty to turn their targets into radioactive craters."

Leaning forward in her chair, Charlize focused on the screen, which was streaming a feed from an aircraft. Clouds blocked the view, and although digital telemetry scrolled across the bottom, she couldn't make out the data.

Diego pointed to the screen. "This is the live video from one of our drones over North Korea. You're about to see what's left of Pyongyang."

The clouds peeled away to reveal a glimpse of hell.

"My God," Loyola said, her face going ashen.

Charlize didn't blame her. She'd flown bombing runs over Iraq, and the knowledge that she'd killed civilians along with militant insurgents weighed heavily on her conscience. But to order a nuclear strike that would kill millions? That was a call she wasn't sure she could make.

The clouds muddied the video feed again—no, not clouds, Charlize realized. The drone was passing through smoke, ash, and the atomized remains of over two point five million people.

Diego moved away from the monitor and took a seat at the head of the table. "I'm showing you this footage so you understand the gravity of our situation. World War Three is well underway," he said, tapping the table with a finger for emphasis. "On our very soil."

A knock rapped on the door, and General Pennington stepped inside carrying a laptop.

"Sir, we have a situation," he said. "We just got a report from the Washington Navy Yard of a container ship on the Potomac River. I had a Marine unit call it in."

Pennington set his laptop on the table and flipped it open. "This feed is being broadcast from a special unit we deployed to keep an eye on the river."

"How are their cameras working?" Loyola asked.

"Several units in D.C. had equipment designed to survive an EMP attack," Pennington replied. "This is one of them. We also have several F-22s in the area that are on standby. They have been notified and are en route."

The camera was positioned on a bridge over the Potomac. Marines shouldered their M4s at a container ship downstream. Several Humvees with mounted M240s rolled onto the bridge and set up position.

Pennington looked up from his laptop. "We just got confirmation that ship was outside of the blast zone of the EMP. It was spotted sailing in from the Atlantic a few hours ago. Pretty convenient timing, if you ask me. The country of origin appears to be China, and whoever is at the helm seems to be ignoring those Marines."

Everyone in the room fell silent but Crosby. He rose from his seat, breathing heavily. "This could be a second attack. I've said it once, and I'll say it again. Container ships are one of the biggest threats to our national security. We already know the North Koreans spoofed the transponder codes of Chinese planes to get their Ilyushins into our air space. They could have hijacked a Chinese container ship much more easily."

"I could have my men fire across the bow," Pennington said.

"No," Diego said. "Order them to board that ship right now."

Pennington nodded and gave the order. Several minutes passed before a video feed was transferred to the main monitor that showed a Zodiac carrying a small fire team of six Marines launch from the shore. The men loaded their suppressed M4s as the boat raced to catch up with the container ship. Audio crackled from the wall-mounted speakers in the room.

"Eagle's Nest, this is Kilo 1, preparing to board bogey."

Kilo 1 directed his helmet-mounted night vision camera at the container ship as the Zodiac ferrying the men came up along the starboard side. Another Marine tossed a rope up to the deck. One by one the team climbed up. Charlize watched the rattling green-hued image as Kilo 1 stormed past the containers and toward the superstructure.

"No sign of contacts," Kilo 1 reported. "We're heading to the bridge."

The team started up a ladder that led to the command room. Kilo 1 was halfway up when the sound of gunfire cracked from the speakers. The Marine looked up at a platform where one of his team lay face down. Another Marine took a knee next to the fallen man and fired at a contact out of sight.

Charlize felt helpless as she watched the battle unfold.

She laced her fingers together to keep from tapping on the table.

On screen, Kilo 1 continued climbing and followed the other men across the platform in stealth movements. He directed his muzzle at a large window peppered with bullet holes, and then bent down to check the pulse of the fallen Marine.

"Kilo 3 is KIA," Kilo 1 said. "Proceeding to the bridge."

The team shouldered their weapons and approached the next corner cautiously. The Marine on point flashed a hand signal and then peeked around the corner. A gunshot sounded, and a round hit him in the helmet. He dropped woodenly to the platform.

Two of the remaining men pulled him back to safety, but Charlize knew it was already too late for the man. Kilo 1 hurried past them just as another Marine pivoted around the corner and opened fire. He took a round to the chest and crashed into a railing.

The crack of automatic gunfire barked from the speakers as all hell broke loose. The feed bobbed up and down while Kilo 1 moved from position to position. He stopped to fire at contacts Charlize still couldn't see, and then continued on. His team was gunned down one by one in front of him until there were only two Marines remaining.

She gripped the side of the table as Diego gave his next order.

"Tell those F-22s to go weapons hot and to prepare to fire on the ship."

Pennington looked up from his laptop, unable to hide his alarmed expression. "But sir, we still have men..."

"That's an order, General."

Kilo 1 passed another dead Marine and followed the only other survivor toward the hatch outside the command room. Three North Korean soldiers lay on the platform. Kilo 1 put a bullet into the skull of one of the men, who was trying to crawl away. Then he put a hand on the back of the other Marine and prepared to storm the bridge.

"F-22s are thirty seconds out, sir," Pennington reported.

Charlize bit down on her lip. Thirty seconds for Kilo 1 and his teammate to take control of the ship. They burst inside the room and were immediately fired upon by a contact inside. The Marine next to Kilo 1 took several rounds and crashed to the deck. Kilo 1 took the North Korean soldier down with a three-round burst to his chest.

"Eagle's Nest, bridge is clear. Kilo 2, 3, 4, 5, and 6 are all KIA," he said heavily.

Pennington didn't reply, but he did look over at Charlize. They both knew Kilo 1 was seconds away from joining the rest of his team. The Marine quickly ran over to the dead North Korean man and pulled a small device from his hand. He held it up toward the camera. It was a clock or timer of some sort. Kilo 1 slowly turned to the windows of the command center as the rumble of F-22s sounded.

The rumble turned into a roar, the speakers in the PEOC crackling as the birds raced toward the Potomac. The fighters swooped low to fire their payloads on the ship. Kilo 1 ducked down just as the missiles streaked toward the ship. Fiery blasts sent containers cartwheeling into the sky.

Charlize held in a breath as a blinding explosion bloomed out of the center of the ship, instantly killing the feed.

"Did we take it out?" Diego asked.

Pennington nodded solemnly. "Target destroyed."

There were several seconds of silence, every head in the room bowed to contemplate the loss of the brave Marines. A deep and raucous roar shattered the quiet. Charlize knew right away the sound wasn't from the F-22s.

At first it was like a screeching runaway freight train, but the sound grew into a growl that made it seem like a hundred trains were headed toward the White House. Loyola's eyes widened in fear, and she grabbed Charlize's hand as they shared a look of terrified realization.

The timer from the container ship had been counting down to a final attack, and it was now screaming straight toward the White House in a fiery blaze that would vaporize everything in its path for several miles.

The room shook violently. The walls, floor, and ceiling were all in motion, and for a moment Charlize felt almost weightless. Dust rained down from the ceiling, and the Presidential Seal affixed to the wall rattled and then fell to the ground. The main screen went next, shattering.

"The PEOC was designed to take a direct hit from a nuclear—" Pennington said. He stopped, all color draining from his face. "Everyone under the table!"

All around her, the top officials of the United States government were screaming and crawling under the table, but Charlize remained where she was, staring at the broken Presidential Seal.

Someone grabbed her, dragging her under with everyone else. To her surprise, it was Crosby. The policy expert was calm in the midst of the chaos, a brave smile on his face.

"Pray with me," he said. Charlize locked her fingers with his. If anyone had asked her twenty-four hours earlier whether she'd ever hold hands with Leon Crosby, she would have laughed in their face. Now she was just grateful for the simple human connection.

This is it, she thought. *This is the moment I die.*

Shockwaves pounded the room. There was a cracking sound, and then a terrible groan as the steel beams that were supposed to hold the bunker together gave way, bending and ultimately snapping like bones.

"Ty, I'm so sorry. I love you," Charlize whispered. In her final moments, those words seemed more important to her than any prayer. She closed her eyes and pictured her baby boy as the ceiling collapsed.

Blood ran down her arm, but she didn't feel any pain.

How odd, she thought, filled with relief that dying did not, apparently, hurt.

Her eyes snapped open as she felt Crosby's hand go limp in her own. In the swirl of emergency lights, she saw what was left of the CIA advisor. There was a chunk of concrete where his head had been. A storm of smoke and dust swirled through the operations room. She covered her mouth, coughing, and tried to move.

From every direction came the cries of her colleagues. Diego's voice was the worst, rising several octaves higher than normal. The grinding of rock against concrete and steel did little to drown out the screams.

She saw a figure make a run for the door, only to vanish into a hole in the floor. The horrified scream was swallowed by the shifting walls and ceiling.

Darkness flooded the room. It was followed by a massive heat wave that stole the air from Charlize's lungs. The exposed skin on her arms, legs, and face prickled with pain, like she was strapped inside the burning cockpit of a jet fighter.

Damn, she thought. *I guess dying does hurt after all.*

The sun didn't rise over Rocky Mountain National Park on Saturday morning. Police Chief Marcus Colton didn't expect it would. Holding his Glock in one hand, he pulled back the curtain covering the window to his bedroom while his wife and daughter slept in the bed behind him. Rain drizzled down the window, and a haze drifted off the rocky slope in their backyard. In the distance, clouds obscured the mountain peaks, blanketing the sky.

It all seemed so peaceful, but Colton knew the truth.

He secured his pistol in the holster on his duty belt. Then he sat on the edge of the bed, trying not to wake his girls. Despite his efforts, Kelly sat up, her braided hair falling over her Estes Park Police Department t-shirt.

"What time is it, Marcus?"

"Little after six."

Risa stirred and rolled from her side onto her back. She blinked and looked at him. "Can we have pancakes?"

The sound of his daughter's sleepy voice almost brought Colton to tears. Rex and Lilly would never hear their daughter speak again, and he vowed never to take a single minute with Risa for granted.

"Not this morning," Kelly said. "Your dad has to go to work."

The excitement faded from Risa's face, her face contorting into a frown. "It's cold in here," she said. "Why's it so cold?"

Colton tucked the comforter around his daughter and studied her in the faint light of dawn—the brown pigtails that matched her mother's, the dark brown eyes, and the freckles on her button nose. She was too young to be told the truth, but just old enough to know something was wrong.

He looked at his wife for support.

"Just a power outage. The lights will be back on in no time," Kelly said.

Risa grabbed a pillow and hugged it. She had given up her teddy bear a year ago when Colton had said she was too old for it. Now he wished he'd let her keep it.

"C'mon, let's have pancakes," he said. Colton didn't really have time for their Saturday morning ritual, but he couldn't bear to say no to her, not today.

Using one of their precious bottles of water and an old kerosene camping stove, Colton managed to whip up some halfway decent pancakes. Risa dug in, smacking and grinning and carrying on like they were the best things she'd ever eaten.

Colton didn't have much of an appetite. He nibbled on a piece of bread as he checked over the kitchen for anything he'd forgotten to do. He'd spent several hours last night making preparations at the house, including filling up the bathtub and sinks and saving what was left in the water heater.

He and Kelly had taken their supply of meat from the freezer in the garage and salted it, too.

While Risa ate, she punched at the home button on her iPad. "It won't turn on," she complained.

"If you're done eating, why don't you go make your bed?" Kelly said.

"But I don't want to do chores. I want to go play."

"Make your bed, and then you can go play," Kelly replied calmly.

Risa narrowed her eyes as if she was being tricked.

Colton forced down the last of his slightly stale breakfast. "Listen to your mother, honey."

Risa carried her plate to the sink, but Kelly stopped her before she could plunge the dirty dish into the reservoir of clean water. Puzzled, she set it on the counter and ran upstairs. Once her footfalls had echoed away, Colton laced his fingers together behind his head and sighed.

"This could go on for months, maybe longer. We don't know how much of the country was affected yet. After Melissa…"

Kelly put a finger to her mouth. Colton nodded, understanding. They still hadn't figured out how to tell Risa that her friend was dead, or that the power wasn't going to come back on anytime soon.

"There's a killer on the loose and the country's been attacked," Colton said heavily. "I don't even know where to start today. The whole town is looking to me for answers, but all I have is bad news."

Kelly grabbed his hand. "You start by going to town hall and doing what you always do. You lead, Marcus."

"Thanks, Kel," Colton said. "I'll find the man that did this to Melissa, and I'll get the town's affairs in order. I just need time. It's going to be a hard winter, love. We need to conserve everything and plan for the long haul. That means rationing food and water."

"How much do we have?"

Colton did the math in his head. He had squirreled away an entire crate of MREs in the basement, plus gallon jugs of water, some kerosene, and plenty of canned vegetables and preserves, thanks to Kelly. His little family would be fine for a few months, but he doubted most residents would be in as good a shape.

"I want you to walk to Safeway with Tim and Linda next door. Take the cash from the safe and buy canned food, water, and anything else with a long shelf-life. We'll also need more batteries, toilet paper…" Colton sighed, frustrated. "You know what to get."

"It's just like preparing for a camping trip," she said, trying to lighten the mood.

"I need to get to town hall and meet with Mayor Andrews."

"Knowing Gail, she's probably already there."

"She's going to be mad."

"Because you declared a state of emergency?"

"Because I didn't consult with her first."

Kelly came up behind Colton and put a hand on his shoulder. Goosebumps prickled up and down his arms. Even after all these years, she could still give him the chills.

"You're going to have to make some very unpopular decisions," Kelly said. "But stay strong and trust your instincts."

Colton kissed his wife, jotted down a few more tasks on his ever-growing to-do list, and then went to his office to get the rest of his hardware. The room was small and furnished only with a desk and a comfortable chair. A bookshelf took up most of the wall to the right, and a window with wood blinds looked out over their rocky backyard.

He walked over to the closet. A Western-Style duty belt hung from a clip on the wall. It was the one his father had carried during his thirty years of service as Sheriff of Larimer County.

Colton removed his duty belt and exchanged it for his father's. After securing it around his waist, he took a knee in front of the gun safe in the corner. Inside were some of his most prized possessions, including an M14 rifle with a scope. He grabbed the rifle and set it against the wall before he turned back for his favorite gun.

The Colt Single Action Army revolver was another gift from his dad. He held the gun across the palms of both hands like an offering, admiring the beautifully engraved metal and scrimshawed ivory grips.

"*Morior Invictus*," Colton said, reading the motto on the barrel. "Death before defeat."

It was his father's favorite saying, one that Colton had adopted after losing the man who had meant the most to him. He holstered the revolver and then grabbed the M14.

When he turned to leave, Kelly was standing in the door. "Be careful, Marcus. Please, by God, be careful out there."

"Do you have your Glock?" he asked.

She lifted up her shirt and turned, cocking a hip. The black grip of the pistol was sticking out of her waistband.

"Good girl," Colton said with a grin. "Got any more moves like that?"

Before she could answer, they both flinched at the sound of a horn honking outside.

"What in the hell?" Colton said. He hurried to the living room and looked through the window. In their driveway was Jake Englewood's red 1952 Chevy pickup.

Colton grabbed his backpack with a smile on his face. Risa came thundering down the stairs a split second later, crying out, "Uncle Jake!"

Kelly and Risa followed Colton out to the driveway.

"Mornin' Kelly," Jake said. He tipped his Stetson at Risa. "How you doin', little lady?"

Colton almost laughed when he saw Jake had shaved most of his bushy red beard, leaving only a handlebar mustache.

"Can't call me a Viking anymore," Jake said.

"You never were good at history," Colton chuckled. "Vikings had mustaches, too."

"Whatever you say, Chief."

"You're a cowboy Viking," Risa chirped.

That earned a bellowing laugh from Jake.

Colton looked over the vintage truck. The windshield had a major crack, but it was at least on the passenger side. The chrome grill was off, and only two of the tires had hubcaps, but the tread was good and the lights all seemed to work.

Jake put his hands on his hips and turned to look with Colton. "She may be old, but she runs," he said. "Rebuilt the engine with my own hands."

"I didn't say anything," Colton said, laughing. "In fact, I think we're looking at our new squad car."

Jake patted the hood fondly. "You're beautiful, baby. Don't let anyone tell you different."

"We better get going. Mayor Andrews is probably on her way to town hall."

"Actually, she's already there. I dropped her off before coming to get you. She isn't happy."

Kelly laughed. "Told you, Marcus."

Colton kissed his wife on the cheek. "I'll see you tonight." Then he crouched down and hugged Risa. "I love you. Be good while I'm gone."

"Love you too, Daddy."

He grabbed his gear and rifle, and forced himself to walk away. Leaving them suddenly felt wrong, but he had a duty to his town. With threats coming from all sides, he had to get to work. Colton climbed into the passenger seat of the truck. Jake wedged his bulk behind the steering wheel and turned the key. The engine coughed to life. Both men waved at Colton's family, smiling as if this was just another ordinary day, but as soon as they were out of the driveway, their conversation became serious.

"You got any updates for me?" Colton asked.

"Detective Plymouth has been checking the Geiger counters every hour. Looks okay so far. Still trying to contact all the reps for the EOC. Other than that, we've got officers stationed at all critical facilities, including the YMCA."

"The YMCA?"

"I thought we could use the pool as an additional water source."

"Good call," Colton said. "But that won't last very long. We need to think long term here."

"I know. Once I drop you off, I'm heading to Bill Catcher's with Major Sardetti. Maybe he can get some answers from his base."

Colton pointed at the dashboard of the truck. "Have you tried this radio yet?"

"Yeah, but I didn't get anything but static."

"You mind?" Colton asked, reaching for the tuning knob.

"Knock yourself out."

Colton spun the dial as they pulled out of the driveway.

"We're going to need to hold a town hall meeting," Jake said. "Tell people what's going on."

"Let the mayor handle it. I have other shit to do."

Jake took one hand off the steering wheel to scratch his mustache. "You've never been a man of many words."

"There's a killer out there, and I—" Colton paused as the sound of a garbled transmission came over the radio. He slowly twisted the knob back to the left. "Pull over a minute."

Jake drove onto the shoulder, kicking up a storm of dust. He shifted into neutral and waited.

White noise broke from the old speakers.

"I don't hear nothing—" Jake began to say.

A robotic voice from the radio cut him off.

"At 5:05 a.m. Eastern Standard Time, a second attack…"

"Second attack?" Jake asked.

Colton raised a finger and waited for the message to continue, but there was only the hiss of static.

"Dammit," Colton said. He fiddled with the knob, turning it ever so slightly to the left. Through the storm of crackling came a beeping sound, and finally a barely audible voice.

"This is a national emergency. Important instructions will follow…"

The beeping returned for several agonizing moments.

Colton stared at the knob. "Come on, come on."

"The following message is transmitted at the request of the United States government. This is not a test. At approximately 7:21 p.m. Pacific Standard Time, three North Korean planes detonated nuclear warheads above Iowa, Virginia, and Colorado. The subsequent electromagnetic pulse knocked out power across the continental United States. At 5:05 a.m. Eastern Standard Time, a second attack took place. A nuclear bomb was detonated from the Potomac River just outside of Washington, D.C."

"Holy shit," Jake muttered.

Colton stared at the radio in disbelief. "D.C. is gone?"

"All residents within a four-hundred-mile radius of the attack should seek a fallout shelter. Fallout is a product of nuclear attack. Prolonged exposure will result in certain death. If there is a nearby fallout shelter, go there now. Otherwise seek shelter in the interior of a building on the lowest floor. Do not leave the shelter until an all clear has been issued."

The annoying beeping began again.

Jake went back to stroking his mustache with his index finger and thumb, muttering a slew of curse words.

"This is an emergency action notification. All networks and cable systems shall transmit this action message."

Colton couldn't believe what he'd just heard. Thanks to Major Sardetti, they'd already had some idea of how bad the situation was, but this? This was Armageddon. How could it have happened? And why had the North Koreans followed up their devastating EMP attack with a direct nuclear strike on Washington?

Jake pounded the steering wheel and then grabbed it with both hands, squeezing until his knuckles were white. The tattooed image of a coiled rattlesnake and the words "Don't Tread On Me" showed on his forearm.

"That's it," Colton said as he noticed that the snake's head was lost in a mass of pink scar tissue from an old shrapnel wound. "Cut off the head of a snake and it can't strike."

Jake's eyebrows drew together in a single, heavy line. "What the hell, man?"

"D.C. was the snake's head. With the seat of our government gone, we will have a hell of a time managing any recovery efforts."

"So what you're saying is that help ain't coming," Jake said. "Shit, Marcus, I coulda told you that. We handled our own problems back in the flood of '13, and we'll take care of ourselves again now."

He pulled back onto the road and punched the accelerator. The metal bones of the old truck groaned.

Colton looked to the mountains in the distance. He had always felt isolated all the way up here away from society. It could be a lonely feeling, but maybe now that isolation wasn't such a bad thing.

As they drove through Estes Park, Colton saw a crowd gathering outside town hall. At the front, facing the others, was Major Sardetti. He had his hands up like he was fending off questions.

"Shit," Colton said. "Should have told him to lay low. Now they're going to want to know why a jet pilot is wandering around town."

Jake waved at the major and pointed to the parking lot. Nathan nodded, said something else to the crowd, and then limped over to the truck. Colton opened the door and stepped out to let Nathan inside.

There were no good mornings or hellos, just a simple nod between three soldiers.

"Good luck today. Bill Catcher's a crazy, paranoid son of a bitch, so I'd bet he's feeling pretty twitchy right now," Colton said. He patted the passenger door of the truck. "Play that message for Major Sardetti on the way up to Prospect Mountain."

"What are you going to do, Chief?" Jake asked.

Colton took a deep breath, still not sure if he was making the right call. "I'm going to tell everyone the truth."

12

As Jake steered up the twisty roads around Prospect Mountain, Nathan held the probe of a Geiger counter out the window and watched the needle while the words of the emergency broadcast repeated inside his head. This was the worst-case scenario. Not only had he lost his brothers from the 120th when their planes fell from the sky, but he'd lost his only sister to a damned nuclear strike on the nation's capital. The only thing keeping him going now was the thought of his nephew. But if the device in his hand detected high amounts of radiation from the first wave of nukes, then Ty would probably be doomed, too.

The big officer picked at the bottom of his handlebar mustache. "What's it say?"

"We're good for now," Nathan said.

Jake drummed his fingers on the steering wheel and then

said, "Look, I know you've been through the wringer in the past twenty-four hours, Major, but you landed in one of the best towns in America. You're welcome to stay if we're not able to get you a radio. We could use a good man like you."

"Thanks, but I have to get to Empire to find my nephew after I reach Buckley AFB," Nathan said.

"I understand. Kids are the light of the world. If my girls weren't safe at home in Estes Park with their mom, I'd be trying to get to them, too."

Jake took a swig of bottled water and offered it to Nathan. "No thanks."

"Suit yourself," Jake said. He set the water back down and pointed up the steep road.

"Bill Catcher lives off the grid up here. He's a paranoid bastard and doesn't care much for law enforcement."

"Or the military?"

Jake grinned. "You got it. Let me do the talking. If I don't end up with a gun pointed at my head, I'm going to offer Bill some diesel in return for his help looking over our recovery plan and letting you use any radio he might have."

He parked on the side of the road and killed the engine. Nathan limped after Jake up the dirt road. That pretty nurse had done a good job wrapping his ankle, considering the circumstances, but it still hurt.

"Remember, let me do the talking," Jake said.

Prospect Mountain towered over them like a castle. A small cabin was set up high on a clearing peppered with rocks and clusters of pine trees. They approached slowly with their hands by their sides, held away from their holstered pistols.

To the east stood a small barn that looked like it had been made from salvaged wood. Nearby was a well with an old wood bucket hanging from a rope. There were rows of solar panels, plots of well-tended crops, and a chicken coop topped with a faded blue tarp. Rain barrels flanked the front porch, but one of them was knocked over.

That seemed odd. Everything on the property was rough and ramshackle, but it was all carefully maintained. Nathan could tell at a glance that this Bill Catcher took a lot of pride in his homestead, so why wouldn't he have righted the rain barrel?

"You see anything?" Jake asked.

Nathan shook his head. "Looks like no one is home. But I've got a bad feeling about this."

"Bill!" Jake said in a loud but non-threatening voice. "It's Jake Englewood and my buddy Nathan."

They stood about a hundred feet from the porch, a breeze gusting against them. Besides the wind, the only sound came from the squawk of chickens.

Two of the birds waddled over and began pecking at the ground by the spilled rain barrel.

"That's weird," Jake said. "Bill wouldn't leave them out here alone. Too many coyotes around."

Nathan squinted at the cabin, trying to see inside. Curtains were pulled across all the windows.

"Bill, you home?" Jake said.

The answering silence was unsettling. A particularly strong gust of wind slammed the screen door on the porch open. It creaked, whined, and then slammed shut again, the impact echoing through the property.

"Maybe he walked into town," Nathan said.

"Doubtful. The guy's practically a hermit." Jake jerked his head toward the porch. "You stay out front. I'm gonna see if he's around back."

Jake walked around the side of the house, leaving Nathan alone.

The screen door opened and slammed shut again. A bead of sweat dripped down Nathan's forehead. He walked up to the porch furnished with a rocking chair and a small table. An empty bottle of whiskey rested next to a pack of smokes on the table.

Nathan reached out to knock on the door when he noticed it was slightly ajar, providing him a glimpse inside the cabin.

"Mr. Catcher? Bill?" Nathan said. He stepped into the single room cabin, holding his arm to his nose at the strong smell of body odor and barbeque, half expecting to get a shotgun barrel pointed at his face. The space was divided in two by a long brown curtain. A kitchen table cluttered with empty bottles sat next to a fireplace on the right. In the center of the room was a desk topped with radio equipment.

What the hell is that smell?

He pulled his M9 with one hand, grabbed the curtain with the other, and yanked it back to reveal a bedroom. A shadow moved in the corner of the room and he almost blasted a cat, which hissed at him from the top of a dresser. The cat jumped onto the floor and dashed around him, vanishing out the front door a second later.

"Major, out here!" Jake shouted.

Nathan looked around one last time, grabbed a ham

radio, and then retreated to the porch. Jake was waiting outside, his face pale.

"Thought I told you to stay put," Jake said. "Doesn't matter now. You're going to want to see this."

Nathan followed him around the side of the house. They halted in the knee-high grass to stare at the body hanging from the branch of a massive ponderosa tree.

Head bowed, the dead man swayed slowly in the wind. The front of his shirt was drenched in blood, and his legs were burned black to the knees.

The scent of charred flesh caught Nathan's nostrils a moment later. He covered his nose with a sleeve, realizing that this was what he had smelled in the cabin.

The remains of a bonfire lay just below the corpse. Blood from a dozen different wounds had darkened his plaid flannel shirt, and his bare feet were charred down to the bone. Whoever had killed Bill had strung him up and left him to burn. Fortunately for the surrounding woods, the rain had put out the fire. Nathan tried not to think about whether the poor man had died from blood loss, suffocation, or the flames.

"What kind of sick bastard did this?" Nathan asked.

Jake shook his head. "I don't know, but I got to get back to the station to tell Colton. Whoever killed Melissa didn't stop with her."

>——

"We're at war," Colton said. He braced himself for the response from the six town officials that were sitting in the Sundance conference room.

Across the table from him was Mayor Gail Andrews, a sixty-year-old woman with long white hair that she wore in a tidy braid. When she wasn't trying to micromanage every aspect of the town, she ran a gallery that catered mostly to rich tourists. To her right was the town administrator, Tom Feagen, a thick-set man with silver hair and a nasal voice that Colton couldn't stand. Tom was officially Colton's supervisor, but most of the time he worked directly with Gail. There was also the city engineer, the town clerk, and several officers from Colton's staff, all of whom were trying to talk at once.

"What do we do?"

"Who's in charge?"

"The government is really gone?"

"The power can't be out everywhere, can it?"

"What about the murderer? If we're stranded here, then so is he."

Colton decided he'd had enough. He raised a hand and said, "Listen up, everyone. What we discuss stays in this room for now."

For the next several minutes he reported everything he knew about the attack. By the time he had finished, the room was in chaos again. Feagen's voice was the loudest of them all.

"What are we going to do?" he kept repeating.

"If you'd give me a chance to explain, I'll tell you," Colton snapped.

Gail glared at Colton. He wasn't normally one to lose his cool, not even with Feagen, who had a law degree from some school in the Midwest and thought he was smarter than everyone in the room. However, the administrator had been hired after the 2013 floods. This was his first disaster, and he was already falling apart.

Well, if the municipal government couldn't handle things, Colton would.

"I've already put my people to work," he said. "I've declared a state of emergency and activated the EOC. We still haven't been able to reach anybody from the sheriff's office, but we're working on it. Now, what I need you to do is—"

The mayor cleared her throat. "Marcus, you know I respect you, but I'm not going to just let you take over the town. There have to be checks and balances," she said.

"I know, Gail, which is why I need you folks to step up. I'll take care of the policing, but I'll need you and Tom to work with Jake on the administrative and recovery stuff. If we all work together, we can keep our people safe, fed, and warm this winter."

"What about the fallout?" Feagen asked. "How are you going to protect us from that?"

"It's technically not fallout," Colton replied. "So far we haven't seen a spike in radiation, and if that changes we have a plan in place to evacuate people to emergency shelters. They're already stocked with supplies. For now, we have to keep everyone calm. We can't let them know what's going on until we're prepared."

A knock pounded the door, and Jake pushed it open without waiting for a response. He took off his cowboy hat and looked at Colton.

"Sir, I need to talk to you," he said firmly.

"Give me a minute," Colton replied. Then he noticed the

blood on Jake's uniform. "Actually, if you'll all excuse me, I'll be right back."

Feagen stood and waved a finger at him. "Whatever news Captain Englewood has, we all deserve to know."

"Tom is right," Gail said.

Colton scanned the frightened faces in the room and then looked back at Jake. Nathan was standing in the hallway, his arms folded across his chest. With a reluctant nod, Colton gave Jake the okay to speak.

"It's Bill Catcher, Chief." Jake let out a breath and cradled the cowboy hat against his chest. "He was murdered. Looks like the same person that killed Melissa."

The room erupted into panicked, angry shouting again. Colton cursed under his breath. If things weren't already bad enough.

"What are you going to do, Marcus?" Gail glared at him over the top of her green-rimmed glasses. "And what do you expect *us* to do? The town needs to know what's going on. We can't keep people in the dark."

"I think we should hold a town meeting," Feagen said. The other city officials began nodding and muttering their agreement.

"Fine," Colton said. "I'll be there, but I have something to do first."

As he turned to leave the room, Gail called after him. "Where are you going? We haven't adjourned yet!"

"Sorry, Gail," he said. "I've got a killer to track down."

Although he hated the thought of owing the man a favor, Colton knew he couldn't do this alone. He was going to have to convince Raven Spears to help him again.

13

RAVEN HAD HARDLY SLEPT SINCE HE GOT BACK TO HIS house. He lay in his bed replaying everything he knew about the attack while Allie played in the other room. Just as he began to doze off, a knock pounded his door.

Creek bolted away from his spot at the foot of the bed and raced down the stairs to the living room. His claws slid as he scrambled for traction on the wood floor. When he got to the door, he started barking.

"Shit," Raven said, rubbing his eyes. Akitas hardly ever barked unless there was something wrong. He jerked upright and reached for the crossbow next to his bed.

"Allie, where are you?" he said.

His niece poked her head around the door. Her hair was pulled back with one of Raven's skull bandanas. He would have laughed if he wasn't so worried.

"Someone's at the door, Uncle Raven," she said.
"Yes, I know."

Swinging his feet over the side of the bed, Raven crept up to the window. With the utmost care, he pulled the curtain back. There were two men on the front stoop. The taller of the pair wore a black suit. The other was in a gray sweatshirt. He was much shorter and heavier set, and he was looking around the property as if scanning for threats.

"Shit," he muttered. They were from Redford's posse, the loan shark he had borrowed money from. He pulled the Glock from under his pillow and tucked it into his pants before Allie could see it. Then he grabbed the crossbow from the wall and said, "Allie, we're going to play a game, okay?"

Creek was scratching on the door now, barking even louder.

"We know you're in there, Raven!" one of the men shouted.

Allie walked into his room, clutching her stuffed animal against her chest. "That man sounds mean. Why is he yelling?"

Raven set his crossbow on the ground, put a finger to his lips, and took a knee in front of his niece. "Go hide in the closet, kiddo. Don't come out until I tell you it's okay. I promise you can feed the chickens later."

Allie tilted her head like she wasn't sure if she could trust him. At last she seemed to make up her mind and climbed into his closet, settling cross-legged on the floor. Raven closed the sliding door and hurried back to his crossbow.

"Open up! I'm not going to ask again!" the goon shouted.

Redford apparently wasn't going to let a little thing like the end of world stop him from collecting on his debts. Raven had planned on paying them with the money he made from finding Melissa, but without any cash in hand, they weren't going to be happy. He couldn't exactly run down to the ATM and get the money, either.

"Creek, get back," Raven said. The dog obeyed and moved out of the way. Raven propped his crossbow beside the door, unlocked the deadbolt, and took a step back.

"Gentlemen," Raven said with a grin.

Neither of the two men returned the greeting. He recognized Redford's enforcers now.

"How's it going, Theo?" Raven asked the taller of the two goons. "And Andy! You're looking…short."

The smaller man growled. "It's Alex," he said. "Cut the shit and pay up."

"We're here to collect what you owe Mr. Redford. And we're not leaving until we do," Theo added.

"Figured that much," Raven said, looking at his feet. He had forgotten to put on shoes, which would make leading these guys away from the house—and his niece—more difficult.

"I'm a little short right now—no offense, Alex."

"You're not funny," Theo said. He nodded to Alex, who punched Raven in the gut with surprising force.

"For a little guy, you pack quite a punch," Raven wheezed. Creek came barreling from his hiding spot, but Raven waved him back. The dog snarled at the two men.

"Call off the dog or I'll put a bullet in his head," Theo said.

Raven got his breathing under control and stood up straight. "You'd shoot a dog? That's low, even for you."

"I said cut the shit," Alex said. "Just give us the cash, and we'll leave."

"Does Mr. Redford understand that cash is no longer going to be of value after last night?" Raven asked. He flexed his abs and waited for another gut punch, but it didn't come. Instead, Alex and Theo exchanged a confused look.

"You walked here, yes?" Raven said, jerking his chin toward the muddy cuffs of their pants. Both men nodded.

"Your cars don't work because an EMP fried everything with microcircuits in the whole state, maybe the whole country," Raven continued. "The banks are closed. The ATMs are useless. And you can't even call your boss because your cell phones have no signal."

"*Bullshit.* You're lying," Alex said, licking his lips. He inched forward, but Raven held his ground.

"You guys can't be that stupid," Raven said. "Look around. The lights are out, and nothing works. Trust me, I was over in Loveland last night, and it's the same deal there."

Theo was still shaking his head. "What's an EMP?"

"Hey, how were you in Loveland last night? You couldn't have walked there and back," Alex said.

Raven's grin faltered. *Shit, I should not have said that. Sandra always told me my big mouth would get me in trouble.*

"Um," Raven said, his mind racing. If they drew their guns, would he be able to take them both down before Creek got hurt? And what if he couldn't stop them? What would they do to Allie?

"You got a working car, huh?" Alex said. "Tell you what, we'll take that old hunk of junk as a down-payment now. Give me the keys."

"Okay, okay." Raven held up his hands like a magician revealing a trick. "Keys are inside, I'll be right back."

He turned, but the click of a hammer being pulled back on a revolver made him freeze. His eyes flitted to Creek. The dog was quivering, anxious to leap at the bastards. All Raven needed to do was blink, and Creek would be on whoever was pointing the gun at Raven's head. There was just one problem: If he started a fight, he couldn't be sure of the outcome. If Raven got himself killed, he wouldn't be able to protect Allie. And there was also the risk of a stray bullet punching through the floor of his closet.

Raven couldn't break his promise to Sandra—but he couldn't lose his Jeep, either.

"We'll come inside with you," Alex said.

"Don't make any sudden moves," Theo added.

Time slowed to an agonizing halt as he heard a round being chambered in a second gun. Raven used the stolen moment to plan his next move.

"What's going on?" asked a high-pitched, innocent voice.

Raven's eyes flicked to Allie. She was standing on the stairs, her stuffed pony still tucked in the crook of her arm.

"Didn't know you had a daughter," Theo said.

Raven gritted his teeth. "She's my niece." He slowly turned to see both men aiming guns at his head. Theo had a Glock, and Alex held a revolver that looked massive in his small hand.

"Come on guys, let's put the guns down. There's a kid here."

"Give us the keys," Alex said, holding out his other hand.

Raven slowly nodded and looked at Allie. "Go back upstairs, kiddo."

Squawking chickens broke the momentary silence that followed. Allie's eyes tracked the birds from the stairs. Then another sound came from the road. A sound Raven wasn't expecting.

Tires were crunching over the driveway.

Theo and Alex both looked away as a red pickup truck rumbled up to the house. In the passenger seat was Raven's least favorite police chief, looking like even more of a hardass than usual.

Raven used the opportunity to whisper a command to Creek. Of the hundred or so commands the Akita knew, about a dozen involved tearing out throats. The dog was on Theo before the man could react. As Alex turned back to the door, Raven knocked the gun from his hand and punched him in the temple. The smaller man crashed to the dirt like a felled tree, and Raven plucked the gun from his fingers.

"Get him off me!" Theo yelled as Creek ripped the sleeve of his jacket with a vicious snarl.

"No can do," Raven said, grinning again. Colton was here to arrest someone else for a change, and it felt great. He kicked Theo's Glock away and had just turned around to deal with Alex when the little debt collector yanked a second gun from an ankle holster and pulled the trigger.

>——>

Charlize stood in the waiting room of the Saint Luke's Hospital emergency room, trembling uncontrollably as she waited for her husband and son to get out of surgery. She never lost it like this. At least there weren't many people around to see her. Just Clint, her right-hand man, and her mother. Both of them were crying, so it didn't seem as shameful for her to fall apart.

Wait, that wasn't right. Clint hadn't been there that night, and her mom had been dead for fifteen years.

The emergency room vanished, replaced by darkness so black it was like her eyes had been plucked from their sockets. At first Charlize thought she was dead, but as the pain swept over her skin like burning acid, she found herself wishing she were dead.

There was so much pain.

She tried to scream, but all that came out was a strangled noise. She tried to move, but just blinking her eyelids required a monumental effort.

Where am I? What happened? Why does everything hurt?

It was difficult to focus on anything but the pain. Her skin was tight on her arms and face, and even the slightest movement resulted in another wave of searing agony. She drew in a breath of hot air that filled her nostrils with the unmistakable scent of burned hair.

She reached up to touch her face. It felt...wrong. Blisters popped as her nails grazed her cheeks. Every inch of exposed skin was burned.

"Hello," she choked, her voice a low rasp. "Hello?"

The only reply was the drip of water and the groan of structural supports in the bunker walls.

The bunker. Charlize remembered now. She was in the

PEOC, deep beneath the White House, along with what remained of the federal government.

She sucked in another hot breath. Exhaling, she steadied her shallow breathing and focused on Ty. Her son was still out there, halfway across the country. He *had* to be. She refused to consider any other possibility. Ty was okay. He would be scared and lonely, but he was okay.

The pain and the terror faded, replaced by determination. She had to get to her son.

Digging her fingernails into the debris-strewn carpet, she began dragging herself across the room, stopping when she bumped into a body. She groped blindly and felt an arm, then a chest, and as she reached for a face her hand brushed the jagged piece of concrete that had crushed Leon Crosby's skull.

She continued on, frantic now to find another survivor. Clint and Albert had been in the other room, and Charlize considered calling out to them. If they'd survived, she knew her loyal team would be helping anyone they could while searching for her. But she couldn't hear anything besides the sporadic crack of concrete or a snapping pipe. If they were still alive, they were on their own for now. She would just have to rescue herself.

A steady flow of water dripped onto her exposed skin as she crawled out from under the broken table. The cool liquid felt good on her burns, but she quickly shivered from the cold. Stars rolled across her vision.

Teeth chattering, she called out a second time. "C-can—anyone—hear—me?"

"Help," someone answered. "God, it hurts. Please, someone help me."

Charlize recognized the voice. It was Acting President Diego.

"Sir, hang on. I'm coming," Charlize said.

She fumbled across the floor on all fours like a blind dog, pulling herself over debris.

"Trapped," Diego groaned. "Please, I can't move."

"I'm coming," Charlize said. As she moved toward the voice, she tried to think of a plan. Even if she could free him, they were stuck down here. And even if they could somehow escape, the surface above would be hell. If the fire and ash didn't kill them, the radiation would.

You have to try, she thought. She pushed herself to her feet and fell, landing on a body. Charlize scrambled to her feet. This time she made it all the way up, bumping her head on something hanging from the partially-collapsed ceiling.

A jolt of pain rushed down her back, but she pushed on, groping the air with her hands. She stumbled over a chunk of debris and then blundered into a curtain of cold water falling from a broken pipe.

"Sir, where are you?" Charlize said. "This is Senator Montgomery."

"Over here." Gasp. "Stuck."

She turned in the direction of his voice. He sounded like he was having trouble breathing.

"I'm almost there," Charlize said. "Just hang on."

The room replied with a tremor that shook the walls. Charlize froze, closing her eyes and waiting again to be crushed. These walls were built to withstand a direct hit from a nuclear weapon, and yet they were falling down around her. What the hell had the North Koreans hit them with?

Charlize carefully waded through the darkness, hands moving through the air in front of her in wide arcs, desperate to save a man she didn't even like.

The walls continued to creak as she moved. With every step, she wondered if it would be her last.

An agonized groan reverberated through the room.

"Hang on, sir. I'm almost there," Charlize said.

She froze as something began pounding against the walls or ceiling—she couldn't tell where exactly it was coming from. Whatever was causing the noise sounded deliberate, like someone was hitting a drum over and over.

Charlize twisted around, straining to see in the darkness. The pounding stopped, replaced by a scratching and then a crunching, like the walls were being pried apart. Then she heard voices in the other room, faint but unmistakable.

Charlize didn't dare breathe as she listened.

"Over there!"

"This one's gone."

The door to the operations room crashed to the ground, and beams of light penetrated the inky darkness. Charlize held a hand up to shield her sensitive eyes, but she kept her gaze on two men in full CBRN suits who came barreling into the room.

"There," one of them said, pointing in her direction. His voice still sounded strangely muffled, and Charlize wasn't sure if it was from her own damaged hearing or the breathing apparatus inside the man's suit. "Ma'am, it's going to be all right. Help is coming."

Charlize's legs began to shake, and with her last ounce of energy, she pointed toward where she'd heard Diego's voice.

"Help the president," she said before collapsing to the ground.

14

Colton and Jake crouched behind the back of the pickup truck as another gunshot rang out. The bullet punched through the fender. Whatever situation Raven had gotten himself into, it was quickly escalating.

"That guy is going to pay for hitting my truck," Jake growled.

Colton reached out and held Jake back, and took in a breath of mountain air that stung his nostrils. He was regretting several things right now, especially his decision to ask Raven for help. He should have brought more backup, but how the hell was Colton supposed to know he was driving to a gun fight? He should have known better—this was Raven, after all.

"Put down your weapon!" Colton shouted. He considered trying to grab his M14 from the passenger seat, but he didn't want to risk moving.

Colton snapped open the cylinder of his Colt .45 and checked the ammo. There were six rounds loaded.

He slammed it shut and cocked the hammer back. The revolver would have to do.

Another shot cracked through the woods outside Raven's house, and the bullet kicked up the dirt by his left boot. Colton resisted the urge to jump from his position and return fire.

Be smart, Marcus. You can't get shot. You have too much to do.

Every move from here on out was the difference between life and death. Not just for him, but for his family and maybe the whole town. Even a flesh wound could end up killing him now that medicine would be hard to come by.

With his back to the truck, he waited for a third shot. In the respite came Creek's snarls and the grunts of the man the dog had pinned down. Raven was somewhere inside the house with his niece. That was good. Colton didn't want him to get in the way of what happened next.

After another long, tense moment, Colton and Jake exchanged a nod. Colton held up three fingers, then two, then one.

Jake fired his shotgun into the woods and then immediately ducked back down. The shooter was momentarily focused on Jake, giving Colton his chance. Moving to the other end of the truck, Colton raised his revolver, aimed the sights at the shooter, and fired. The shot went wide. A short man in a gray sweatshirt roved his gun toward Colton, and Colton squeezed the trigger again. The shot clipped the man in the shoulder. He let out a screech of pain and took off running in a hunch toward a cluster of trees.

"After him!" Colton ordered.

Jake was already on the move.

Keeping low, Colton bolted in the direction the shooter had run. He still wasn't sure exactly what the hell was going on, but his guess was that Raven had pissed off some bad people.

"Stay in your house, Raven!" Colton shouted.

There was no reply and Colton glanced at the man wearing a suit to the left. He was on his back in the dirt, hands up in a defensive position. There wasn't time to put him in cuffs, but Colton could see the guy wasn't going anywhere. Not if he wanted to keep his throat. Saliva dripped from Creek's maw as the dog snarled at the man.

The ground, slick from the rain the night before, mushed under Colton's boots as he ran into the woods. They moved for several minutes side by side in combat intervals, just like they were trained.

Colton flashed a hand signal and Jake took up position behind a rock a few hundred feet to the right.

Silence washed over the woods. Colton listened for the crunch of footfalls or the groans of their injured chase, but there was nothing besides the wind rustling the canopy and a bird calling out in the distance.

He signaled for Jake to take point. An instant later, Colton saw a flash of gray moving on the ridgeline right toward Jake.

"Watch out!" Colton shouted.

There was an earsplitting crack, and Colton knew the

short man had gotten off the first shot. The retort from Jake's shotgun never came. Colton watched his friend crash to the dirt.

"NO!" Colton shouted. He aimed his Colt .45 toward the man, but by the time he found his target, the shooter was already on his knees, pawing at his neck as blood drenched the front of his shirt. An arrow protruded from the center of his Adam's apple.

Colton raised his pistol at an approaching figure. As soon as he saw it was Raven he lowered his gun and ran toward Jake.

The burly officer was on his back, clutching his gut and sucking in labored breaths. Colton holstered his pistol and dropped by his friend's side.

"Son of a bitch, that bastard got me," Jake wheezed.

"Don't talk." Colton felt around Jake's chest and stomach for the wound so he could apply pressure, but Jake slapped his hand away.

"It's okay," he grumbled. "I'm wearing a vest today."

Colton pulled his hand away. "Jesus, Jake. You about gave me a heart attack."

"Hey," Raven shouted from the top of the hill. "Is he okay? This little prick is dead."

Colton helped Jake sit up and then ran over to Raven and the dead man. Dark, wide eyes glared up at cloudy sky, a look of shock still painted on his face.

"Thanks, I owe *you* one," Colton said to Raven, hardly believing the words as they left his mouth.

Raven nodded and rose to his feet. "Actually, I owe you one. You got here just in the nick of time. This guy and his friend would have killed me and my niece if it weren't for you two."

"What happened to the other guy? Did you—"

"No, I didn't kill him. Creek is still watching him."

Colton had a dozen questions running through his head, but instead of asking them, he reached down and grabbed the dead man's pistol. He wedged it in the pocket of his jacket.

"Goddammit, Raven," Colton said. Now that they were out of danger, he found his usual impatience with Raven returning. "Why can't you stay out of trouble?"

Jake staggered over to them, gripping his chest. "Nice shooting," he said to Raven. "But how about you explain why this guy just tried to kill me?"

"I swear I didn't start this shit. They came for some money I owe their boss." Raven slung the crossbow over his back. "When I told them about the attack, they tried to take my Jeep, and then they pulled guns on me right in front of Allie."

Colton's eyes flicked to Jake. The hulking officer looked okay, but he'd probably have a hell of a bruise come morning.

"Look, if you came here to arrest me, then just get it over with, man," Raven said, holding his wrists out. "Go ahead, put the cuffs on again."

Colton sighed. "I didn't come to arrest you, Raven."

"Oh? Did you come for my Jeep?" He lowered his hands. "Sorry, I'm not handing it over for good…but you can borrow it if you really need it."

"I didn't come for your Jeep either," Colton said. "I came for your help. We found Bill Catcher's body this morning, hanging from a tree in his backyard."

"Oh shit," Raven said. He patted his jacket pocket, drew out a crumpled pack of cigarettes, and then seemed to think better of it.

"Bill's legs were burned, like Melissa's," Colton said quietly. He paused, listening to the wind rustle the branches of the ash trees. "We've only got two bodies so far, but I fear we might have a serial killer on the loose, and with everything else going on, I need your tracking skills to find him."

The world was burning.

Charlize was lying on her back, too hurt and exhausted to move, in a place that looked a lot like hell. Fires raged in every direction, flames licking at a sky the color of bloody mud. Or was that the ceiling?

I'm dead. I've gone to hell for all those innocent civilians I killed during the war.

Intense terror ripped through her. She could sense the rush of adrenaline, but she still couldn't feel her limbs. She couldn't feel any pain either, and somehow the numbness was worse than the burning agony.

You're dead. You failed Ty, and you won't ever see Richard again.

But if this was hell, shouldn't she feel pain? Wasn't she supposed to suffer?

The blurry forms of other sinners were moving around her. Their skin looked like dark plastic, wrinkled and deformed.

Burned. Everyone was burned.

Lightning flashed overhead. So that was the sky after all. And she seemed to be rising toward it. The burning pyres seemed to be falling away, growing ever smaller as she rose out of hell. She could see other shapes now, skeletal things like the bones of whales jutting out of the scorched dirt.

The sensation of motion grew stronger, and a fierce, hot wind whipped at her body. Beyond the dull ringing in her ears, she heard a strangely familiar sound.

This wasn't hell, but she wasn't ascending into heaven either.

I'm in a chopper, she realized. How had she gotten here? All she remembered was burning pain and then darkness. Had her F-15 crashed? Was she being airlifted to safety?

She sucked in a breath of sharp air that stung her lungs. A hand touched her shoulder, and she turned away from the burning world to see a man in a space suit looking down at her.

Her vision suddenly sharpened. It wasn't a space suit; this was a soldier in a CBRN suit.

"Ma'am, can you hear me?"

"How...?" she started to say. Her mouth was so dry. She licked her lips and tried again. "How did my plane crash? Where's the rest of my squadron?"

To the masked man's right was a familiar face—a face that reminded her she wasn't in some foreign warzone. She was in D.C. What was left of it.

Albert nudged the soldier out of the way and managed to open his cracked, bloody lips. A single tear rolled down his face. It was the first time Charlize had ever seen the big man cry.

"You're going to be okay," Albert said. "We're going somewhere safe."

Charlize tried to respond, but all that came out was something that sounded like a witch's cackle. She tried to move again, managing to palm the metal floor with her burned hands. Her skin stuck to the surface.

Two more soldiers in CBRN suits closed the door to the helicopter, sealing off the view of the burning landscape below. Charlize scanned the troop hold, trying to see who had made it. Diego was on a stretcher with two soldiers working on him. There was another person in the corner of the troop hold whose flesh was so badly burned she couldn't tell who it was.

"Where's Clint?" she asked.

Albert's mouth moved in reply, but a raucous clap cut him off.

Charlize twisted to look out the window, half expecting to see North Korean fighters tearing through the skies. Instead of hostile jets, there was only the electric blue crackle of lighting.

She made herself sit up to look out the window. Her body seemed distant, like it had been unplugged from her brain. Probably morphine, she realized. Either that or shock. The view outside really was like looking down into hell. Fires burned across the horizon. Husks of buildings were all that remained in some areas, but ground zero was a flat, smoldering field. The shockwaves from the strike had pounded the city into a blackened pancake.

Near the epicenter of the destruction lay what remained of the Washington Monument. Blackened blocks of stone littered the smoking dirt not far from where the other symbols of American democracy and freedom had once stood. The White House, the Capitol, the National Mall …they were all gone. From now on, Washington would be nothing more than a radioactive night light.

"Ma'am. Can I look at your arm please?"

She forced her gaze away from the window. The soldier in the CBRN suit was back, holding a medical kit.

Charlize ran a hand over her head, and a clump of hair came out in her burned fingers. She held it up and examined the shriveled ends of what had been her favorite feature. Charlize wasn't a vain woman, but she had loved her long, glossy black hair.

A tear crept down her cheeks, the salt searing her skin. Lips trembling, she looked to Albert and asked again, "Al, where's Clint?"

Albert wiped his forehead and then slowly pointed toward the horribly burned body in the back of the troop hold.

―――▶

Raven was late.

That normally wouldn't have surprised Sandra, but today she needed her brother more than ever before. It had been a rough morning, with several new patients showing up throughout the early hours. One man had suffered a mild heart attack on the walk into town after being stranded on Highway 34. He claimed to have trekked ten miles to get to the hospital. They had him stabilized now, but another man who had gone into cardiac arrest hadn't been so lucky.

Sandra sat next to Teddy's bed, her hands tingling from the constant motion of pumping air into his breathing tube. She had traded off the duty with other nurses and doctors throughout the night, but they were all busy with other patients now.

Everything that required power was offline: ventilators, feeding tubes, dialysis machines. Feeding tubes and saline drips could work by gravity, but the pumps were offline. ECG monitors were dead. The labs, the CT and MRI machines…none of their expensive equipment worked. Sandra and the other nurses and physicians were practically working in the blind.

The doors were propped open to let in light from the outside. It also helped with the airflow. Without ventilation, it was already getting hot despite the chilly temperatures outside. And the smells…

Sandra breathed in through her surgical mask. It helped block some of the stench, but not everything.

The curtain cordoning off the small space peeled back and Newton looked in. He closed it and asked, "How is he?"

"The same," she said.

Newton examined Teddy. Sandra wasn't sure what was going on in the doctor's mind, but she could tell by his calculating look he was probably factoring Teddy's chances of survival.

He looked away and tapped his iWatch several times before giving up.

"Damn thing still doesn't work. Does anyone know what time it is?"

"Little after noon," someone yelled back.

Newton wiped sweat from his forehead with a sleeve. "Doctor Duffy and I have asked Kayla to put together a handwritten schedule for the staff. We're going to need everyone to work double shifts until the power comes back on."

Sandra wanted to tell him that the power was never coming back on, but she held her tongue. Instead, she pumped another breath into Teddy's lungs, his chest rising with the oxygen. He looked so peaceful, drifting in his medically induced coma. Sandra realized with a jolt that she hadn't slept for more than a few minutes for over thirty hours.

"My daughter is with her uncle, but I'm sure he can watch her longer. I just need some rest, maybe an hour."

"Of course," Newton replied. "Everyone is going to get—"

The sound of a commotion in the lobby cut the doctor off. Several raised voices echoed into the ICU. One of them was Kayla's, but Sandra didn't recognize the others.

"I better check this out," said Newton.

"Does anyone know where I can find Sandra Spears?" someone called.

Sandra nearly forgot to help Teddy breathe. She carefully squeezed the bag, but her heart was running wild. Had something happened to her little girl?

Newton glanced at her and reached out for the bag. "Looks like you have visitors. Why don't you let me take over?"

Coordinating the shift with the utmost care, Sandra and Newton changed places. She stepped onto the floor of the ER, terrified about what she would discover.

"Momma!"

Allie was standing at the entrance to the room, holding Police Chief Marcus Colton's hand. She came running and grabbed Sandra around the waist.

"Allie! What are you...?" Exhausted and confused, Sandra looked to Colton for an answer.

"Ma'am," he said, inclining his head. Before she could ask him what he was doing there, Doctor Duffy approached. Sandra hugged Allie and then knelt to look her over.

"Are you okay?"

Allie nodded.

"Where is Raven?"

She nestled her head against Sandra's shoulder and whimpered.

Hospital staff watched Colton as Sandra worked to calm Allie. People from the lobby tried to follow the police chief into the ER, but Kayla shooed them away before sending the curious nurses back to their tasks.

"What can you tell us? Will the power be back on anytime soon?" Duffy asked Colton. Then his eyes went wide. "Damn, Chief, what the hell happened to you?"

Colton glanced down at his uniform, which was covered in blood.

"There was an incident," he said dryly, before reassuring the doctor that the blood wasn't his. He looked toward Sandra and said, "Ma'am, we need you to come outside."

"What did my brother do now?"

Colton jerked his chin toward the exit. "You can ask him yourself."

Sandra grabbed Allie's hand and led her through the lobby

and outside into the parking lot. Between the lack of sleep and her rapidly firing heart, Sandra felt like she was going to faint.

The first thing she saw was Jake standing next to Raven's Jeep, guarding the rear door with a shotgun. A man in a black suit that Sandra didn't recognize sat inside.

Raven was sitting on the tailgate of a red pickup truck next to Nathan. Sandra wasn't sure what to think when she saw the two men fiddling with a radio. She had expected to see her brother in handcuffs.

Creek trotted over and nudged up against her leg. He let out a whine and then sat on his haunches.

"Sis!" Raven shouted when he saw her. He jumped onto the pavement and strode over. Nathan carefully set the radio down and then limped over.

As she walked over to meet them, she noticed the shape covered in a bloody blanket on the bed of the truck. She moved in front of Allie to block her view.

"What happened? Who is that?" she asked.

"Stay calm," Colton said. "Your brother was attacked at his place. One of the men didn't make it."

"Attacked by who? And why?"

"Redford's goons," Raven said. "Don't worry, they didn't hurt Allie."

Anger boiled up inside of Sandra, warring with the relief she felt at having her daughter back. If Raven had needed money so badly, why didn't he ask her or get a loan from the bank like a normal person? No, he had to get in deep with a loan shark and put her little girl in danger.

She would have yelled at her brother, but she didn't want to scare Allie any more than she was already.

"We're just here to drop Allie off," Colton said, looking nervously at her. Sandra hoped she looked as furious as she felt. "Sorry for the trouble, ma'am, but I need your brother's help."

Sandra regarded Colton with a scowl. "Help? I figured you'd be taking him off to jail again. Maybe he deserves it."

Colton looked around, seemingly checking to see who else was in earshot, and then stepped closer to Sandra to whisper, "Someone murdered Bill Catcher sometime this morning or last night. I think it's the same person that killed Melissa. I need your brother and Creek to help me find him."

Sandra wasn't ready to be friendly or forgiving. "Don't let him get you shot," she said.

Colton nodded as if this was good advice. "Yes, ma'am. Is there someone else who can watch your daughter while you're at work? If not, my wife could—"

"That won't be necessary," Sandra said. "I'd rather keep her with me."

Colton nodded, smiled warmly at Allie, and then made his way back to the vehicles. He gestured for Nathan and Raven to join him.

"This man needs medical attention," Sandra said as Nathan started to walk away. "Come here, Major, let me take a look at you."

The handsome pilot actually blushed. "I'll be fine, Ms. Spears."

She gave him her best nurse's glare. "You're going to permanently damage yourself if you keep running around with my fool brother."

"I heard that," Raven said. "I swear, I didn't do anything wrong."

"You never do anything wrong, Raven," Sandra said with a sigh. "You never take responsibility for anything either. What if those men had hurt Allie, or Creek?"

Raven stuck his hands in his pockets, and his eyes flitted to the ground. He wore the same wounded look that Sandra remembered from their childhood after their dad would yell at him. Her heart hurt at the sight, but her brother was going to have to grow up sooner than later.

She joined the men by the trucks as Colton gave them orders. Nathan would take Jake's battered truck and see if he could get the ham radio working. Colton and Jake would transfer the corpse to the morgue in Raven's Jeep, drop off their prisoner at the jail, and then head out to the high school, where Colton would address the people of Estes Park at a community meeting.

He pointed at Raven. "What do you need?"

"Well, since you're borrowing my Jeep, I could use a million bucks, a couple cases of top shelf whiskey, and a couple of supermodels." Raven glanced up at Prospect Mountain. "And how about a helicopter?"

Colton flared his nostrils, clearly not amused.

"I'm just kidding, Chief," Raven said. "I just need Creek, my crossbow, and a ride up to Prospect. I'll try to pick up the trail at Bill Catcher's place."

"I'll send an officer with you," Colton said.

Raven shook his head and looked at Sandra. "I'm better off on my own. Don't want anyone else to get hurt."

The dig was aimed at her, but she wasn't going to apologize

for her earlier words. Raven had promised he would protect them, and instead he had gotten her daughter mixed up in a gun fight that ended with at least one man dead.

"Suit yourself," Colton replied. "Let's move out."

Raven hesitated and then put his arms around Allie. "I'm sorry, *Agaliga*," he said.

"Sunshine," Sandra said after a snort. Her brother always was the charmer. He pulled away from Allie and reached out for Sandra. The knuckles of his hand looked even more swollen, and a bruise was coming up on his cheek. She clicked her tongue, remembering all the times she'd held makeshift ice packs against his bruised face while they were growing up. Their dad had thrown a lot of punches in that house.

"I'm sorry," Raven said again, turning to her. "Seriously. I'm really sorry, Sis. I promise I'm going to change. I'll be a better man."

Sandra wrapped her arms around her brother as her anger at last thawed. "You're still the best man in my life. Be careful, okay?"

15

Nathan drove the Chevy up Trail Ridge Road, following a map Chief Colton had drawn him. He hoped that the higher elevation would help him get a clear signal. The old pickup was having a hell of a time with the climb, rattling and shaking. Going from an F-16 Viper to this old clunker was one hell of a change. He wasn't used to seeing the snow-kissed mountains and evergreen forests from the ground, either. Was this what his sister had felt like when she gave up her wings for a seat in Congress?

The long, winding road provided him plenty of time to think. He realized how lucky he'd been to run into Sandra in the woods. Her face appeared in his mind's eye with her proud, high cheekbones and dark eyes full of compassion and fire. Although they looked nothing alike, something about her reminded him of his sister.

It didn't seem likely that he'd see Charlize again, at least not in this life. His poor nephew was almost certainly an orphan now. Ty was the bravest kid he'd ever known, but he was still just a kid, and Nathan wished more than anything that he'd ignored orders and gone on to the Easterseals camp.

At least he had finally found a radio. The battery-powered analog shortwave radio was his best shot at reaching the outside world. He just hoped it worked. So far the damn thing wasn't getting a signal. His plan was to rig up the antennae he had borrowed from the police station. The highest point of Trail Ridge Road was just over twelve thousand feet. If it still didn't work there, then he was shit out of luck.

Then again, if there was a radioactive cloud from the high-altitude nuclear blast, they were all out of luck. He didn't know much about how the radioactive particles were spread, but he knew it was highly dangerous in the short term. If they blew east, then Estes Park might be okay, but he wasn't sure about Empire. The small city was much closer to the blast zone.

The truck chugged along, and he had to weave around several abandoned vehicles. The drivers were long gone. He didn't envy them the long trek they must have made into town.

As the road looped around the peaks, Nathan looked out over the valley below. His heart stuttered when he saw the black pockmark on the sheer face of a nearby mountain. Below, the burned skeletons of pine trees poked out of the ground. Nathan couldn't see the debris from his wingman's wreckage from this vantage, and part of him didn't want to.

He pressed down harder on the gas pedal. The truck

jolted forward, the chassis protesting with a shriek. Ahead, the road cut through a narrow pass in the mountains. On the other side, snow carpeted everything from the treetops to the pavement.

"Almost there," he said, patting the wheel.

The road curved past a large open meadow with drifts of snow. A herd of elk raced away from the sound of the truck. In the distance, a storm was moving in. Dark, bulging clouds rolled over the mountains. Lightning flashed in their swell.

Nathan parked the truck on the side of the road and looked for a place to set up. After a quick scan, he picked the slope to the east. He would make the easy trek across the snow and rig the antennae up there.

Lugging his bag over his shoulders, he limped across the road and into the snow. He was still wearing his rumpled, dirty flight suit, topped with an Estes Park Police Department sweatshirt. He'd never cared much about his appearance, but this was bad even for him. He made a mental note to find some clothes when he returned to town.

The snow was only shin-deep at first, but it quickly got deeper as he made his way across the meadow. By the time he reached the top of the slope, it was halfway up his legs. His ankle throbbed in the cold, and he wished he'd taken Sandra up on her offer to rewrap it.

A gust of wind bit into his side, nearly throwing him off balance. The cold crept through his layers. He raised his cupped hands to his mouth and blew in them before setting up the radio. The sharp peaks of the Rocky Mountains lined the horizon. It was a beautiful sight, but the storm clouds were growing in size and strength.

Nathan bent down and unloaded his gear. He spent the next few minutes attaching the antennae. When he had finished, he set the radio on a rock and pulled the receiver. Then he dialed to all the even numbers to listen for chatter. There wasn't much, and what he did hear wasn't helpful. Just a lot of panicked-sounding civilians asking for information or begging for help.

"CQ, CQ. This is Sierra Tango Foxtrot Niner in Iowa City, Iowa. We've got refugees streaming in from I-80 with signs of radiation poisoning. Is anyone out there? We need help. FEMA, the military, anybody. Someone, please answer!"

He decided to search for a clean frequency instead and see if there was someone out there from Colorado that would respond to him. After he found one, he checked to make sure it was open. Since he didn't have a ham call sign, he used his rank. "CQ, CQ, Major Sardetti, US Air Force, CQ, CQ. Is this an open frequency? This is Major Nathan Sardetti calling CQ and listening."

He waited a few minutes but didn't hear any chatter. He continued his call. "CQ, CQ this is Major Nathan Sardetti, United States Air Force. My Viper was shot down over Estes Park, Colorado. Anyone out there?"

"That's affirmative, this is Whiskey Foxtrot Zero Zero Niner. Located at Colorado Springs. Sorry about your Viper, Major. Glad you made it out."

The wind howled, and he covered the receiver to protect it from the gust.

"Say again? My noise level is horrendous," said the other operator. "I hope you're not outside, Major. There's a radioactive storm heading your way."

Nathan's eyes darted to the bulging storm clouds on the horizon. "Come again, Whiskey Foxtrot Zero Zero Niner?"

"Radioactive cloud heading your way, Major. I'm holed up at Cheyenne Mountain. We're tracing the radioactive patterns, and I've been tasked with relaying that information over analog."

Nathan allowed himself a breath and tried his best to remain calm while the operator continued speaking.

"You all need to stay indoors for at least a couple of days just to be safe, and even after that the radiation might be too high to leave shelter if it's as bad as we're predicting."

Nathan pulled the mic away from his mouth and looked out over the valley. Colton was down there somewhere preparing to talk to a high school gym full of civilians, all of them unaware of the threat barreling down on them.

"How long do we have?" Nathan asked.

"Two and a half, maybe three hours."

"Is Empire, Colorado, in that storm pattern?"

"Afraid so, Major. They have been for the past few hours."

Nathan's bottom lip quivered. He held the mic away, hesitated, then brought it back to his lips. "Whiskey Foxtrot Zero Zero Niner. I need you to do me a favor. Two actually."

"Why don't you call me Jeff, sir? Senior Airman Jeff Main at your service."

"Okay," Nathan said. "Right now I have to get back to town to warn everyone, but please see if you can contact anyone listening in Empire and warn them. Tell them there are kids and staff at the Easterseals camp that need help. I also need you to reach Senator Charlize Montgomery in D.C. She's my sister."

"Sir, that's not going to be easy." There was a pause, and then the airman continued, "Washington was destroyed in the second wave of the attack. I'm sorry, Major."

Nathan fell to his knees in the snow, his body giving out as all hope faded. Charlize was really gone. He missed the next several messages as his mind filled with grief.

A beeping sound drew his attention back to the present. He glanced at the radio, but the noise wasn't coming from the device. The Geiger counter in his bag was chirping as the needle ticked higher toward the red zone.

Nathan pushed the radio's receiver back to his mouth. "I have to get back to town. I'll transmit again as soon as I can."

"Copy that, Major. Good luck."

Nathan stuffed the radio back in his bag and hurried back to the truck, his eyes on the growing storm. One thing was certain: They were going to need more than luck to survive this.

Two hours after throwing Theo in jail, Colton stood in the high school gymnasium, staring at the purple Bobcats flag hanging from the wall. Over a thousand people had shown up, despite having to walk there. The natural light coming in from the open doors was hardly enough to illuminate the entire gym.

Looking out over the crowd, he saw people of all ages ranging from a baby clutched against her mother's chest to an elderly woman hanging on the arm of her son. There were plenty of faces he didn't recognize in the dim lighting, probably tourists who were stranded here. If the worst came to pass and the power grid was never restored, those strangers would probably become permanent residents of his town.

No matter where he looked, everyone had the same fearful gaze. What he said next would need to reassure these people enough to prevent them from panicking, but he couldn't bring himself to lie to their faces, either. The burden of his position began to sink in as he walked toward the platform to face the crowd.

Sergeant Aragon and Mayor Andrews' entire staff were standing on the platform. Kelly and Risa were up there with them. Colton smiled at his wife and then nodded at the Mayor. She had convinced him that whatever was said today needed to come from him.

The chatter in the room died down as he stepped up to the podium, but some conversations continued. He stuck his fingers in his mouth and whistled, a trick he'd learned in the National Guard from his commanding officer. It took several more seconds before the room was silent.

Over sporadic coughing, Colton could hear the wind howling outside the gym's open doors. The sound seemed fitting for what he was about to say.

"We are at war," he said in a commanding voice. "Today, we stand together in the aftermath of a devastating attack. North Korea set off a series of nuclear weapons in the skies above the United States, triggering an electromagnetic pulse that knocked out our power grid and crippled our electronic devices."

The gasps, shouts, and voices that followed didn't surprise Colton. He could feel Gail glaring at him, and he didn't blame her. He wasn't following the narrative they had discussed, but part of being a leader was knowing when to improvise.

"Many of you remember the 2013 floods. This is much, much worse. Estes Park is a small but proud community. We will be one of the last cities in Colorado to receive aid, if help is even available. You deserve to know what we face in the coming days, weeks, and months. It may sound like this is the end of the world, but I assure you, if we stand together as one, we will get through this. Our isolation isn't a bad thing. We have plenty of clean water up here, and we can hunt, fish, and forage when our food supplies run out. But..."

It wasn't the best time to pause, but his words trailed off when Colton saw Rex and Lilly Stone standing near the front, holding on to each other.

Don coughed into his hand, a subtle message to get on with it. Colton grabbed the sides of the podium and leaned forward.

"But we need to follow some basic rules or else there will be chaos in our streets. Anyone who breaks the peace will answer to me."

"What are you going to do about the murder of that little girl, Chief?" someone shouted.

"I heard Bill Catcher was murdered too!" yelled another man.

Colton held up his hand. "As many of you have obviously heard, we have had two homicides in the past twenty-four hours, but I promise you that I will find the person or people responsible."

He could still feel Rex staring at him, and he didn't avoid

the grieving father's gaze. Colton held it for several seconds before continuing.

"Make no mistake. We are at war, and life is going to dramatically change. That's why we need to stick together and help one another."

Several shouts rang out through the room, and Colton heard more than one person crying. Terrified faces stared back at him. Families clustered together. Children were sobbing, and some parents seemed too shocked to comfort them.

The burden of Colton's duty to protect these people was nearly overwhelming, but instead of slouching, he stiffened and looked to the American flag hanging from the northern wall, a symbol of freedom and justice that he had fought and bled for. It gave him the strength he needed to finish his address.

"I know you're all scared," Colton said. "I'm scared too, but we're Americans. We have overcome great adversity in our history. We have come together to fight for our independence, we healed after a devastating Civil War. We united after Nine-Eleven, and we must remain united now."

The room quieted.

"We have survived attacks in the past, and we will survive this."

Several heads began to nod.

Colton pointed at the flag. "We're all citizens of this great country, and as long as we work together we will prevail."

The sounds of panic and crying in the audience faded. People wiped away their tears. That was the American way. Grieve, and then get up and fight. These people were ready to do just that.

"Moving forward, I'm going to need your help protecting our town. I'm talking to all of you, residents and visitors alike. Last night each tourist became a citizen, too, and we need your help."

John Palmer, a volunteer firefighter, stepped forward from the crowd. "I've got your back, Chief!" he shouted.

Within seconds, half of the gymnasium was offering their help and support.

Even Dale, the belligerent soldier he had disarmed the night before, was pumping his fist in the air and bellowing *Ooh Rah*. Colton couldn't help but smile at that.

Don began clapping, and others soon joined in. But there was also another noise, a commotion coming from the side of the room. A sea of bodies parted to make way for two men rushing to the platform.

"Chief," Jake said, gasping for air. "Chief, we need to talk to you."

Looking back over the crowd, Colton said, "Can't this wait?"

Jake stared back, eyes blazing with something he didn't usually see in the burly police officer.

Fear.

"What is it?" Colton asked, keeping his voice low.

"I made contact with a senior airman out of Cheyenne Mountain," Nathan explained. "He said there's radiation heading our way in that storm. We have to get everyone to shelter."

Colton's heart hammered as he glanced back over the crowd.

"How long do we have?" he asked.

Nathan shook his head. "Not long. A little over two hours at this point."

"Shit," Colton said. He waved Gail over and relayed the news.

"We have a shelter here at the high school, another at the hospital, and a third back at town hall," she said. "But what about people in the rural areas?"

"Jake, go get the bullhorn from the station and take your truck out to notify people they need to get indoors. They should put plastic sheets and tape over their windows, if they can, and get their livestock and pets under cover. They should protect their water wells, too. Tell them to stay put until we give them the word."

Jake nodded. "I'm on it."

The large officer kept his hand on his cowboy hat as he hurried away.

Colton stepped back up to the podium. The only good news he had to offer was that these people wouldn't have far to go to reach the nearest shelter. He took a deep breath and spoke in a calm, deep voice.

"Everyone, you all need to listen to what I say next very carefully."

He felt the stares of a thousand people like a physical onslaught, but Marcus Colton would not let that deter him. What these people needed was a leader, and he was the best they were going to get.

"There's a storm heading our way, and it could produce radioactive rain," Colton said. Then he explained the basic steps to secure their homes for the people who wanted to return to their families. Everyone else would take shelter in the well-stocked basement of the high school. People began moving right away, and he stepped away from the podium to give orders to his officers. He'd need all of them on the streets, directing people to the closest shelters. He asked Don to remain behind at the school, and he directed Mayor Andrews to head back to town hall with her staff.

Kelly and Risa rushed over to him, and Colton reached for their hands.

"Dad, was that little girl you were talking about, Melissa?" Risa asked, tears welling up in her eyes. "One of my friends said she was killed."

Colton shared a stricken look with Kelly. They'd wanted to protect their little girl from the harsh truth—and, if he was honest, to protect themselves from the heartache of seeing her innocence fade. But by doing so, they'd ended up hurting her even more.

"Sweetheart, I'm so sorry..." Colton realized he didn't have time to explain anything to Risa right now.

"Chief Colton," said Nathan, limping over to them. "What about Raven?"

"What about him?"

Colton cursed when he remembered that he had sent Raven out to Prospect Mountain. They had left him up there without a vehicle, and he was likely deep in the woods, out of range of the bullhorn. Raven was a cunning son of a bitch and a former recon Marine, but that wouldn't save him from radiation-laced rain.

Wet gravel crunched under Raven's boots. He was in tracking mode, completely alert and aware of his surroundings. He had put every other concern out of his mind, including the guilt he felt for the North Korean attack.

The spectacular views up here helped, with the Rocky Mountains to the west and Lake Estes to the east. But the oncoming storm ruined the picture. It was rolling west across the horizon, and Estes Park looked to be directly in its path.

"Great," Raven muttered. He was itching for a cigarette, but he pulled his Seattle Mariners hat and his poncho from his backpack instead. He threw them on and then jogged after his dog. The road twisted up the mountain, curving off onto private drives that he hadn't even known existed. Many of the properties were blocked off by high fences with elaborate metal gates, but he could make out the enormous houses beyond.

So this is how rich people live, he mused.

Not everybody up here was rich, of course. For every mountaintop mansion, there were trailers and ramshackle cabins tucked onto parcels of heavily wooded land. He continued to climb, and soon he reached a black metal gate across the road. Pulling out the laminated map Colton had given him, he checked his location. The road beyond led to the aerial tramway on the other side of the mountain.

He was a tracker, but if he was going to find the killer, he was going to need to think like a cop. Melissa was seen getting off her bus near here before she vanished, and Bill Catcher's place wasn't far. It seemed likely that the killer had a base around here somewhere, but there were too many possibilities. He could be squatting in someone's summer vacation home or holed up in a camper out of sight from the main road.

He forced himself to see the world as a two-dimensional canvas again, summoning up his force recon training. So far he had found nothing. No sign of the blue F-150, or a camp. Without any other clues, he was at a loss.

No way in hell am I going back to Colton empty-handed, he thought.

He raised his crossbow and whistled at Creek. They turned and made their way back down the road toward Bill Catcher's place. Thunder boomed in the distance, and lightning flashed in the black fortress of clouds.

A yellow mist seemed to lead the mass of clouds as they rolled over the mountains. It reminded him of a dust storm in Iraq, but the odd part of this storm was the black swell in the meat of the clouds.

Raven stopped to listen as something that sounded like a bullhorn squawked in the distance. The noise continued for another minute, but it was so faint he couldn't make out any of the words.

He started walking again, and then fell into a jog with Creek by his side. They ran for nearly twenty minutes, keeping low and quiet along the side of the road. Raven put every worry out of his mind and focused on the hunt. His first stop was Bill Catcher's place to search for clues that Colton's people might have missed.

The distant clap of thunder followed them as they ran down the road leading to Bill's house. Raven crouched by the fence and scanned the area. There was no movement other than a few loose chickens.

Creek sat on his haunches, waiting for orders. Raven gave a low whistle, and the dog took off running into the woods framing the property. He trusted the Akita to leave the poultry alone; the dog had more self-discipline than most people he knew, including himself.

Raven shouldered his crossbow and ran across the front yard. When he got to the porch, he took a deep breath and kicked open the door.

The cabin was clear.

He hurried back outside, checking the sky. Sheets of rain were coming down on the mountains now. If he wanted to stay dry, he'd have to wait the storm out here.

Raven continued to the field behind the house where Jake and Nathan had discovered Bill's body. Creek was sniffing the ground under a tree, exploring the remains of a bonfire. Overhead, a severed rope hung from a thick branch, swinging in the wind. Creek moved on to another, smaller tree nearby. The dog sat beneath it and looked at Raven expectantly.

"What? What did you find, boy?"

Raven checked his six and then walked over. Creek pawed at something on the ground, and Raven knelt to check it out. A square of paper, grimy at the edges, was half-hidden in the tall grass.

Setting his crossbow on the ground, Raven knelt and picked the paper up. It was a crude drawing, partly obscured by a tear near the top. Raven glanced around and noticed a hunting knife sticking out of the hanging tree; the killer could have used it to pin the paper beside the dead man, but the wind must have ripped it away.

He returned his attention to the drawing. Two male stick figures stood in the center, and he could clearly make out their long, dagger-like teeth. More figures lay at their feet, their prone bodies riddled with arrows. A wavy line curved around them, and he realized it was supposed to be a stream or river.

Goose flesh rose across his arms and legs when he realized what the scene meant.

This chase wasn't just a killer. He was acting out a story from Raven's childhood, a story that had haunted him for years.

The Water Cannibals had come to Estes Park.

16

Charlize Montgomery stood at the top of a grassy hill, gripping the handle of her son's toy truck. Ty sat inside, holding onto the steering wheel, his eyes glued to the slope that probably looked like a mountain to him.

"Go, go, go!" he shouted.

Smiling, Charlize growled to mimic the sound of an engine. Ty slapped the side of the steering wheel with delight.

That was her signal to get moving.

She pushed, and the plastic wheels rolled over the fresh-cut grass toward the playground below. Charlize kept a strong grip on the handle and sped up. The other kids were playing and laughing. Some were climbing on equipment, others were running and throwing a football. All things Ty would likely never do, but for a few moments he was having more fun than all of the other kids combined.

"Faster, Mom!" he yelled.

The truck jerked up and down over the lumpy ground, but Charlize kept up their speed. Whenever Ty spun the wheel to the right or left, Charlize turned the car in that direction. She continued growling to imitate the sound of a motor. Overhead, a jet echoed the noise, roaring across the heavens. She searched the sky out of habit to see if she could identify the aircraft.

They were almost to the bottom of the hill when a flash of blinding light bloomed over the Denver skyline. Charlize nearly lost her grip on the handle at the sight of a fireball climbing into the air. She dug her heels into the grass to stop their descent and fell on her butt.

The truck fishtailed, and Ty screamed. She had to let go to shield her eyes from the light. A wave of blistering heat pressed her body to the ground as Ty continued screaming, his voice rising into a high, eerie wail like a klaxon.

"Ma'am, can you open your eyes?"

The voice was unfamiliar, and it sounded both far away and close at the same time.

Charlize forced her burned eyelids open, squinting at several blurred figures standing above her.

"Where…where am I?" she asked. The words came out as a whisper.

"You're safe, Senator," said the voice. It was familiar. Richard? No, Big Al! Her fingers quested over the blanket covering her body, and they found the huge, warm hand of her bodyguard.

"Where's Clint?" she asked. Charlize had a vague memory of asking the question before, but she couldn't remember the answer. She struggled to sit up. She had to find her chief of staff. They had to get that bill filed before the next session of Congress, and she needed him to set up a meeting with the agriculture board.

"Don't try to move," a woman's voice said. "You were severely injured."

Her vision finally cleared enough to make out the faces of the people looking down on her. Albert was wrapped in so much medical gauze that he looked like a mummy, but he was smiling at her. Not his usual megawatt grin, but a smile nonetheless. The other two people were strangers. A man and a woman, both of them wearing scrubs and lab coats.

"Where am I?" Charlize repeated. "And who are you?"

The woman answered. "You're aboard the USS John C. Stennis," she explained. "I'm Dr. Huppert. This is Dr. Rodriguez."

"Where's Clint?" she asked.

Albert's smile faded away. "He didn't make it, ma'am."

Charlize took in a long breath and winced. "No," she whispered.

"I'm sorry," Albert said. "They did everything they could for him, but he was just too badly burned."

Charlize pushed the grief aside for later. For now, she had to focus. But her body hurt so badly, and stars moved across her vision. She felt like she was going to be sick.

"Where are we?" she managed to say.

"Three hundred miles east of Maryland, sailing south to avoid fallout from the ground detonation," Huppert said.

"My son, he's in Colorado. I have to get to him." She

palmed the bed and attempted to sit up again, but she was immediately hit by a wave of agonizing pain.

Huppert raised a hand. "Ma'am, you're not going anywhere. You have first degree burns on over twenty percent of your body, second degree burns on your face, and third degree burns to your right hand. You're also being treated for radiation sickness. You're lucky you were evacuated when you were, or you might not have made it."

"I have to get to Ty. He can't run from the fire." In her mind, she was back in her nightmare as the hellish flames of nuclear blast swept toward her son. She struggled against the hands now holding her down. Why didn't they understand? She had to get to her baby.

"Calm down, Senator," Huppert said. "I'm going to sedate you now for your own safety."

"My baby," Charlize mumbled. "I have to…"

A heavy numbness began to spread through her body. She fought to hold her eyes open for a few minutes longer before giving in to the darkness.

Colton felt like a bus driver as he drove through downtown. The Jeep was packed full. Mayor Gail sat in the passenger seat beside him, while his wife and daughter huddled in the back seat with Nathan. Tom Feagen had gallantly volunteered to ride back in the cargo area, but he seemed to be regretting the decision now.

Risa was crying, and Kelly was stroking her hair in an attempt to calm their daughter.

"It's okay, Risa," Colton said, wishing he could pull over and hold his baby girl. "Everything's going to be fine."

His words felt like a lie. The town he was sworn to protect was falling into chaos. Citizens ran toward the shelter at town hall. An old man fell, but no one stopped to help. People were yelling and trying to wave his vehicle down. To the west, the storm was growing.

"This is madness," Feagen said.

"We'll be okay," Colton said, trying to sound as though he believed his own words. "The shelters are well stocked. They can take care of the whole town for a few days."

"And if we have to stay longer than that?" Feagen asked.

"We make do," Gail said.

Colton caught her gaze in the rear review mirror. The mayor was handling this surprisingly well. They'd clashed often, but he was beginning to think that she might actually be a capable leader.

"Okay fine, but what about when we come out? What if everything is poisoned?" Feagen asked.

Colton tried to remember the FEMA certification he'd done several years ago, but he couldn't recall the specifics for dealing with the aftermath of a nuclear event. Honestly, he'd thought the scenario was so far-fetched that he hadn't given it enough attention.

"That's a possibility, but we will figure it out," he said. "Everything outside will need to be scrubbed down, and we're going to have to clear the soil before we can plant anything in the spring."

Suddenly, Gail screamed. Colton whipped his head around to find her pointing at the storefronts that lined the main street. Somebody had thrown a rock through the window of her art gallery. The plate glass window lay in shards across the sidewalk.

"I'm sorry, Gail," he said, returning his focus to the road just as a woman darted in front of him. He slammed on his brakes, and the tires skidded to a stop, the bumper just a foot away from her. She gave him the bird and then continued after the mob of people running for town hall through Bond Park.

Colton took in a long breath and said, "Is everyone okay?"

Kelly nodded and put her arms around Risa. Slamming on the brakes seemed to have shocked their daughter so much that she'd stopped crying. Colton drove around the throng of citizens toward the rear of town hall. The back door to the station opened as soon as he pulled up to it, and Detective Lindsey Plymouth rushed out to meet them.

As everyone got out of the Jeep, Colton prepared for more bad news.

"We're headed to the shelter," Gail said, casting a backward glance at her store. She took off with Feagen, leaving Colton with his family and Nathan.

Lindsey brushed a lock of red hair away from her face as she approached the Jeep. "We have a situation at the grocery store, Chief. People are trying to stock up on food before the storm, and apparently things are out of control."

"Who do we have stationed there?"

"Just Nelson," she said. "We're spread pretty thin."

Colton thought of the rookie officer with a wife and a newborn at home. Then he looked at his own family.

"I need to go check this out, Kelly," Colton said. "Make sure everyone gets to the shelter safely, Lindsey."

The detective nodded and motioned for Kelly and Risa.

"Marcus…" Kelly began to say. Her dark eyes pleaded with him to reconsider.

"I'll be right behind you." He kissed her on the lips and then Risa on the forehead before jumping back into the Jeep. The passenger door creaked open, and Nathan looked in.

"You need some backup?" he asked.

Colton nodded. "Hop in, Major."

They squealed out of the parking lot and raced up the street. He took a left toward the Safeway. Colton had been afraid to ask Nathan what else he had heard over the shortwave on the drive from the high school, and Nathan didn't seem to be up for talking right now. His features were set in a stony mask. He stared out the window, his hand gripping his chest like he was in pain.

"You good, Major?"

It took Nathan a long moment to reply. "Not really. My nephew is in the middle of the radiation zone, my sister was in D.C., and I'm trapped here."

Colton had been through some heavy shit in his life, but if he lost his family, he wasn't sure he could go on.

"If we make it through this storm, I'll find you a working vehicle and give you enough food, gear, and ammo to make it to Empire," Colton said. "I've got a few CBRN suits at the station. After the flood, we applied for a grant and bought all kinds of disaster equipment."

Nathan pulled his hand away from his chest and patted Colton on the arm.

"Thanks, brother."

Colton would have replied, but when he pulled into the parking lot of the Safeway, he saw Officer Rick Nelson standing with his shotgun shouldered. He jerked the muzzle back and forth at two rail-thin men and an even skinnier woman dressed in a tank top and denim skirt despite the cold. Colton didn't recognize any of them.

He assessed the situation quickly as he drove toward the crowd. The man on Nelson's left wore a red poncho and was twirling a baseball bat. His friend had on an Old Navy sweatshirt covered in mud and held a large duffel bag. The woman was carrying a pair of bulging plastic shopping bags.

Behind them stood a group twenty- or thirty-strong. More people filed in and out of the front doors, some of them pushing carts loaded to the brim with food and supplies. He didn't see any Safeway employees.

"Goddammit," Colton said. "Looters. *Just* what I need right now."

"I've got your back, Chief," Nathan said. He un-holstered his M9 and pulled the slide back to chamber a round.

Colton parked the Jeep and pulled his Colt .45. The three civilians surrounding Nelson all looked at Nathan and Colton.

"Drop the bat and the bags," Colton said.

"They raided the pharmacy," Nelson said, his voice shaky. He kept his shotgun aimed at the man with the bat.

"We took our fair share," the man in the poncho said. He twirled the bat in one hand.

The other man smirked, revealing blackened teeth. He centered a crazed gaze on Colton. There was no mistaking the wide eyes and sweat pouring down the man's forehead. These three were all opiate addicts—dangerous, unpredictable, and an increasingly common sight in Estes Park. People like this were going to be a problem as their supplies of prescription drugs dwindled.

"You better do what Chief Colton told you to do," Nelson said. The guy with the bat stepped toward the officer. Both of his friends followed, but Nelson held his ground.

Behind them, another group of shoppers pushed full shopping carts out of the store. Colton couldn't let this situation continue. With the storm approaching, they had less than an hour to get these people to safety. They couldn't afford to leave the food out where it might be contaminated by the storm, either.

"Drop your bat and your bags, last warning," Colton said. He pulled the hammer back and directed the Colt's barrel at the man's head.

The bat clattered on the ground and Colton nodded at Nelson, who lowered his shotgun.

"Watch them, Officer Nelson," Colton said. "Nathan, follow me."

Side by side, they approached the entrance, weapons angled at the ground.

"Turn those carts around and get your asses to town hall. There's a radioactive cloud coming!" Colton yelled. He didn't bother telling them what radiation did to a body; there wasn't time for a public service announcement.

He didn't know most of these people, and many of them simply stared back at him or kept pushing their laden carts toward the street.

Colton raised his gun and fired it into the sky.

Every person in the parking lot froze as the crack reverberated through the town.

"Carts back inside, and then get to a shelter!" Colton yelled.

There was no movement at first, the shock of the gunshot having paralyzed the residents of Estes Park. Colton almost felt bad. Instead of yelling, he said, "Now, everyone. Get those carts back inside."

He corralled everyone back to the store with Nathan's help, while Nelson stood guard. Inside, they discovered two store employees who helped push the carts together near the cash registers. Just as Colton felt like he'd gotten a handle on the situation, the glass front door shattered.

People in the parking lot were shouting, and then a woman screamed.

A shotgun blast rang out.

Colton and Nathan ran back outside to find Nelson twitching on the ground, blood pooling around his head. A brick lay next to his body, and a halo of glass surrounded a second brick near the entrance to the store. The baseball bat was gone, and so was its owner. Colton bent down next to his fallen officer and saw the meth heads running away, bags of drugs still in hand.

Nathan limped after the trio but they were already halfway across the parking lot, and in another moment they were lost in the fleeing mob.

"Nelson?" Colton said. "Nelson, can you hear me?"

A few of the civilians that had remained hovered around them, blocking Colton's light. He didn't need much to see the officer was in bad shape. His skull was cracked open.

"Stay with me, Nelson."

Colton glanced up and recognized Lisa and Brad Banks, the owners of a t-shirt shop on Main Street. "Help me get him to the Jeep, and be careful."

Together, they cautiously picked Nelson up and carried him over to the vehicle. Nelson's skull was Colton's primary concern, but he was also worried about the man's spine.

"That guy in the poncho just picked up a brick and brained Officer Nelson with it," Lisa said.

"There wasn't anything we could do," Brad added, panting from the weight. "I'm sorry, Chief."

Nelson groaned feebly as Lisa opened the back lift gate and Brad helped Colton set him inside.

"Get to the shelter at town hall," Colton said, wiping the blood on his pants. He shut the door and looked for Nathan. The pilot was already limping back across the parking lot. He sucked in a breath when he saw the severity of Nelson's injuries.

"Jesus," he said. "I'm sorry, Chief, but the bastards got away."

Colton cursed, but he had bigger problems on his hands. The storm was almost overhead. It wouldn't be long before the skies opened up and killer rain began to fall.

Nathan jumped in the back to ride with Nelson, while Colton climbed into the driver's seat. As soon as Nathan pulled the gate shut, Colton pushed down on the gas and raced toward the hospital. There was less than an hour left to get Nelson some help and return to his family at town hall before the storm hit.

"Be strong, Nelson," Colton said. "You can't die. That's an order."

Rain battered the cabin's roof and streaked down the windows. Raven sat on the bed with Creek, slowly stroking the dog's fur. Eight hours earlier, the first drops had begun to fall on Prospect Mountain.

He had decided to return to Bill Catcher's cabin to search for clues, and the decision had saved his life. Raven had discovered an old, home-built radio tucked away in one of the kitchen cabinets and fired it up. The thing couldn't send messages, but it did pick up a station playing an emergency message:

Seek shelter immediately. Put plastic and tape over the windows and doors. Don't go outside until the storm has passed.

It had taken an entire roll of Duct tape and all the tarps and plastic sheeting he could find in Bill's well-stocked cabin, but in the end, Raven had sealed the place tight. There were definitely benefits to riding out the storm in a crazy old prepper's stronghold. Bill had laid in plenty of water and food, although he seemed to favor brisket MREs that tasted like dog food. At least Creek hadn't seemed to mind it when Raven gave most of the meal to the dog.

He had also discovered a small Faraday cage built out of an old microwave tucked under the bed. The cage had protected a pair of walkie-talkies from the effects of the EMP blast. He turned on one again to the sound of static.

What Raven really wanted right now was a cold beer and a cigarette, but there wasn't a drop of booze in the house—just a bunch of empty bottles.

He got up from the bed and walked over to the window. Creek followed him across the room. Pulling back the tarp an inch, Raven looked at the sky. Lightning cut through the darkness, backlighting the mountain and the gondolas of the Estes Park Aerial Tramway stranded mid-air. At least it was the off-season, so no tourists had been riding on the damn thing when the power went out. He'd ridden it once with Allie and Sandra, and there was a breathtaking panoramic view of Rocky Mountain National Park, Lake Estes, and the Big Thompson River Valley when you got to the top.

Raven longed to be up there again, looking out over a place he loved. There was something about the mountains that had always called to him. But instead of being out there, or sheltered with his family, he was trapped in this cabin because of Police Chief Marcus Colton.

No, you're here because of your choices, Raven thought. *You didn't have to volunteer for this mission. Colton had nothing to hold over your head this time.*

As he went to sit back down, he heard a rattling from the chimney. He walked over and bent down to put his ear against the tarp.

The sound didn't come again; all he heard was the pitter-patter of radioactive rain. He paced back and forth in the cabin's small main room, hoping to wear himself out so he could get some sleep. Creek watched him from the floor, his head on his paws, eyes following Raven back and forth.

He sat on the bed again and closed his eyes, but his head

was filled with stories of the Water Cannibals. As a kid, he'd been so scared of them that he'd slept at the foot of Sandra's bed on nights like this, when the storms raged and the demons walked the earth, looking for human meat. At the time, he'd pretended he was only doing it to protect her, but they both knew the truth. It had always been him and Sandra against the world, ever since their mom had left them, and he liked to think that they took turns protecting each other.

He walked back to the kitchen to search the bottles of liquor again but stopped halfway there. Deep down he knew booze couldn't save him from his tormented thoughts. He felt like his world was closing in around him and there wasn't anything he could do to stop it. And it was all his fault. He couldn't save Billy Franks in North Korea, he couldn't save Melissa, and now he was trapped here while his family was out there, with nothing to do but wait, like he had so many times as a child, for the Water Cannibals to come snatch him and his sister.

Only this time it wasn't just the irrational fears of a child. There were real demons out there. He pulled the cryptic drawing from his pocket and studied the stick figures. There was no way he was going to share this detail with Colton. The officer wouldn't understand the story. White people never did. If anything, Colton might somehow try and pin this on Raven or say he was making shit up.

This time Raven had a feeling he was going to have to face the demons on his own.

He turned back to the window and patted his leg to signal Creek they were leaving. He grabbed a tarp and prepared for the trek. Radiation or no radiation, he had to get out of here and protect his family before it was too late.

17

"There's someone outside again, Major," Detective Lindsey Plymouth said quietly.

Nathan put the shortwave radio receiver down on the desk. The signal was way too weak down here to reach anyone. He followed the detective through the shelter under town hall, past sleeping civilians. There were a lot of people down here and the room was hot as hell. They couldn't stay locked up forever or they were all going to suffocate.

Colton was already at the bottom of the stairs, listening as someone pounded on the door outside. Neither of them had slept much through the night, and he guessed that he looked about as ragged as the police chief did. After nine hours, the rain had finally stopped coming down, but that didn't mean it was safe to go outside unprotected.

"Second one in the past three hours," Colton said,

keeping his voice low as Nathan approached. "We better check it out."

They both walked up the narrow staircase toward the blast door. Nathan squeezed next to Colton and pressed his ear against the reinforced steel. It was the main entrance to the shelter, but there was another hallway beyond and a second door to the outside of town hall. They couldn't hear much of anything, and shouting was only going to scare everyone inside the room.

What Nathan did know was that high-level radiation could kill within hours. It was going on nine hours since the storm rolled over the town, so if someone was outside, then it stood to reason that the radiation wasn't that bad.

"Reckon we should get out the Geiger counter," Colton said as if reading Nathan's thoughts.

"I'll put on one of those space suits and go out there to take a reading," Lindsey offered.

Nathan glanced down at the detective. She was young and reckless, just like he'd been once upon a time. When the hell had he gotten so old?

"No," Colton said. "We need to wait longer."

"I can't wait much longer," Nathan said. "Remember your promise at the Safeway?"

Colton leaned closer. "We can't compromise this shelter, Major. My family and a hundred other people are down here. We have enough air to last for another twenty-four hours or so, even without the HVAC systems. I understand you want to get to Empire, but—"

A howl from outside cut Colton off.

"Was that a wolf?" Lindsey asked.

"I think that's a dog," Nathan said.

"Creek," Colton whispered, reaching for the door handle. "Holy shit."

Feagen approached them, shaking his head. His hair was sticking up on one side from where he'd slept on it, but he still managed to look disapproving. "Do not open that door," he said.

"I can't leave them out there. It's my fault Raven was on the mountain in the first place," Colton said.

"Do not open that door," Feagen repeated. "Whoever's out there is contaminated!"

Colton pointed a finger at the town administrator. "Keep your voice down. You're going to scare people."

"I'll wake the mayor!"

The police chief wanted to tell Lindsey to lock Feagen in a closet, but decided to give her other orders. "Lindsey, get the CBRN suits and the Geiger counter."

Nathan nodded and put his hand on Colton's shoulder in a silent show of support. They went back to listening with their ears against the door.

"Raven couldn't have survived out there for nine hours without shelter, right?" Colton asked.

Nathan shrugged. "I get the sense there's no telling what that guy can or cannot do."

A shrieking sound came from below as Lindsey dragged a crate with a biohazard sign to the staircase. The mayor followed on her heels, looking annoyed at being woken up.

"You're not seriously thinking about going out there," Gail said. She pushed her green glasses up her nose and frowned. "Chief, with all due respect…"

"I have to," Colton said. "Someone's got to go out there and take a reading, anyway."

Nathan grabbed a suit and started putting it on. All he needed was gear and a vehicle to get him to Empire. Would the chief try to stop him? Colton seemed like a man of his word, but if he tried to back out of their deal, Nathan would just have to steal the keys to the Jeep.

"All right, let's move," Colton said. He accepted an AR-15 from Lindsey and slammed a magazine into the gun.

Nathan picked up his M9. They walked up the stairs single file, their bulky suits crunching. Nathan hated these things. They made everything more difficult, muffling his senses and hampering his movements.

"I'll go first," Colton said. "You open the second door and then cover me just in case there's someone else out there besides Raven and Creek."

Nathan nodded.

Colton eyed Feagen. "Don't give Detective Plymouth any problems."

Lindsey, standing guard at the bottom of the stairs, raised her shotgun with a smile.

Nathan took in a breath that smelled like plastic and grabbed the door handle.

"Okay," Colton said.

Nathan unlocked the door and pushed it open. Colton strode into the hallway toward the second steel door with his rifle shouldered.

"Who's out there?" Colton said, his voice muffled by his suit.

They listened for a response but Nathan couldn't hear much of anything.

"Get ready," Colton said.

Nathan grabbed the door handle and waited for the order. At Colton's nod, he unlocked the bolt and pushed the door open.

A thick mist was rolling over the parking lot. Overhead, the sky was the dull grey of newsprint.

"About time someone opened the door!"

Nathan moved toward the voice to see Raven leaning against the building with his arms crossed in a relaxed pose. Creek was at his feet, sheltering under the narrow overhang of the roof.

As soon as Raven saw they were armed, he held up his hands. "Hold your fire!"

Creek wagged his tail at Colton.

"That you inside the moon suit, Chief?" Raven asked, squinting in the dull light.

"You're okay?" Colton asked, stepping forward to get a better look at Raven. The rain had finally tapered off, and a mattress of thick gray clouds rolled overhead.

"Yeah, I'm good, Chief," Raven replied. He pulled off his hat. "My hair hasn't fallen out yet, and my insides aren't melting as far as I can tell."

Nathan grabbed the Geiger counter from the top step and then closed the door behind them.

"You sure?" Colton asked. "Any nausea or diarrhea?"

Nathan turned the device on and stepped up to Raven, the probe held high. Static hissed from the machine.

"Careful where you put that thing, Major," Raven protested.

"Just hold still and shut up," Nathan said. He held the

device against Raven's arm and watched the needle move. It stopped at the border of the danger zone.

"Well, I'll be damned," Nathan said, exhaling a hot breath against his visor. "The rads are higher than before, but not too bad."

Raven's smile widened. "See, I told you. It's a miracle. The storm dumped whatever radiation was up there before it hit us."

Nathan lowered the Geiger counter and scrutinized Raven. "How do you know that?"

Raven reached into his pocket and pulled out a walkie-talkie that he handed to Nathan. Then he pulled another walkie-talkie and tossed it to Colton.

"Found a radio at Bill's place. I was listening to a broadcast about the storm. I also found those walkie-talkies in a Faraday cage under the bed."

"They work?" Colton asked.

Raven smirked like a kid that had just finished his chores. He pulled off his baseball cap and wiped his wet forehead clean with a sleeve. "I got to be honest, Chief. Your officers did a really shitty job searching that place. I also found a clue that you guys missed."

"That's because we haven't had time to search his place or follow proper protocol. Hell, we just barely had time to recover Bill's body and—"

"Did that broadcast say anything else about the southern part of the state?" Nathan interjected.

Raven avoided Nathan's gaze, then looked up and said, "The radiation was mostly dumped on the Southern part of the state. Sounds like it was hit hard, too. I'm sorry, Major. I know your nephew is down there."

"I have to go. Colton, are you still going to loan me a vehicle?" Nathan said.

Colton turned toward him. "You'll die. You know that. Just stay here a few more days until the radiation lessens to the South."

"Chief, you made me a promise."

"It's suicide, and all due respect, but we both know your nephew is probably..."

Raven held up a hand. "Guys, sorry to interrupt, but there's something else you should know."

"What?" Nathan and Colton said at the same time, pivoting toward Raven.

Raven smiled again and pulled out a cigarette from his vest. He jammed it between his lips, lit it, and took a long drag. Nathan was really starting to dislike the guy. He seemed to be enjoying the attention as they waited for him to deliver the rest of his briefing.

"I've been waiting for a smoke all morning."

"That's your news?" Colton asked.

"Oh right, sorry," Raven said. "After you guys left me on that mountain to fend for myself in the storm—thanks for that, by the way—I found that blue F-150 we've been looking for."

"That's the clue?" Colton asked.

Raven took another drag and nodded. He exhaled several puffs of smoke and watched them climb into the sky, avoiding Colton's gaze. The small mannerism told Nathan that Raven wasn't being completely honest, but Raven was Colton's problem now. Nathan was heading out to find Ty as soon as he could get a ride.

First the planes fell out of the sky. Then all the lights went out.

Brown Feather didn't mind; Water Cannibals hunted better in the dark.

People lost their minds, abandoning their cars in the middle of the road and walking into town, as if someone there would save them. These people were no better than sheep, and their shepherd was a fool who couldn't control his own flock. There would be riots soon. Chaos in the streets, neighbors fighting each other to the death over a loaf of bread.

"Your time will come soon," said his demon brother.

Brown Feather replied with a smile. "I know, Turtle. Our hunt will come to an end soon with our prize."

He loved watching these people fight amongst themselves. It was as though the world had given him a gift. He didn't give a shit about cell phones and supermarkets. He knew how to live off the land. All he needed was his knife, his woman, and the other demons to keep him company.

The rest of the world could go to hell for all he cared.

But tonight the world had given Brown Feather another gift. She was tall and slim, with hair the color of a crow's wing that fell to her shoulders in a black wave. He'd spotted her earlier that evening, outside the town hall. At first, he had mistaken her for his woman. The bronzed skin and dark hair were the same as hers, but this girl was younger and more supple.

He was on foot tonight, moving like a shark through a shoal of fish as the crowd dispersed. His truck was safely hidden where the looters wouldn't find it.

She wasn't alone. That was more challenging, but he liked it when his prey played hard to get. Walking slowly with the herd, she made her way across the park, her sneakers leaving distinctive diamond-patterned prints in the soft, wet earth. He could have tracked her by those prints alone, or the scent of her sugary perfume.

She didn't know it yet, but she was already his.

The girl stopped to tie her shoe, waving the others on, insisting that she'd catch up. She wouldn't. He watched her prop a foot up on the park bench, her lean muscles tensing as she bent over to knot the laces.

It was time. He moved swiftly, silently. Approaching from the side rather than behind so he didn't startle his prey, he held his hands spread wide and said, "Can you help me?"

She looked up, her eyes curious but not yet frightened. They were the eyes of a doe, soft brown and sensitive. "Uh, sure. What's wrong?"

He let out a good-humored chuckle. "Seems like everything's wrong. But right now, I can't find my dog. My little girl loves that mutt."

"I love dogs, what's yours look like?" she asked as she finished tying her shoe. Her hair had fallen over her eyes, and she swept it back with a copper-brown hand.

He thought fast, the lie running smoothly from his mouth. "Chocolate lab. Her name is Candy. I'm Brown Feather, by the way."

"I'm Mollie," she said, smiling and eager to help. "Let's find your dog."

It took only a moment to draw her away from the crowd, into the soft darkness of the wooded park. She didn't realize what was happening until it was too late. One step from light to dark, one step from life to death. He clamped a massive hand over her mouth, his palm easily covering the lower half of her face. She struggled like a fish on a hook.

"Hold still," Brown Feather said, pressing the tip of a small knife into her side. "I won't hurt you if you hold still."

She went limp, and he almost laughed. What a stupid girl. It almost wasn't worth killing her.

Once they were far enough from the crowds to risk moving his hand, he gagged the girl and bound her hands with zip ties. She must have realized then what her fate would be. Tears streamed down her face as she dug her heels into the turf, but in the end, he brought her to the river's edge. In the old stories, the demons lived beneath the surface of lakes and rivers, coming out only at night to stalk and burn their prey. If he followed in their footsteps tonight and proved that he was one of them, he would finally be ready to unleash the horror of the Water Cannibals on these pathetic sheep.

"You can't do this here," said his demon brother. "We can't risk being seen yet. It's too early for the world to know what we're doing."

Turtle was right. The other demon was always right.

The girl's eyes widened, and Brown Feather smirked with excitement. He knocked her unconscious with a butt of his large head. For the next hour he carried her over his shoulder through the woods until they reached his lair where he set her on the ground. Next he looped a length of thick nylon rope over a tree branch and then tied one end into a simple but effective noose that slipped easily over the girl's head. A small fire was soon burning merrily below her feet. She writhed and kicked as she regained consciousness, but all her efforts did nothing more than tighten the noose.

Soon—too soon—she died. He watched the fire for a while longer, staring deep into the heart of the flames as if it might reveal secrets to him.

Once the flesh had been charred, he would cut her down and feast. That was the Water Cannibals' way, so that's what he had to do too. Squaring his broad shoulders, he strode forward and examined the body. Where should he start? The air was rich with the scent of barbecue as he contemplated his options.

He had tracked, killed, and eaten just about everything, from squirrel to elk, but this was new to him. The legends weren't clear on which parts were the best to eat. The flash of a diamond on the ring finger of her left hand caught his eye.

Okay, Brown Feather thought. *I'll start there.*

Sandra peeled off her gloves and tossed them in a trashcan overflowing with medical supplies. It was morning of the third day after the attack, and only one of the cleaning staff had showed up earlier that morning. He was doing his best to keep up, but it wasn't enough.

She grabbed another pair of gloves and strode to the ER. Inside, Doctor Newton was hovering over Rick Nelson. Rosy spots of blood had formed on the bandages covering the four burr holes Newton had drilled in Nelson's skull. Sandra could still hear the crunching sound as the hand drill broke through the bone.

"Check his vitals," Newton said without looking up at her. "Then check the drainage."

Sandra stepped up to the bed and gently took Rick's wrist. She took his heart rate by placing her index and middle finger over the radial artery. Then she counted for fifteen seconds and multiplied by four.

"Heart rate is ninety-two," she announced. That wasn't good. Next, she took his blood pressure with a manual cuff and a stethoscope. It had dropped since she had taken it last.

"Blood pressure is now ninety-six over fifty."

"Shit," Newton replied. "His breathing is getting worse, too. We might have to get out the BVM."

Sandra opened Rick's eyelids and shone a flashlight at his pupils. She raked the light back and forth, but there was little movement.

"He still isn't responding," Sandra said. "His pupils are equal in size, but not reactive to light."

"We need to do everything possible to keep him calm and pain-free or we're going to be looking at a higher probability of brain herniation," Newton said. He doused his hands in rubbing alcohol, which was the best they could do for sterilization without hot water. "How are those burr holes?"

Sandra examined the four small holes in Rick's skull. Three of them were left open for pressure relief, but the fourth had a tube draining a mixture of blood and clear fluid into a sterile bag.

"Looks good," Sandra said. "Relatively speaking."

She checked them a second time just to make sure. The drip was slow, which was hopefully a good sign. Drilling was an archaic method that Newton had never performed before. Sandra wasn't sure what was normal.

"The drain doesn't look like it's putting out much cerebral spinal fluid," she said.

"Let me take a look," Newton said, bending down next to her. She moved out of the way, giving her a full view of Rick's buzzed skull. A bloody dent marked the top of his head where he'd been struck with a brick. Judging from the placement wound, he never saw the attack coming.

Standing, Newton shook his head and put his hands on his hips. "I'm not sure what else we can do for him. Check on Teddy, please."

Sandra sucked in a long, deep breath. She needed an entire day of sleep, maybe two, to catch up. But there was no time for that. She tried to put the officer's fate out of her mind for now, but Sandra couldn't help thinking of Nelson's wife, Maggie, and their infant daughter. She'd been Maggie's nurse, and she remembered how delighted the young officer had been to be a father for the first time.

She approached Teddy's bed, where a nurse named Jen was pumping the bag that allowed him to breathe.

"I thought he was trying to open his eyes, but it might have just been involuntary movement," she said when Sandra asked for an update.

Sandra threw her gloves in a trashcan and put on another pair. "Thanks, Jen. I'll take over now."

"Take an extra ten minutes," Jen said. "You look

exhausted. When was the last time you ate something? Go get a drink of water at least."

Sandra hesitated until she heard Allie's voice from the lobby.

"I'll be back in a bit," Sandra said.

Jen continued pumping precious air into the little boy's lungs. Teddy's parents were sitting in the lobby, as they had been ever since their son was admitted. They had been watching after Allie, who sat on the floor in front of them playing with a puzzle.

Outside the window, a police officer was pacing with his shotgun. Creek lay on the pavement, protecting the hospital while his handler got better inside. He wagged his tail when he saw Sandra, and she waved at the dog before turning back to Teddy's parents.

"Mr. and Mrs. Brown, thank you so much for watching my daughter," she said.

"Momma!" Allie cried, delighted. She came running over.

"How is Teddy?" Marie Brown asked.

"He's doing okay," Sandra said. "Your son is a very strong boy."

"When will they have the power back on?" Michael Brown asked.

"I…I'm not sure," Sandra lied. She avoided their gazes by kneeling in front of Allie. "How are you, sweetie?"

"I want to go home. When is Uncle Raven coming back?"

"Soon, baby." Sandra hugged Allie and then stood. She drew in a breath before turning to face the Browns.

"What have the doctors told you?" she asked.

Michael rubbed the back of his neck. "They said that there's no further sign of the bacterial infection, but that's it."

Sandra picked her next words carefully. "There is no sign of the Necrotizing Fasciitis infection, but Teddy needs a constant regimen of intravenously fed antibiotics."

Allie looked up at Sandra, tilting her head slightly as if she was trying to understand. She put a hand on Allie's shoulder and pulled her close.

Michael did the same to Marie.

"My baby," Marie whimpered. "My poor baby."

Sandra gave Allie a final squeeze and said, "You'll have to excuse me, but I need to go see my brother."

Marie nodded and returned to her seat with Michael.

"You stay with these nice people, sweetie," Sandra said.

"But I want to see Uncle Raven."

"He's resting, baby, but you can see him soon."

Sandra left the lobby and cut through the ER to get to Raven's room. He was sharing it with an older man who had been caught outside during the storm for much longer than Raven. The man seemed to be doing okay, but only time would tell.

She pulled her mask over her face and knocked on the door. Once inside, she nodded to the first patient and then slipped between the curtains to her brother's bed.

He was sitting up, a mischievous grin on his face. Seeing him smiling made her heart nearly burst with joy—until she saw him quickly pull his sheet up to his chest to hide something.

"Sam Spears! What are you up to?"

"Nothing," he said. "I'm a model patient, Sis. Ask that good-looking nurse with the tattoos on her—"

She held out a hand palm-up. "Hand it over, Raven."

"I don't have anything to hand over!"

She pulled the sheet back and grabbed the can of beer that he was attempting to hide.

"Where the hell did you get this?" she asked.

"Cut me some slack! I nearly died."

"Yes, you could have died, and you have been exposed to radiation, which means you need to rest and take in fluids."

"Beer is a fluid. Can't I drink just a little?"

She poured the remainder of the can down the drain and then perched in the chair beside his bed. "I still can't believe you walked all the way into town in the middle of the storm. What were you thinking?"

At her words, his face turned grave. All trace of humor had vanished.

"Raven, what is it?"

"Remember the Water Cannibal story?"

Sandra smiled behind her mask. "I remember you used to crap your pants over it."

"I think someone's trying to bring it to life," Raven said coldly.

"What? What do you mean?"

"The man who killed Melissa and Bill Catcher seems to know the story, like they're trying to act it out. I found a picture near the tree they found Bill Catcher hanging from. And both victims were burned."

"Picture?" Sandra asked. "Like a photograph?"

"No. Someone drew the scene on a piece of paper. They

were just stick figures, but it was definitely a scene from the Water Cannibal story."

"Have you told Chief Colton?"

Raven shook his head. "He won't understand."

"You can't keep this from him. It makes you look guilty," Sandra said. "You don't need him to be any more suspicious of you. Besides, whoever is doing this is a sick person, but they aren't carrying out some story our parents told us when we were kids. That's just crazy."

A knock on the door echoed through the room, startling Sandra. She pulled her mask up and stood as Colton and Jake stepped into the room. Nathan waited in the hallway behind them. She smiled at the pilot, and he returned it with interest.

"Ma'am," Colton said, taking off his hat. "We need to speak to your brother."

"This can't be good," Raven said.

"Can you give us a few minutes?" Colton asked Sandra.

"No," she said, surprising them both.

Colton and Raven both stared at her.

"Whatever you have to say to him, you can say in front of me, Chief. I'll just make him tell me later."

Nathan chuckled from the hallway.

"Raven, we need your help," Colton said.

"Of course you do," he said.

"There's been another murder."

Raven stopped grinning, and Sandra held her hand to her mouth.

"A college student named Mollie Harms was found in Fall River this morning, right in the middle of town. She was hacked up pretty good—missing a hand, and her legs were burned down to the bone."

Raven let out a sigh and threw off his bed sheets. "Then I guess you really do need my help. It's a shame; I was starting to like these digs."

"No, this is not happening," Sandra said. "Raven, you need to stay put and rest."

"And take in fluids. Yeah, I know," Raven said. He grabbed his Seattle Mariners hat from the table and put it on. "Don't worry, Sis. I'm good."

"I'll keep an eye out on your brother, ma'am," Colton said.

Raven joined Colton and Nathan at the door.

"Tell them," Sandra said.

All three men stopped and turned.

"The drawing, Raven," Sandra said. "Tell them about it."

Colton pivoted slightly to stare at Raven, but Raven kept his gaze on Sandra.

"Either of you ever heard the Cherokee legend of the Water Cannibals?" Raven said. "'Cause I got reason to believe our chase is trying to bring the story to life."

18

A BRILLIANT SUNRISE STRETCHED ACROSS THE HORIZON over the Atlantic Ocean. Charlize sat in a wheelchair outside the command center of the USS *John C. Stennis*. Albert stood by her side. She shielded her eyes with a hand to look at the other vessels of the strike group cutting through the sea behind the flagship.

The salty breeze rustled her newly trimmed hair. That slight friction was enough to make the back of her neck flare with pain. She had suffered one of the worst burns among the survivors from the PEOC, and a healthy dose of radiation poisoning on top of that.

Senator Sarcone had also made it out, but countless others weren't so lucky. Secretary of Defense Smith, Secretary of State Loyola, and Clint were among the ranks of those that had perished.

"Beautiful," Albert said as they stared out over the water. Rays of light sparkled on its surface in a mesmerizing dance.

"It is," Charlize said.

Charlize looked up at her bodyguard and longtime friend. He offered a reassuring smile. A gentleman, no matter what they faced. They both knew that his family was almost certainly dead. His wife and kids had been on their way out of D.C., but it wasn't likely that they had made it out of the blast zone in time. She considered saying something reassuring, but the words wouldn't come. What could she possibly say right now to make him feel better?

Instead, she reached up and touched his arm with her left hand. The other lay curled in her lap, still swaddled in bandages. She hadn't been brave enough to look at it yet.

Nearby, a Black Hawk was preparing to take off. Six Marines ran toward the chopper, keeping low as a crew chief waved them into the troop hold. As soon as they were aboard, the bird rose into the air and curved away from the ship. The Navy had been running missions all morning and returning with troop holds full of civilians. Many of those shell-shocked survivors were in bad shape. It was amazing how quickly civilization collapsed without the infrastructure to support it.

The hatch to the command center opened and Captain Victor Dietz stepped onto the platform.

"Senator," he said with a nod. "How are you feeling?"

"The radiation treatment seems to be working, but I still feel like a hotdog that spent too much time on the grill."

The hint of a grin formed on his lips. He strolled up to the railing to watch the Black Hawk.

"Where are they headed?" Charlize asked.

"Evac op," Dietz said. "We're still tracking down several members of the cabinet. Plus about a thousand other high-ranking individuals. President Diego has provided us with a list."

The captain's words reminded her of Senator Ellen, chasing desperately after the convoy of black SUVs. Ellen hadn't been important enough to make the list, and Charlize wondered if the woman had survived despite being left behind. Maybe she'd been taken to someplace safer than the PEOC—but Charlize doubted it.

Her mind seized on something else Dietz had said. "*President* Diego? When did he get promoted? Last I checked, he was Acting President of the United States."

Dietz shook his head sadly. "We've confirmed that President Drake, Vice President Pederson, and Speaker Hamilton are all deceased. You missed out on the formalities, but it's official. Diego is the forty-fifth President of the United States. The injuries he sustained in the PEOC were relatively minor. He's one hell of a lucky man."

Charlize looked up into his eyes. The captain's sunburned forehead was a map of creases. They had only met once before, years ago when she was still a pilot. He hadn't aged well, and recent events seemed to weigh heavily on him.

You're not looking so hot these days, either, she reminded herself. After seeing her reflection in the mirror for the first time after the bomb, she'd thrown up. She was still struggling to accept the massive damage that had been done to her body.

"We need you healthy, Senator," Dietz said. "You're one of the highest-ranking government officials left."

Charlize looked back to the deck as a second Black Hawk took to the sky. An Osprey was preparing to take off farther down, and a flight crew was preparing several F-18 Super Hornets. The deck of the super carrier was alive with activity, and all Charlize could do was sit in her chair to watch.

Just give me a fighter jet, she thought, the fingers of her good hand twitching as if they were anxious to wrap around the flight controls.

The hatch opened again, and Janet Marco, the ship's XO, slipped outside. She was a stiff, alert woman with the physique of a long-distance runner and sharp, never-resting eyes.

"Senator," Marco said, inclining her head. "Glad to see you out and around."

"Thank you," Charlize said without taking her eyes off the fighter jets.

"Captain, we still haven't been able to reach the Seventh Fleet, but I do have an update for you on the Second Fleet. They're two hundred and fifty miles north of us. Admiral Doyle has requested we send F-18s for CAPs while civilians are evacuated from the East Coast."

"They're worried about more attacks?" Charlize asked.

"Yes, ma'am. Apparently, the North Koreans also hacked some of our satellites. We're mostly blind north of the Mason-Dixon line."

Dietz nodded. "Get it done."

Marco saluted and returned to the bridge. A few minutes later, a dozen pilots were running across the flight deck toward their birds. Charlize gripped the armrest of her wheelchair and leaned forward to watch them.

"Goddammit," Dietz muttered. "We're already low on aircraft, but the Second Fleet are sitting ducks out there."

"Is there any indication the North Koreans are capable of hitting us again?" Charlize asked.

"After seeing some of the drone footage of the northern part of the peninsula, I don't see how they could mount another attack. North Korea is so pockmarked with radioactive craters that it looks like the surface of the moon."

"I'm not convinced they didn't have help," Albert put in. It was unusual to hear her bodyguard speak up, but he was a smart man and she valued his opinion when he chose to give it.

Charlize nodded. "I've considered the same thing, Albert, but who would have helped the North Koreans start World War Three? Iran? Russia? China? No one is that crazy."

"So far there is no evidence of collaboration," Dietz said.

The last pilot closed the canopy over his cockpit and gave a thumbs up sign. She pushed at the grips on her chair, trying to rise to her feet.

"Senator, you should really stay in the chair," Dietz said.

Albert put a hand on her shoulder, but instead of insisting she sit down, he helped her to her feet.

Dietz gave them both an exasperated look. "I won't snitch to your doctors, Senator, but you should really take it easy. As I said, you're one of the highest-ranking officials left, and I'm sure President Diego will be looking to you for a position in his cabinet."

One by one the F-18s were moved into position. She shuffled over to the railing and grabbed the cold metal in her burned hands. "Captain, how far inland are those rescue missions?"

Dietz scratched his chin. "I'm not sure. Why do you ask?"

"My son is in Colorado. If President Diego won't authorize a rescue op, I'm going to steal a Black Hawk and fly out there myself."

"If I didn't know you, I would think you were kidding," Dietz said. "But your reputation precedes you. I'll put in a good word…however, if you try to steal one of my birds, I'll have you thrown in the brig." The ghost of a smile returned, and then Dietz left them to return to the command center.

Charlize tilted her face to the sky, watching the jets streak toward the mainland. Three days earlier, she had thought she would never see the sky again, but now she had a feeling she would be flying across it soon enough.

"I don't like this, Raven," Sandra said. "Colton is using you."

Raven took a drag of a cigarette as he approached town hall with Sandra and Allie in tow. Creek trotted alongside them.

His sister rubbed at her eyes. Raven had never seen her this exhausted. She'd been working herself to the bone at the hospital. How could she expect to help her patients if she wouldn't take care of herself?

"You're the one that said I need to make better choices, Sis. I'm trying to be one of the good guys here."

It was almost three in the afternoon, and for the first

time in days the sky was clear. The sun beat down on them as they walked to town hall.

Raven's Jeep was parked next to Jake's Chevy pickup and an old VW van with tie-dyed curtains in the rear windows. A technician was working on the engine of a VW Beetle at the front of the new Estes Park police fleet.

"Uncle Raven, why do you have to go?" Allie said.

"I promise I'll be back soon."

Allie stroked Creek's coat and frowned. "Can Creek stay with me? He's my friend."

"Sorry, but I need his nose. We won't be long, kiddo," Raven said.

Colton, Nathan, Jake, and a half dozen police officers stood in front of the vehicles, looking at a map spread over the hood of Raven's Jeep. The men were armed to the teeth with semi-automatic rifles and pistols.

"They're not playing around," Raven muttered.

"What did Colton say about the drawing?" Sandra asked.

"Not much."

Sandra halted and grabbed his arm. "You did tell him everything, right?"

"Yeah," Raven said quietly.

"You're somethin' else," Sandra said, sensing his lie.

Colton called out before Raven could reply. "Sandra, I'm glad you're here. How's Officer Nelson?"

"He's hanging in there," she said.

"Good, I'll come see him when we get back."

"In the meantime, you better keep your promise about watching after Raven, or you're going to have to deal with me when you do."

"And me," Allie said with her hands on her hips.

Nathan limped over and smiled at them. "I promise to personally watch out for Raven," he said.

Sandra thanked him, but Allie hid behind her back, peering out at the pilot.

"How's your ankle?" Sandra asked.

"It hasn't snapped yet." He stopped a few feet away and bent down to Allie's height. "I'm Nathan. What's your name?"

Allie didn't answer. She pushed her face against Sandra's back.

"I'm sorry, she's really tired," Sandra said. "And a little shy, too."

"It's okay. I don't blame her."

Raven left his sister to talk, or flirt, or whatever it was she was doing with the major. Creek followed him and Colton to the Jeep.

The chief had a serious, hard look on his battle-scarred face. "Get ready to move out. We have another lead. Detective Plymouth found the signs of a camp at the top of Prospect Mountain, not far from the aerial tramway and that truck."

"What the hell was she doing up there?" Raven asked. Privately, he was also wondering how the big city cop had managed to find something he had missed.

"She was checking on the folks with homes up on the mountain," he said. "And she found this."

Colton handed him a pink mitten.

Raven didn't need to ask whose it had been. He recognized it immediately; in fact, he still had Melissa's other mitten in his Jeep somewhere.

Colton gave an ear-splitting whistle, and the officers, along with Raven and Nathan, gathered around the Jeep.

"We got lucky with the storm, but we still have major problems. One major problem in particular." Colton paused and scanned his officers before continuing. "Our suspect has killed three times so far. I've been able to keep the third homicide quiet for now, but if our citizens catch wind of it, we're going to have more than riots at Safeway to worry about. Nothing is more important right now than stopping this man."

"Is it true the killer is acting out some Cherokee folk story?" Lindsey asked. "Water Snakes or..."

"Water Cannibals," Sandra corrected.

"Anything else we should know, Raven?" Colton asked. "You and Sandra are both half Cherokee. If anyone can tell us more, it's you two."

Every officer glared at Raven and his sister. This was exactly why he didn't want to say anything. All of a sudden he felt like a suspect. He resisted the urge to scratch his neck and stiffened instead.

"Our chase is a hunter," Raven said. "A damn fine hunter. You may think you're out there tracking him, but make no mistake, whoever this guy is, he's good. The best I've ever tracked. He got the drop on me and Chief Colton back at Ypsilon where we found Melissa. I could feel him out there. Watching."

"This dude is crazy," Lindsey said.

Raven nodded. "Psychotic, actually."

"He's just one man," Colton said. "Together we will find him and we will kill him."

"We're with you, sir," Lindsey said.

"To the end," Jake added.

Colton raised his hat to rub his forehead. "All right, let's gear up and prepare to move out. You all have your assignments."

Jake slammed a magazine into his AR-15 with a click. After chambering a round, he pushed the scope to his eye and scanned the tree line on Prospect Mountain. Nathan loaded the M14 that Colton had given him and then reached down to retie his boot, wincing as he struggled with his injured ankle.

Colton turned on one of the walkie-talkies Raven had brought him and said, "Margaret, you copy?"

"I'm here, Chief," she replied.

"We're heading out soon. Keep in touch."

Colton clipped the radio on his belt and checked the ammunition in his various guns. The man looked more like an Old West outlaw than a modern-day lawman, but Raven had to admit it was a good look on the chief. Raven was packing light today, with only a crossbow and his hatchets strapped across his back.

Nathan limped past Raven and started loading bags into the VW van. Sandra drifted over a moment later and leaned against the vehicle.

"You going somewhere after this?" she asked.

"Yup, as soon as this is over, Colton is giving me this beauty and a CBRN suit to go track down my nephew in Empire." He paused and then added, "You take care of yourself, Ms. Spears."

"I told you not to call me that." She smiled and took the

hand he offered, holding it for just long enough to make Raven's older brother protective instincts go into overdrive.

"I hope I get to see you again," she said.

"I'd like that," Nathan said.

Raven thought his sister might be more worried about Nathan than she was about him, but as soon as she threw her arms around Raven, he knew the truth. Her eyes were filled with unconditional love.

"You be careful, too, Raven," she ordered.

"I will, Sis." Raven hugged her back, harder this time, as if she was the only real thing in this increasingly crazy world.

19

T EDDY SLOWLY OPENED HIS EYES.
Sandra almost forgot to pump the next breath, but she quickly regained her composure. She had seen patients do this before, especially those in a chemically-induced coma. He'd already closed his eyes again.

"Teddy, can you hear me?" she asked.

His eyelids fluttered, but this time they didn't open.

Doctor Newton had pulled Sandra back into the emergency room as soon as she had returned to the hospital. Jen had reported a possible infection in Teddy's wound. They had upped his dose of antibiotics and were continuing to monitor him closely.

Still exhausted and worried about her brother, Sandra decided to talk to Teddy, even if he couldn't hear her, just to stay sane.

"You're going to be out of here in no time, buddy. Your parents are right outside, and I promised them I'd help smuggle in your dog the day you wake up. What's his name again? Baylor?"

Teddy's eyelids fluttered once more. His forehead was sweating, and Sandra wiped it clean with a cold rag in between pumps.

She looked at his dressings. The stump just below his elbow was clean, but his temperature bothered her. It was 102.5 and rising. If the antibiotics didn't start working soon, they might lose him after all.

"I know you're in there, Teddy. I know you can hear me," Sandra said. "I need you to keep fighting, honey."

A jolt shook his right arm. That was normal, too, but each of these involuntary movements gave Sandra hope.

Sandra continued pumping air into the little boy's lungs and watched his chest rise up and down.

"Your mom and dad said you're already reading and that you like the Harry Potter books. I've been trying to get my Allie to read, but she would rather play on her tablet." Sandra laughed ruefully. "I guess I don't have to worry about that anymore, huh? I bet books will be making a big comeback. When you wake up, maybe you can talk to her..."

Teddy let out a low groan, and his chest convulsed.

"It's okay, sweetie," Sandra said. She tried to think of something else to say, eager to keep up the steady, soothing flow of words in case it helped Teddy. "My brother has an Akita named Creek. Maybe Baylor and Creek will become friends."

Sandra pumped another breath into Teddy's lungs as

Doctor Duffy and Jen pushed a gurney out of the room, a white blanket draped over the form of another patient lost. This time it was Jack Parker, a WWII veteran. He had been as tough as nails, but in the end, pneumonia had killed him. He had turned down the medicine that would have saved his life so patients like Teddy could live.

Sighing, Sandra turned back to the boy.

"I think you would really like Creek. He's a good dog. Very smart, too. What kind of dog is Baylor?"

Teddy began to cough, struggling to breathe around the tube, and his eyes were now wide-open and filled with panic.

"Doctor Newton!" she shouted. "Doctor Duffy! Somebody come over here!"

Newton rushed over and assessed the situation. He checked Teddy's breathing, listened to his lungs with a stethoscope, and then removed the endotracheal tube.

Teddy coughed and sputtered. His dry lips pursed as he took his first voluntary breath of air in over two weeks.

He whispered something, and Sandra had to lean down to hear him. "What was that, sweetheart?"

Teddy tried again. "Momma."

"Your mom is just outside," Sandra said.

Teddy tried to use his right hand to reach out for her. The realization set in on the boy's face. His eyes widened with shock.

"You were sick, Teddy. Very sick," Newton explained. "Jen, please go notify his parents that Teddy is awake."

The nurse scurried away, and a moment later the doors to the ER swung open and ecstatic voices filled the room. Marie and Michael ran across the space to their son's bedside.

Sandra left to give the family some space. She realized that if the Browns were in here, then Allie was alone in the lobby.

She pulled off her gloves, tossed them in the trash, and looked at Jen.

"Where's Allie?"

She shrugged. "I didn't see her."

Sandra's heart froze into an icy lump.

"Your brother came to pick her up," Marie said without taking her eyes off Teddy. "He said they were going for a walk."

"My brother?"

Michael chimed in. "Yeah, a Native American guy, right?"

Sandra turned and ran toward the lobby, her frozen heart shattering.

"Where are you going?" Newton shouted after her.

She burst through the ER doors into the lobby. "Allie! Allie, where are you?" she shouted. "Has anyone seen my daughter?"

The duty officer was Tom Matthew today, and she grabbed the front of his uniform, holding on as if she might start shaking him. "Where's my daughter?"

Tom pulled himself free. "Calm down," he said, straightening his shirt. "She went for a walk with her uncle."

"Her uncle is on Prospect Mountain, you idiot! You let her wander off with a stranger."

Sandra ran into the street, yelling her daughter's name over and over again. Kayla jogged out to meet her a few minutes later, something brown and fuzzy in her hands. It was

Allie's stuffed pony, the toy she had refused to go anywhere without ever since Raven had given it to her.

"This was in the lobby," Kayla said, handing it over. "Sandra, there's a note attached to it."

A piece of paper was pinned to the plush fur. Sandra's hands were shaking so badly that she nearly crumpled it into a ball before she could read it. In blocky, horribly familiar handwriting, were words that chilled her to the marrow.

THERE IS A MOUNTAIN ABOVE THE ENTRANCE TO THE UNDERWORLD. FOLLOW THE WINGS TO THE NEST AT THE TOP. COME ALONE, OR YOUR DAUGHTER BURNS.

Colton dipped down to look out the windshield at the bulging clouds creeping across the sky.

"Looks like another storm," he said.

"Then I guess we're going to get wet," Jake replied.

With a jerk of his chin toward the rearview mirror, Colton said, "Not as wet as those poor bastards."

Nathan, Raven, and Creek were in the bed of the pickup, heads bobbing up and down as the truck jolted over the highway.

Colton unclipped his walkie-talkie. "Margaret, this is Colton. Do you copy?"

"Loud and clear," the administrative assistant replied.

"We're headed to the first road block on Highway 7 by the Scott Avenue turnoff. Then we're checking out Prospect Mountain."

"Roger that, sir," Margaret said. "I'll keep you updated if anything happens in town."

"There it is," Jake said. He pointed to a fort of cars positioned strategically on the highway. To the left was a red minivan, the windows smashed out on all sides. A volunteer marksman sat in the back seat, face pressed to the scope of a rifle aimed up the road. To the right was a panel truck from an appliance store. Two wood barriers blocked off the small passage between the vehicles. Officer Sam Hines waved when he saw Jake's truck. Three other men carrying high-powered rifles and shotguns fell in to watch.

John Palmer had followed through on his promise to help keep order in Estes Park; he was standing in the bed of a pickup with a shotgun trained on the road. It felt good to have men like John watching over the town. Colton was going to need a lot more like him in the days to come.

The men stationed here were under orders to stop and search any vehicle attempting to enter Estes Park, as well as people on foot, and turn away anyone who didn't have a legitimate reason to be there. Although he didn't feel good about the decision, Colton had also ordered his men to turn away refugees unless they possessed a skill that would benefit the town in the coming months. Those people would be welcomed, but he had to be realistic about how far the town's limited resources would stretch.

Sam Hines strolled up to the pickup and ducked down to look in the driver's window. "Morning."

"How are things?" Colton asked. "Any problems?"

"Pretty quiet night. We had a few refugees this morning.

We turned a family away, but let a man through who said he was a mechanic."

"Good, we need more of them," Colton said.

"Heard about Mollie Harms," Sam said. "You really think it's the same person that killed Melissa Stone and Bill Catcher?"

"We know it is," Jake said.

"Focus on holding this road, Sam. I'll focus on finding the person responsible for these murders."

"You got it, sir," Sam said. He signaled to his men, and two of them jogged over to the barriers and moved them out of the way.

Colton watched the roadblock recede in the passenger side mirror. In some ways it wasn't much different than those he had guarded in Afghanistan, but he'd never expected to see something like that in America.

They drove in silence for several minutes until they reached their turn off. Colton rolled the window down manually to let in the cool breeze. Brown grass and ponderosas framed the road on both sides. Jake put the truck into third gear and climbed toward Prospect Mountain Drive. Detective Lindsey Plymouth had found the camp up there, about a half mile to the west of Bill Catcher's place.

The walkie-talkie on his hip crackled. "Chief, do you copy?"

Colton pulled the radio and brought it to his lips. "Roger that, Margaret, go ahead."

The white noise from the radio made it hard to hear what came next. They were already too far out of range for a clear transmission.

"Chief, Sandra Spears is here." Static. "She says someone—"

Colton tapped the side of the radio.

"Come again," he said. "I didn't catch your last."

Another squawk of static and then the signal cleared. "Chief, Sandra Spears claims someone kidnapped her daughter."

Colton swallowed, his gaze instantly flitting to the rearview mirror. Raven was smiling and bantering with Nathan in the back.

"Pull off," Colton ordered.

"Where?" Jake asked. "Not really a great place—"

"Pull off now!"

Jake slammed the brakes and twisted the wheel. Colton opened the door and jumped onto the dirt before the truck had come to a complete stop.

Raven was standing in the bed of the truck, looking down at Colton.

"What's wrong? Why did we stop here?" Raven's smile slowly faded away as he took in the expression on Colton's face. "Chief, what's wrong?"

"Allie has been kidnapped," he said, keeping his voice low.

"What?" Raven said quietly, like he couldn't believe it.

"Your niece has been taken," Colton said. He pulled his radio off his belt and held it up. "Margaret called it in. Apparently, your sister showed up at the station and said someone took Allie from the hospital."

Raven gritted his teeth and kicked a rock over the side of the ledge. It tumbled down the bluff, dust swirling into the air. "I was supposed to protect them. I was supposed to keep them safe."

The crackle from Colton's radio cut him off.

"Go ahead," Colton said, grateful for the interruption.

"Sir, Ms. Spears said she found a note with Allie's stuffed animal. She's hysterical."

"Tell Sandra to hold on. We're headed back to the station."

Raven reached for the radio, but stopped at the crackle of another transmission.

"Sir, she ran out of here right after I called you," Margaret said. "Sandra Spears is already gone."

Raven's hand wobbled as he reached out for the radio. Colton handed it to him.

"Margaret, this is Raven," he said, his voice shaky. "What does the note say?"

There was a hard pause of static followed by Margaret's reply. "There's a mountain above the entrance to the underworld. Follow the wings to the nest at the top. Come alone or your daughter burns."

Raven's eyes widened and he lowered the radio as if he had just realized something awful.

"You know what that means?" Colton asked.

Raven didn't reply, but he didn't really need to. The truth of it was written all over his ashen face.

20

The flag bridge on the USS *John C. Stennis* felt like a freezer. Charlize fidgeted in her chair, goose flesh prickling across her burned skin. She and Captain Dietz, along with several other officers, had already been waiting nearly forty-five minutes by the time President Diego limped into the room. Rear Admiral Robert Luke followed him, holding a briefcase in one hand and a stack of folders under his other. Luke was the commanding officer of the strike group, and it appeared he was already trying to curry favor with the new president.

"Sorry to keep you all waiting," Diego said, not sounding sorry at all. "I was on the horn with the British Prime Minster and the Secretary-General of the United Nations about aid shipments."

"No problem, sir," Dietz said. "Thank you for meeting with us."

Luke handed the folders to Dietz, who in turn passed them out to everyone in the room. Diego didn't waste any time. He cracked the seal on his folder. Charlize followed suit, opening hers to find a dozen sheets of satellite imagery and several pages of documents inside. She rifled through them, wondering why she hadn't already seen these reports.

Luke said, "You will find the current international locations of all branches of the military, including troop counts, equipment, armaments, and so on, in your packets. There are also reports detailing the recovery efforts in the United States."

The admiral licked his index finger and thumbed through the documents until he found the one he was looking for. "Page twenty, everyone," Luke said.

Charlize flipped to the page to find a map of the United States and several diagrams.

"We estimate over a quarter of the population will die in the next two weeks as a result of the radioactive fission products from the air detonations and the fallout from the ground blast in Washington D.C. From our models, the safe areas appear to be shown on this diagram," Luke said. "It's hard to know how accurate these models are, though. The radioactive fission products and the fallout can be difficult to measure."

Charlize could hardly bring herself to look at the predictions for Colorado. Empire was right in the middle of a red zone. She felt like crying and screaming and running for the hatch, but instead she swallowed her despair and listened to the briefing.

Luke walked them through the report on the following

page, which showed how much of the country had gone dark following the EMP. Almost the entire map was shaded gray, and parts even extended into Mexico and Canada.

"Ladies and gentleman," Diego said, taking over the briefing. "Moving forward, there's good news and bad news. I'll start with the good."

He clasped his fingers and rested his elbows on the table. "As you can see from these documents, recovery efforts have begun. Working closely with the military and FEMA, we're setting up SCs in all major cities."

"SCs?" Charlize asked.

"Survivor Centers outside the radiation zones," Diego said. "Water, food, and medicine is being heavily guarded and distributed appropriately at these locations. The Army has also established FOBs to help combat the rioting and destruction in major population centers."

Diego paused to take a sip of water before continuing.

"Now comes the hard part. Two of the most important assets we have are the FEMA generators located in Southern Florida and the fleet of semi-trailers that were not damaged by the EMP. Using military escorts, we will be shipping these generators to priority SCs in the coming days and weeks."

Charlize understood now. The good news was they had resources in Florida that had survived the attack, but the bad news was they would have to prioritize which SCs received those resources—in other words, who lived and who died.

Diego continued the briefing. "We have recalled over one hundred thousand active duty troops serving overseas. They will be returning to the states in the next few weeks to help with the recovery efforts."

"How about our allies, sir? You mentioned you spoke to the UK and the UN?" Charlize said.

"Mexico and Canada are dealing with their own problems as a result from the attack, but England, France, Germany, and a dozen other allies have committed and or already deployed hundreds of aid ships to help," Diego replied. "Many of these shipments will include high protein food, medicine, fuel, and generators. However, I'm afraid they won't arrive in time for many of our citizens."

Diego looked down at his folder and turned the page. "Anyone living west of the Mississippi River who survives the radiation is going to suffer for several months before we can get these supplies to them. Highways are already impassible due to abandoned vehicles, and we simply don't have the capability to ship supplies."

He looked up from his folder, eyes as cold as ice. After a short pause, he added, "We expect fifty million Americans will starve to death by winter. Another twenty-five million who are dependent on medicines will die, and an additional twenty-five million will be killed in the violence and disease that follows."

There was an uneasy silence as everyone in the room did the math. A hundred million dead in addition to those who had already perished or would perish from the radiation made Charlize sick to her stomach.

"There's more bad news," Luke said. "Take a look at page thirty-three."

Charlize had to hold her folder to the light to see the image. Where there should have been the nuclear-powered super carrier, the USS *Ronald Reagan*, and the rest of Carrier

Strike Group Five, she only saw blackened sheets of metal floating in the teal water of Yokosuka Harbor.

"The North Koreans hit Yokosuka Naval Base with intercontinental ballistic missiles shortly after the initial attack with their commercial airliners. We didn't see it coming because they took out several of our satellites, leaving us in the dark across key areas. This is more evidence that the Supreme Leader believed he could destroy us before we could hit back. They actually thought they could win this war."

"All due respect, Admiral, they *have* won this war," Charlize interjected. "The war is over. They won it the moment they violated our airspace."

The hatch to the room opened before anyone could reply.

Lieutenant Marco stepped inside. "I'm sorry to interrupt, but we have a problem, sir." Her gaze was directed at Rear Admiral Luke.

"Speak freely," he said after Marco paused.

"Our anti-submarine warfare officers have caught some passive sonar hits that could be enemy subs."

Dietz stood. "Have we been able to track them?"

"Negative, sir, the hits fade in and out too often to accurately track."

"Put the fleet on high alert, Lieutenant," Luke said.

>——

Sandra wasn't sure where she was going, but she was running there as fast as she could. Her mind was a complete mess. The note said to come alone, but she had hoped the police could help her. When had she started trusting them? Kids from the Rez knew better than to trust the cops. They wouldn't save her daughter and Raven was too far away to help right now. She would have to do it herself.

Looking up, she realized that she'd run all the way through the station and into the parking lot. Raven's Jeep was still parked there. Detective Lindsey Plymouth was leaning against the passenger door, chewing bubble gum as if she didn't have anything better to do.

I have to find Allie. I have to find my baby. I should never have come here!

Her vision clouded and her stomach rolled. She bolted for the green trashcan outside the building, doubled over, and puked in the grass.

Lindsey rushed over. "Ma'am, are you okay?"

"No, I'm not fine," Sandra said. "I need the keys to my brother's Jeep."

Lindsey shook her head. "I'm waiting for Detective Ryburn to go check out an incident at the YMCA camp."

Sandra brushed the curtain of hair from her face and wiped her mouth off with a sleeve. "My daughter was taken." She was gasping for air now—hyperventilating, she realized.

"Just calm down," Lindsey said. She put a hand on Sandra's shoulder, but Sandra backed away.

"No, I *won't* calm down, Officer. I need my brother's Jeep."

"I'm sorry, but…"

"Chief Colton said it's fine, and if you don't believe me, you can go ask that girl at the front desk."

Lindsey glanced toward the door and then back at Sandra with a skeptical look.

"Stay here, then. I'm going to check with Margaret."

Sandra waited for Lindsey to enter the building. Then she rushed to Raven's Jeep. She opened the door, reached under the front seat, and searched for the extra key he kept taped to the floorboard.

"Come on, come on," she muttered. Her fingers scraped against the metal key, and she plucked it off the floor, jumped into the car, and slammed the door.

"Stop!" shouted Lindsey. The door to town hall swung open and footsteps pounded the ground. By the time the detective reached the parking lot, Sandra was already gunning the engine through Bond Park. The oversized off-road tires ripped through the green sod, leaving wide tracks. She squealed onto Riverside East and pushed down harder on the gas pedal.

She recited the note from memory. "There's a mountain above the entrance to the underworld. Follow the wings to the nest at the top. Come alone or your daughter burns."

There were so many mountains in this place. Tears fell from her eyes as she scanned the sky, searching the peaks for anything that might give her a clue.

Birds had wings. Maybe there was an actual bird's nest she was meant to find?

Think, Sandra, think!

She sped up the road, raising a hand to shield her eyes from the brilliant sun. The glow reflected off the glass of one of the tramway gondolas strung across Prospect Mountain.

Sandra was staring at them so hard that she almost ran into a sign that read *Tunnel Access CLOSED*.

It was then she finally understood. On the tramway tour she'd taken with Raven and Allie, their guide had mentioned an old tunnel under Prospect Mountain that ferried water from Mary's Lake to Lake Estes, where it then fed into Big Thompson River.

The underworld was that tunnel, the gondolas were the wings, and the nest was the top of the tramway. Now she just had to figure out how to get up there. The road forked ahead to the right and left. She jerked to the left at the last moment.

A dusty cloud of exhaust trailed the Jeep as she sped up the winding mountain roads. For several minutes she swerved up the west side of the mountain. Ahead, Turquoise Trail ended at a cul-de-sac. She slammed on the brakes and killed the engine.

Wiping the tears from her face, she stared at the top of the mountain. It wasn't far to the tramway, but the woods were dense and steep. She would have to hike the rest of the way up.

Without another thought, Sandra sprinted into the forest.

It took everything in her not to scream Allie's name, but she resisted the urge.

Be strong, Sandra. You can do this. You have to do this.

Gasping for air, she pushed on, sweat dripping down her face, calves burning. She could still taste the bile from throwing up earlier, but nothing was going to stop her now. She would find her baby and then tear the kidnapping bastard apart with her bare hands.

That was when she realized that, in her panic, she hadn't brought a weapon. She really would have to use her bare hands.

She ran harder through the minefield of mossy rocks and fallen logs. Somewhere in the distance, there was the caw of a crow. Another bird answered it, and then another.

Ravens were good omens in some Native American legends. They could be tricksters, too, which was how her mischievous brother had earned his nickname. But it was strange to find so many in one place. When a turkey vulture swooped high overhead, she realized that there was only one reason so many carrion birds would have gathered.

Something was dead at the top of Prospect Mountain.

The pain was deep and raw, but there was something else inside her now, something that would fuel her even when hope and adrenaline failed.

Anger.

A deeper rage than she had ever felt in her life.

Pawing at the branches that scraped her skin, she burst through the final stand of ponderosas at the edge of the woods and stumbled onto a dirt road. The concrete lookout of the aerial tramway towered above her like a castle. Sandra eyed the stairs leading to the tramway platform overhead.

She took a deep breath and prepared to climb.

"Mommy!"

The single word seized all the air from Sandra's lungs. She looked up to see two figures behind the metal safety fence surrounding the raised platform.

Sandra raised her hand and squinted into the sunlight.

"Hello, Sandra," came a voice. "It's been a long time."

She would never forget the cold, calculating, monotone voice. She didn't need a cloud to pass over the sun to know the man that had taken Allie wasn't Mark or some love-struck patient.

It was someone much, much worse.

———

Light as a feather, Raven told himself. He couldn't believe Sandra had run off to find Allie without him. *And* she'd stolen his Jeep.

No, on second thought he could definitely believe it. He just wished that Sandra had waited for him. Now they were searching the mountain for Sandra and Allie, and he could only hope they'd find his family before they became the next victims of the madman acting out the Water Cannibals story.

He ducked under a tree branch and then stopped, waiting impatiently for the rest of the search party. Colton held up a hand to the right. He raised two fingers to Raven, then to Jake and Nathan, then pointed to his eyes, and finally to a clearing ahead.

The scent of smoke caught Raven's nose and he signaled for Creek to hide with a quick hand motion. The dog scurried into the underbrush and vanished under a moss-covered log.

An eerie silence passed through the forest. A bird took off from the canopy, but Raven kept his eyes on the clearing. He caught the strong scent of beans. Someone had definitely been cooking. There must be people ahead, camouflaged by the foliage, and hidden by a fortress of trees. Surely their chase wouldn't be foolish enough to camp out in the open like this, though.

Colton lowered his AR-15 and flashed an advance signal to Nathan and Jake. He gave Raven the same signal and, forming a perimeter, the four closed in on the camp.

After scanning the woods with the scope on his bow, Raven followed the order. He kept low, almost in a hunch, his finger on the outside of the trigger guard.

Colton vanished behind a tree in Raven's peripheral. He lost sight of Jake and Nathan a moment later. Keeping to the left, Raven caught his first glimpse of the camp. There were several t-shirts and pairs of pants drying on a clothesline strung between two pine trees. A fire pit with a grate and a pot on top was smoking in the center of the camp.

He worked his way closer, step by step, and hugged the trunk of a tree. Pushing his scope to his eye, he followed a man with shoulder-length blond hair, his back turned to the trees. As soon as he grabbed the lid of the pot, Colton shouted and burst into the camp with his rifle pointed at the man's face.

"Freeze!" Jake shouted.

Nathan limped out of the foliage, the men closing in from opposite directions to trap their quarry. Raven followed with his bow raised.

The man at the pot held up his hands, one of them still holding the lid. He backed away from the fire, eyes roving from side to side. "What the hell?" he shouted. "I wasn't trying to steal it, I swear. We're just so hungry!"

"Shut up!" Colton yelled back.

Raven caught a glimpse of a second person emerging

from the woods to his left. He aimed his crossbow at a woman that dropped the bundle of sticks she was carrying.

"Don't shoot!" she yelled.

Raven lowered his bow and pivoted back to the man at the fire pit. The officers and Nathan were closing in, weapons held steady.

"On your knees," Colton ordered.

The blond man slowly got down as instructed. "Take it easy. If this is your camp, then I'm sorry. Like I said, we were just looking for—"

Nathan plucked a pistol from the back of the man's jeans. He tossed it to Colton, who snatched it expertly from the air and looked it over.

"Nice piece," he said. "You planning on shooting someone today?"

Jake motioned with two fingers to the woman. "Ma'am, please come over here and get down on the ground with your hands over your head."

"What the hell is this about?" she asked. "We didn't do anything wrong."

"This guy isn't our chase," Raven said.

The man looked up from his knees. "Chase? What the hell are you talking about? We weren't chasing anyone."

"Shut up," Colton said.

It was obvious these people weren't killers, but clearly Colton wasn't taking any chances. He handcuffed the man, despite the guy's continued stream of protests, while Jake did the same to the woman.

"What are your names?" Colton asked.

"Kirk. This is my wife, Sally." He glanced up, blue eyes

pleading. "Please don't arrest us. We were just looking for something to eat."

They were both filthy, faces and hands covered in dirt. They looked like they'd been through a tough ordeal.

"We're wasting time," Raven said, agitated.

"Hold on a second," Colton snapped.

Raven whistled for Creek and circled the camp as Colton interrogated the couple. Two sets of clothes, both men's, and a couple of old towels and a single sleeping bag. Nothing much to tell him who had been living up here. Idly, he peered into the pot.

"C-colton." Raven choked out.

"What?" The chief looked over at him, and something about Raven's expression must have shaken him. "Christ, Raven, you look like you've seen a ghost."

Not a ghost, he thought. *A spirit. I was right all along. The Water Cannibals are here.*

Inside the pot, floating above some mushy, overcooked vegetables, was a livid human hand that ended in a ragged, blackened stump.

Colton looked in the pot and then grimaced in horror and disgust. "Jake, I think we just found Mollie Harm's missing hand."

21

"What do you mean you found a hand?" Kirk asked for the fourth time.

Colton spat on the ground as he unlocked the cuffs on Kirk's hands. "Get out of here and don't come back. It's not safe up here."

"Where are we supposed to go?" Kirk asked. "We were robbed at gunpoint yesterday. Bastards took our bicycles. We walked here, but your people turned us away this morning. We hiked through the woods and found this campsite."

Kirk massaged his wrists and walked over to his wife. She was sitting on a log, whimpering and rocking back and forth.

Colton placed the cuffs back on his duty belt and took a moment to think. According to Raven, their killer had to be a Native American. Probably Cherokee, given the origin of the legend, but he was less certain on that point. This couple had just been in the wrong place at the wrong time.

"Go to the Stanley Inn," Colton said. "Tell Jim that Chief Colton sent you. Know how to get there from here?"

"Thank you," Kirk said, nodding enthusiastically. "Oh God, thank you!"

Sally stopped rocking. "You can't just send us out there alone!" Kirk tried to soothe her, but she shouted, "We almost ate someone's hand, you asshole! Do NOT tell me to calm down."

Kirk looked hopefully at Colton. "Can I have my gun back?"

With a grunt, Colton tossed it to him, and the terrified couple sprinted into the trees without a backward glance.

Raven was prowling the camp, sometimes crouching down to examine the dirt, sometimes studying a snapped tree branch or other, less obvious signs. He knew the man must be desperate to find his sister, but Colton didn't want to run off into the woods half-cocked. Things weren't adding up. If this was their killer's lair, why had he let these people live?

"We need to keep moving, Chief," Raven said. He jogged over, Creek at his heels.

Colton gestured for the other men to join them. Raven pulled off his baseball cap and folded the brim before putting it back on his head.

"I found three sets of tracks leading into the mountains," he said. "Two belong to that couple, and one is a large man's boot print. But it doesn't look very fresh, and Creek hasn't found any trace of Allie or Sandra."

"Do you think this is our killer's camp?" Jake asked.

"I do, but he's not here." Raven said. He shot a glance at Colton and then continued. "We might need to split up. The note said something about the underworld. I think that means the tunnels beneath the mountain, but I could be wrong."

"Those have been closed off for years," Colton said.

"The other possibility is the tramway. That could be the nest. I think we should cover both places, just in case," Raven said. Beside him, Creek whined and pawed the ground.

"No," Colton said, holding up a hand to cut off Raven's protests. "We stick together. The tramway sounds more likely than the tunnels. We'll head there."

"Fine, but let's move now," Raven said. He motioned for Creek and led the way out of the camp. The team worked their way through the forest for fifteen minutes. Colton's boots sank into the damp pine needles with every step, leaving behind clear tracks. If someone had been here before them, surely they would have left a trail.

He looked up to see Raven crest a hill and freeze like a statue. Colton carefully walked up the ridge until he was standing a few feet behind the tracker. He slowly took a knee, his joints creaking. They were almost to the tramway. From here, the pine trees thinned out, allowing Colton to see farther. Fallen trees and boulders covered in moss dotted the terrain. He scanned the area systematically, just like he'd been trained. Glancing over at Raven, he realized the man was doing the exact same thing.

The storm had rolled to the east and the cloudless sky was ocean blue over the mountain that was a collage of changing colors. His gaze moved from left to right, but there was no sign of anything out of the ordinary. No glint of metal or smoke, and no people other than themselves.

Raven stopped at a tree and motioned for Colton. Creek was sitting on his haunches, looking up at his handler.

"Creek's picked up a scent," Raven said quietly. "It could be them. I think we're getting close."

Colton flashed an advance signal to Nathan and Jake. Both men were one hundred feet to the east, using the cover of trees on the ridgeline.

Raven moved north, raising his crossbow as he scanned the tramway. Colton would always prefer a gun to a bow, but he had to admit that Raven was pretty good with the thing.

Creek prowled through the foliage, muzzle sniffing the dirt. He weaved back and forth, picking up the invisible skin rafts blowing on the wind. Maybe, when this was all over, Colton would see about enlisting Raven and Creek as Estes Park's K-9 unit.

Colton stepped over a fallen tree and jogged through a patch of yellow wildflowers. Raven stopped again, squatting to check a pair of tracks. Colton did the same.

"Looks like they separate here," Raven said. "See that?"

Colton checked the footprints. Both appeared to be male, judging by the size. The two sets curved off in different directions.

"Either of these could be our chase," Raven said. "But I don't see any smaller prints. Nothing to indicate Sandra and Allie came this way."

Colton stood and waved at Nathan and Jake. They met under the cover of a grove of pine trees. A cool breeze shifted the branches around them, the canopy whispering to itself. Normally, the sound was reassuring, but Colton was too on edge to appreciate it.

"Nathan, Jake," Colton whispered. "We're going to have to split up after all. The tracks split off in two different directions."

Nathan looked up at the tramway. "Whatever we do, let's hurry."

"You and Jake continue west," Colton said. "Raven and I will head east."

Nathan and Jake nodded and had turned to go when the sharp pop of gunshots rang out. Colton spun in that direction with his AR-15. He put the scope to his eye and roved the crosshairs across the southern stretch of forest. Unless he was mistaken, the shots sounded like they'd come from the campsite.

"Head west with Nathan," Colton told Jake. "Raven and I will check this out."

Colton took off into the trees, hoping that Kirk and Sally hadn't returned to the camp instead of heading to the Stanley. Raven whistled at Creek and fell into a run. It only took a few seconds for the Akita to overtake them both. He moved with graceful ease over the steep terrain, dodging rocks and springing like a rabbit on his powerful back legs. Colton, on the other hand, could hardly breathe. He wasn't used to running like this. Kelly was always trying to get him to exercise more, but he had gotten out of the habit after coming home from his last tour of duty.

Loose rocks tumbled down the hill as Colton ran down

the slope. He threw the strap of his rifle over his back and pulled his Colt .45.

Raven leapt nimbly over a rock. He ran with the grace of a trail runner. Vultures continued to circle overhead. Their calls were growing louder as the raptors swooped lower. The pop of gunfire hadn't sounded for several minutes. Whatever had happened, Colton feared he was too late to help.

I shouldn't have sent Kirk and Sally away on their own.

If something had happened to the couple, it was on him.

Colton ran faster, ducking under branches and scraping against tree trunks. Lungs straining for air, muscles burning, and sweat pouring down his face, he felt like he was back in Afghanistan. A branch caught him in the face. He swatted it away with his hand and bolted toward the clearing of the campsite. When he was clear of the trees, he realized Raven and Creek were nowhere in sight.

Colton tried to steady his breathing. He slowed to a walk, his pistol angled slightly downward. He scanned the path in front of him, looking for hazards and planning each footstep before he made it. He halted and raked the barrel over the camp. A figure was moving in the tall weeds, crawling on its belly.

It was Sally.

"Oh god," Colton whispered. He ran full-speed toward her. As he moved, he caught a drift of smoke, familiar and rank, like charred beef left too long on the grill.

He knew then, but he still forced himself to look at the fire pit.

Kirk lay face first beside the flames, his legs still burning. There was no question that he was dead. A living man, even one with a mortal wound, would have crawled away from such torture.

As Colton ran across the camp, he swept his revolver back and forth. Where the hell were Raven and Creek?

Sally continued dragging her body using only her elbows, dazed and moving like a maimed animal. A choking sound came from her mouth, but Colton couldn't see her face.

An overwhelming wave of anxiety hit Colton. He felt like he was being watched. He spun, raking his pistol across the trees surrounding the camp. The branches swayed in the wind, movement coming from every direction. Seeing nothing, he bent down and put a hand on Sally's back.

"It's okay," he whispered. "I'll get you out of here."

She dug her elbows into the dirt again and pulled herself forward another foot like she hadn't even heard him. She left a swath of blood behind her in the grass, like some kind of nightmarish snail trail.

Colton kept his gun on the trees and touched Sally's shoulder with his other hand. Using the utmost care, he rolled her onto her back.

Wide brown eyes locked onto Colton as if he was the devil in the flesh.

Blood was pouring out of her mouth, and as she opened it to scream or beg for help, he realized that the sick bastard had cut out her tongue.

There was so much blood that at first he didn't notice the second wound, lower down on her neck. Her throat had been slit, just shy of severing her arteries and granting her a mercifully quick death.

"It's okay," he repeated, but he knew it was a lie. "I won't let anyone else hurt you. I'm going to find the man who did this to you."

Sally croaked again, trying to speak, and began to choke on her own blood.

"Don't try and talk," Colton whispered.

Her eyes widened again, but this time they weren't looking at him.

A copper-skinned man with a dark, scraggly beard ambled into the clearing, a gun in one hand and a blood-stained knife in the other. His yellow grin stretched from ear to ear.

Everything that happened next seemed to occur in slow motion. Colton raised his gun just as the man pulled the trigger of his own weapon. A bullet hit the dirt by Colton's right boot, and a second punched into his upper chest, knocking the gun from his hand and sending him backward. A third whizzed by his forehead as he fell. He raised a hand to protect his face, knowing that he had failed, and worst of all knowing that he wouldn't see Kelly or Risa ever again.

Colton collapsed to his back next to Sally. He opened his eyes again, expecting to be looking down the barrel of a gun, but instead he saw Raven and Creek behind the man who'd shot him.

The killer was on his knees, an arrow sticking out of his left temple. He was still staring at Colton, his smirk just as wide as before, as if he didn't notice or didn't care that he'd just been shot in the head.

Raven fired a second arrow not long after, and the killer crashed to the dirt with a thud.

Gasping for air, Colton pawed at his chest where the

bullet had hit him. He felt for blood, but he had been lucky. The vest had stopped the bullet. It still hurt like a son of a bitch, but hurt was better than dead. Wheezing, he rolled over to look at Sally.

"We got him," he said, trying to smile at the dying woman. Blood bubbled in her throat as she tried again to speak. Her eyes rolled up into her head, and then she was gone.

Colton let out a sigh and reached over to close her eyelids. The hunt for the serial killer had ended, but it had cost two more innocent lives. Pushing himself to his feet, Colton looked at the man responsible for this evil. He lay face first in the dirt across the camp, his reign of terror finally over.

Raven felt like his world was falling apart. And deep down, he believed it was his fault. He eyed Kirk and Sally's bodies. He was sorry for their deaths, but he was more worried about his sister and his niece.

He'd sworn to protect Allie and Sandra, and instead he'd let them get taken by a demon from his childhood nightmares. That demon was dead, but his family was still missing.

He'd promised Billy Franks that he'd watch his back, but the Marine had saved Raven's life instead and caught a bullet in the face for his trouble.

Raven couldn't shake the feeling that the North Korean nukes were his fault, too. Everything he touched seemed to turn to shit.

No more, he thought. *You can't mess up again. You have to find Sandra and Allie.*

Creek let out a whine that pulled Raven from his thoughts. The dog sat guarding the killer. Raven walked over to check the corpse for any clues that might tell him where his sister and niece were.

He thought he would feel something at the sight of the dead man, but he was numb. It had been like that during the war, sometimes. He knew from experience that the pain and fear and grief would come later. He still hadn't gotten a good look at the killer's face. Bending down, Raven grabbed his shoulder and rolled him onto his back.

"Holy shit," Raven said. He stood quickly and took a step back, his heart lodged in his throat.

Colton walked over, a hand on his vest. "What? Do you recognize him?"

Raven could almost feel the blood quickening in his veins. He wasn't sure if it was from adrenaline or anger, but whatever it was, he had to control it before it overwhelmed him.

"Raven, what's the matter?" Colton asked. There was genuine concern in the chief's voice. It was almost like he cared. When had that happened?

"That's Turtle," he said, still trying to process what he was seeing. "His real name is Billy Tankala. He and his brother, Mike, used to live on the Rez with me and Sandra."

"Are you sure?" Colton demanded.

Raven leaned down just to make sure, pulling back the man's collar to reveal a tattoo of a turtle.

"Yeah," he said.

"Please tell me you didn't owe him money too," Colton said.

"What? No, I didn't owe him money, Marcus. Mike Tankala—we called him Brown Feather, back on the Rez—used to go out with my sister, but I haven't seen him for years."

"You tellin' me this is just a coincidence? That some asshole from Rosebud came all the way to Estes Park to kill Melissa, Bill, Mollie, these people, and kidnap…"

Colton's words trailed off, realization apparently sinking in. "That's why he's here, isn't it?"

"He came for my sister," Raven said, feeling sick to his stomach. He placed his crossbow on the foot stirrup and used the crank system to load another bolt in the groove.

"Nathan and Jake had to have heard those shots. They're probably on their way. We should stay put until they return," Colton said. He looked around the campsite, his face a grim mask.

No wonder there had been two sets of prints. They were tracking not one but two murderers. That explained the other night at Mount Ypsilon, too. One of the killers had been watching Raven and Colton with Melissa while the other had been busy with Bill Catcher at Prospect Mountain.

"If he was here for Sandra, then why kill Melissa and Mollie?" Colton asked.

"I don't know," Raven said. "Sandra had a thing with Brown Feather a long time ago, when they were practically just kids. Brown and Turtle went to prison after they robbed a liquor store on the Rez and assaulted an officer, along with a shit-ton of other things. He used to write her letters, but after a while they stopped coming. I figured he finally got over her."

What he didn't say was that although he'd hated both the Tankala brothers, Brown Feather was the one he had truly feared. He wasn't just a criminal; he was a madman—and he had Raven's family. They couldn't wait here and hope that Jake and Nathan would return. They had to move out now before Brown Feather could finish his reenactment of the Water Cannibal story with Sandra and Allie.

22

Nathan limped through a fort of trees. He hadn't been able to reach Cheyenne Mountain since that first transmission from the top of Trail Ridge Road. Every time Nathan had tried the shortwave frequency since then, it was silent. But that wasn't the only thing that was quiet. The lack of noise on Prospect Mountain gave him pause. He hadn't heard anything from Colton, Raven and Creek, or Jake for over ten minutes.

Raising his M14, Nathan moved the crosshairs across the trees. The radio tower and aerial tramway were just ahead, but there were no voices, just the whistle of the wind and creak of branches swaying in it.

Where the hell was everyone?

He continued west up a steep slope lined with a fence of aspen trees, their white trunks like bones jutting out of the rocky earth. Nothing moved inside the forest, but Nathan felt like he was being watched.

A quick scan revealed nothing. He shouldered his rifle and moved quickly toward the concrete base of the aerial tramway. The thick trunk of a ponderosa provided cover, and he ducked down next to its base to survey the lay of the land.

There was still no sign of Sandra or Allie, and he didn't see Colton or anyone else trekking up the slope, but the view was magnificent. The entire valley was visible from his vantage.

Nathan carefully edged around the safety of the tree and checked the tramway platforms again, moving the crosshairs across the safety fences for contacts. Seeing none, he ran for the base of the first observation deck. When he reached the bottom of the wall he put his back against the concrete and stopped to listen. There was still only the rustle of falling leaves and the sigh of the wind carrying them to the ground.

Then he heard something else. It was a girl, and she was crying.

Nathan looked up at the higher platforms. The noise was coming from somewhere up there, but it was hard to pinpoint a location. Hugging the base of the lookout, he slowly made his way around the corner toward a cluster of trees growing along the side of the compound. At the top, an empty red gondola hung from the cables.

"Don't do this. I'm begging you, please just let Allie go."

Nathan recognized Sandra's voice, but there was a panicked edge to it that made him want to charge up the slope. He gripped his rifle tighter and forced himself to proceed with caution until he saw the second cart. Sandra was standing inside, hands bound, next to Allie.

Pushing the scope to his eye, Nathan finally saw the bastard that had kidnapped them. The man was tall and powerfully built. He ran a hand over his shaved skull and moved out of sight before Nathan could get a clear shot.

He moved the crosshairs back to Sandra and Allie to see them more clearly. They were tied up inside the bright red tramway gondola closest to the platform. The terrified little girl was sobbing, but her mother's expression was as defiant as a cornered wolf.

Nathan roved his rifle back to the kidnapper, but there was no way he was going to get the drop on the guy from here. Shooting from this angle put Sandra and Allie at risk, so he was going to have to find another path around the tramway and work out a plan from there. Gritting his teeth against the pain in his ankle, he began to search for a way to rescue them.

———

Sandra struggled against her restraints and looked for some way out of their situation. She was tied to the metal handlebar inside the gondola docked at the top of the tramway. Red paint flaked off the bar as she worked the rope back and forth. Allie was lying on the seat, wrists and ankles bound by rope.

A concrete walkway curved away from the platform where tourists boarded. To the left, a staircase led to a coffeehouse, gift shop, and second lookout with a terminal that looked like a cross between a greenhouse and a bunker. Straight ahead, another walkway led to an observation area that looked out over the Rocky Mountains to the west. The familiar shops, houses, and even the red roof of the Stanley Hotel appeared as a miniature skirt of toy buildings at the bottom of the mountain. Although she couldn't see them, she could imagine the town's residents walking the streets aimlessly, no job to go to, no purpose but to survive.

And not one of them was going to help her.

Even if she screamed, no one would make it up the mountain in time. Her only hope was Raven. If anyone could find them, it was her brother and his loyal dog.

She pulled on her restraints again, making the gondola sway. Allie's eyes widened in fear. She had always hated heights, and the one time Raven had taken them here for a family day, Allie had been too scared to enjoy the scenery.

Brown Feather stepped away from the railing. He had been staring at the sea of trees below since the gunshots had rung out.

"Turtle," he hissed. "Where the *fuck* are you?"

"Please, please let us go," Sandra begged.

He slowly turned in her direction, his brown eyes focused hungrily on her face. He was tall for a Sioux, over six feet, with wide shoulders and ropy muscle that had always reminded her a bit of a praying mantis. Feather tattoos ran up his neck on both sides, the tips nearly touching his earlobes, which were pierced with black studs.

"I told you to shut up. You could never keep your mouth shut." He put a hand on his shaved head and muttered something under his breath. Sweat poured down his leathery skin. How had she ever, in a million years, found this man attractive?

Because he's just like your father, only worse, she thought.

"You remember that night when we talked about the future? When I told you about my dream for us?"

Sandra swallowed and nodded, trying to smile. She had blocked out most of their relationship, and she had no idea what he was talking about.

"We're supposed to be together, Sandra. We were going to start a family. You promised me we would. When I got out of jail, I thought you'd keep your promise and we'd be happy. I tracked you all the way here, but when I saw that half-breed brat, I witnessed your betrayal in the flesh."

"You have it all wrong, I still want those things we talked about," Sandra lied. She'd had a lot of practice lying to men to avoid a beating.

"You want me," she continued. "And you can still have me."

Brown Feather blinked, seemed to consider it for a moment and then shook his head slightly. His eyes turned flat and predatory.

Sandra remembered that look, too. It always happened right before he hurt her.

"After I saw you with your daughter, I thought I should have my own daughter, too, but the girl I chose was weak," Brown Feather said.

"So that's why you killed her?" Sandra blurted out without thinking.

"No," Brown Feather snapped.

"Why then?" Sandra whispered.

"Practice," Brown Feather said with a wide smile. The teeth he still possessed were black with rot.

"Please, I'll do anything, just don't hurt my baby," Sandra said. She pulled on the ropes binding her wrists, the coarse material cutting her skin.

"Shut up!" Brown Feather pulled a buck knife from a sheath on his belt and put his other hand on his head, rubbing it back and forth. "I told you to shut your mouth!"

He stopped at the open door to the tramway cart, grabbed the frame and leaned in, examining Sandra and then Allie. His stench washed over them in a fetid wave.

"We could have been a family. But instead you chose to betray me. This is your own fault," he said.

Motion behind Brown Feather drew her gaze. A dark-haired man was scaling the side of the observation deck. He rolled onto the platform, raised his rifle, and took aim.

"Please," Sandra said, trying to keep Brown's attention on her. "Don't hurt my daughter."

"You had your chance." Brown Feather leaned down toward Allie with the knife, the smile on his face expanding into an alligator's hungry grin.

Crack!

A bullet shattered the window of the gondola to the right of Brown Feather. He fell backward onto the platform.

"Nathan!" she yelled.

The pilot fired again, this time clipping Brown's ear and blowing it clean off, onyx stud and all. Screaming, Brown Feather pushed himself up and ran at Nathan. He aimed, but then pushed the muzzle up when Brown Feather moved in front of Allie and Sandra. Nathan raised the butt of his rifle just as Brown Feather barreled into him. The force of the blow slammed Nathan into the guardrail. He let out a grunt of pain as his rifle cartwheeled away. It landed a few feet from the gondola where Sandra and Allie were trapped.

"This another one of your lovers?" Brown Feather said. He turned and snarled at her. "I'm going to gut him while you watch, whore."

He pulled his hand away from his missing ear, his fingers gloved in blood. Both men eyed the gun, which lay roughly halfway between them.

They bolted for the rifle at the same time, but Nathan was faster. He bent to scoop it up as Brown Feather slammed into his side. Nathan stumbled toward the end the platform. He lost his balance at the edge, scrabbling for a handhold on the metal side of their gondola. Allie screamed as the cabin rocked violently.

Brown Feather grabbed Nathan's belt, and for a moment Sandra had the crazy hope that he was going to haul the pilot back onto the platform. Instead, Brown Feather grabbed a pistol from his holster and then shoved Nathan over the side.

"NO!" Sandra shouted.

He didn't scream or even cry out as he tumbled out of view. Brown Feather smiled again, blood running freely down his face as he looked over the side and spat.

"Piece of shit," he said.

Sandra felt her insides sink. Brown Feather had just killed one of the only good men she had ever met in her life. She closed her eyes, but this time there were no tears. She didn't have any left. Footsteps advanced down the platform and into the metal cabin. When she opened her eyes, Brown Feather was standing in front of her.

He tucked the pistol into his belt, licked his lips, narrowed his eyes, and focused once more on Allie and Sandra.

"I told you nothing would keep us apart." He picked up Nathan's rifle and then stepped into the cart. She gagged at his rancid breath and fought to get away as he leaned in to kiss her. That's when she saw motion on the platform behind Brown Feather. A large police officer wearing a cowboy hat approached slowly with a rifle shouldered.

It was Jake and he winked at Sandra.

"Don't fucking move," he said in a deep bass voice.

Jake pressed his gun into Brown Feather's back.

"Get out of the cart, you piece of shit."

Brown Feather grinned at Sandra and then turned around. Jake tore the rifle from his hands.

"On your knees," Jake said.

As soon as Brown Feather obeyed, Jake kicked him in the solar plexus so he would stay down. He let out a deep gasp and collapsed to the platform.

"Are you okay, Sandra?" Jake asked.

"Yes, but he pushed Nathan over the side!"

Jake eyed Brown Feather to make sure he was down and then walked over to the rail. While the big lawman's back was turned, Brown Feather jolted up with the pistol Jake had overlooked. Sandra screamed, and Jake turned just in time to return fire.

She blinked reflexively with each deafening pop. A round buried itself in Jake's vest, and a second hit him in the unprotected gut. Despite the wounds, he kept firing. His next shot grazed Brown Feather's shoulder with such force he jerked to the side and fell against a wall.

Brown Feather dove for cover, rolled, and took off running up the staircase that led to the main lookout. Jake kept firing wildly with one hand, his aim off from his injuries. The bullets punched into the stairs as Brown Feather escaped.

Jake staggered and then dropped to his knees. He pulled a bloody hand away from his stomach.

Sandra sucked in a breath, trying to find her strength. Allie had started crying again, but at least she couldn't see Jake bleeding out on the platform.

"Allie, are you okay?" She scanned her daughter when Allie didn't reply. "Are you hurt, baby?"

Allie managed to shake her head, but her sobs never let up.

"Ma'am, are you and your daughter hurt?" Jake said. He tried to stand up, but he coughed and fell again, landing hard on one meaty palm. He smiled at her, his teeth bloody. "Don't worry, I'll be fine. Just a little unsteady."

The sound of a gunshot rang out, and his smile twisted into a grimace as a bullet knocked off his cowboy hat. As it flew into the air Sandra saw the top of Jake's skull was missing.

She heard a scream, but didn't realize it was her own until she started gasping for air. Jake crumpled to the ground. Through the blur of tears, she watched Brown Feather on the platform above theirs, still holding the pistol he'd used to kill Jake. He gave Sandra a jaunty wave before vanishing down the terminal.

23

THE BIG COP GOT WHAT HE DESERVED FOR INTERFERING with Brown Feather's hunt. Same with the black-haired son of a bitch who'd shot his ear off.

Sandra was close to being his again. This time, they would be together forever. But first Brown Feather had to find his brother and figure out who else was tracking him before he could claim his prize. He gripped the pistol and scanned the woods below the platform.

"Turtle, where are you?" Brown Feather said quietly. He should have never told his brother to return to their camp to kill the dumb hippy couple.

Sandra's screams forced Brown Feather back into action. There wasn't time to go back and silence her. He was done hiding. It was time that the Water Cannibals came out into the light.

Turtle was one of them now, having feasted on the stew containing human flesh. They'd laid a trap to separate the police officers, planning to hunt them like game through the woods, but the hippy couple had ruined their plans. Now he feared his brother was either dead or injured so badly he couldn't help Brown Feather finish the most important hunt of all.

It was the bitch's fault. Sandra had ruined everything, distracting him when he should have been focused on bringing the legend of the Water Cannibals to life. Her lies and betrayals were going to cost her. As soon as he'd finished his hunt, he would sacrifice her half-breed daughter and eat the girl's heart right in front of her mother.

He spotted one of the police officers as he moved around the base of a tree. The man was walking slowly, sweeping an assault rifle over the terrain. Brown Feather was probably too far away to shoot the cop with his pistol. He would have to get closer. That was fine; he preferred to kill up close.

Brown Feather ducked under a branch and silently made his way to the next tree for cover.

Motion farther to the east commanded his attention. Not far from the officer was a man carrying a crossbow. A dog trotted alongside, sniffing the ground.

Brown Feather smiled. Now *that* was prey worth hunting. Raven Spears was coming to rescue his sister, just like he had all those years ago. But this time, he wouldn't succeed. This time, Brown Feather would gut the bastard and spread his entrails through the trees like Christmas lights.

He was going to enjoy this.

Raven's heart kicked when he saw Jake's broken body, and it nearly stopped when he saw Sandra and Allie in the swaying gondola.

They were alive!

Colton burst from the trees a moment later. Raven watched his features transform as Colton realized Jake was beyond helping. The raw expression of grief and fury lasted for only a second before Colton schooled his emotions.

"I think the son of a bitch ran up there," Colton said, pointing to the upper observation platforms. "You find this Brown Feather, and I'll get Sandra and Allie."

Colton jogged toward the gondola without waiting for a response, and to his surprise, Raven found that he trusted the chief to take care of his niece and sister while he tracked down Brown Feather.

Drenched in sweat and driven by rage, Raven followed the blood trail up the stairs. Somebody had hit Brown Feather, but he couldn't tell how badly the bastard was hurt yet.

It wouldn't matter in a few more minutes, because the man who'd hurt his family and killed innocent people would be dead.

Raven thought about discarding his crossbow and using his bare hands to kill Brown Feather, but he'd rather win the fight first and then smack around the corpse. He halted and motioned for Creek to get behind him. There was no sign of Nathan anywhere, and with Jake dead, Raven had to assume he was on his own.

He signaled to Creek, and the dog took the path to the right, which curved around the other side of the tramway. The area was massive, but the idea was to flank Brown Feather and box him in. That way, if he did have a gun, Brown Feather wouldn't be able to shoot both of them.

But if the sick fuck shot his dog, Raven really would tear him to pieces.

The blood trail continued around the corner of the observation deck. Raising his bow, he followed the trail. He listened for Brown's breathing or anything else to determine his location, but all Raven heard were the distant voices of Colton and his family.

Bursting around the corner, he aimed his bow toward a stand of trees that shaded the concrete walls of the tramway like soldiers guarding a castle.

There was no sign of Brown Feather.

Raven checked the trail of blood, but it ended in the dirt by his boots. Bending down, he examined the last drop of red. Dirt, pine needles, and pebbles had been kicked over the path.

Son of a bitch.

Raven's guts dropped like he was standing on the edge of a thirty-story building. He rose to his feet and spun around, but it was already too late. Brown Feather had been hiding behind him among the tall trees. It was an ambush, and Raven had walked right into it.

Brown Feather knocked the bow away, grabbed Raven by the face, and pushed him into the concrete wall. The back of Raven's skull hit it with a crack. There wasn't much pain, mostly just pressure, followed by a warm feeling and a flurry of stars that broke before his vision.

"Hey, Sam," Brown Feather said. "Been a while. I've been waiting a very long time for this."

Dazed but determined, Raven threw a clumsy punch that went wide and hit Brown Feather's bloody shoulder instead of his face. Brown screamed in agony and grabbed Raven by the shirt as he lost his balance. They crashed to the ground in a heap.

Raven launched another blow as Brown Feather climbed on top. This time, Raven was aiming for his wounded shoulder, seeing as how bad it hurt Brown Feather the first time. His fist connected with a meaty thump.

Brown Feather shrieked like he'd been stabbed with red-hot iron. Raven flipped to his stomach and crawled away, elbows digging into the bed of pine needles beneath a towering ponderosa. Pushing himself to his feet, he reached back and pulled his twin hatchets.

When he turned, Brown Feather was standing, too. He pulled the buck knife from his belt and sank into a fighting stance with the blade held high in one hand. He balled his other hand into a fist. Blood flowed from his missing ear, and a rosy patch blossomed from the bullet wound on his shoulder. His jaw snapped and then opened into a wide grin.

"You ready to die, half-blood?" Brown Feather snarled.

Raven remembered the taunts in school. Coming from a mixed family on a Sioux Reservation, he was always teased about his Cherokee background.

"For a Sioux, you sure liked the Cherokee stories," Raven said.

The statement seemed to light up Brown Feather's dark eyes. Saliva webbed across his lips like a wild animal frothing at the mouth. "Then you understand," he said huskily. "The Water Cannibals *are* real, Sam. I've released them into the world."

Raven spat on the ground. "You always were a crazy bastard. I should have killed you the first time you hurt my sister."

"I'm going to enjoy sticking you like a pig." His jagged black teeth clanked together at Raven. "And after I'm done hacking and burning you, I'm going to roast that mutt dog of yours alive and then go to work on your sweet little niece. I bet she's tender."

Raven howled in a voice he didn't recognize as his own. He darted forward, swinging his hatchets in long arcs. The blades whooshed through the air in front of Brown Feather. He was fast and easily dodged the blows. Then he swiped at Raven with his blade. The edge slid along Raven's ribs, drawing blood. That just made him more furious.

He moved his left arm as if he were about to strike, then swung the axe in his right hand. Brown Feather parried the attack with a slap of his palm. He nicked Raven again with his knife, flicking the blade against his cheek.

Raven backed away and touched the cut. Warm blood trickled down his fingers as he pulled them away. He used the stolen moment to get his bearings. The mountain was huge and easy for a man to get lost on, but where the hell was Creek? Surely the dog hadn't deserted him.

He looked back at Brown Feather, and decided he was glad they were alone. His gut had been right before. Brown Feather was Raven's demon to face alone.

"Come on, you ugly bastard," Raven muttered. He strode

forward and swung both hatchets at Brown Feather in wide arcs. The right blade found the soft flesh deep in the back of Brown Feather's right leg as he turned away. The wannabe Water Cannibal dropped to his left knee.

"Raven, get out of the way!" a woman's voice shouted.

He glanced up to see Colton and Sandra, both aiming guns at Brown Feather from the observation deck above.

"Don't shoot, he's mine!" Raven shouted.

Brown Feather seized the opening to strike. He charged and speared Raven in the gut with his bald head. The blow knocked Raven on his back again. More stars danced before his eyes. He blinked, trying to clear his vision. He couldn't see his sister or Colton from this angle, which meant they didn't have a clear fire zone to hit Brown Feather as he loomed over Raven.

Good. I'll kill him myself!

Raven raised his right axe, but the bigger man knocked it from his hand and bent down with his blade. Before he could stab Raven, a blur of fur slammed into Brown Feather.

"Creek!" Raven shouted.

He watched helplessly as Brown Feather picked the Akita up and threw him into a tree. The dog slumped to the ground, letting out a low whine.

Brown Feather staggered over with a smile on his face and kicked Raven in the leg. As he moved in with his knife, Raven brought his knee up into Brown Feather's belly. The bigger man fell on top of Raven.

"I'm going to kill you!" Raven yelled. "I'm going to *fucking* kill you!"

Brown Feather thrust his knife at Raven's throat as

he gasped for air. Raven caught his wrist and pushed, but Brown Feather was stronger and had gravity on his side. He slowly inched the knife down. Raven watched the tip of the blade descend, arm shaking as he tried to push it away.

A massive vein like a fat leech protruded out from Brown Feather's forehead. His eyes were wide, crazed, and full of bloodlust. Maybe if Raven held out long enough, the bastard would have a stroke. He pushed back harder. Sweat and blood dripped off Brown Feather's head onto Raven's face.

"Give up, Sam," Brown Feather muttered between breaths.

The blade was just centimeters from Raven's throat now.

He tried to squirm, but that just made things worse. His breath was driven out as Brown Feather dug his knees into Raven's gut. He gasped, but he couldn't get enough air. His vision began to fade in and out, in sync with the thunderous beating of his heart.

"Die, you fucking half-blood," Brown Feather hissed. He glared at Raven with eyes as dark as black holes.

Raven pushed back with all his strength. He couldn't fail. He couldn't let his family down. He had to fight, he had to kill this demon on his own…

No matter how hard he pushed, it wasn't enough. Pain flared as the blade punctured the muscle above his rib cage. He closed his eyes and offered up a silent apology to his sister for failing her when it mattered most.

And then, suddenly, he could breathe again. Brown Feather had been hauled backwards like a fish caught on a hook. There were muffled shouts and the crack of a fist on bone.

Gripping his chest and gasping for air, Raven sat up. He blinked and tried to make sense of the scene. Brown Feather appeared to be fighting a man-sized pine tree near the edge of the bluff that overlooked Estes Park.

Then he recognized the sweatshirt Nathan had borrowed from the police department. The pilot looked worse for wear. His tattered clothes were plastered with mud and blood and other things Raven couldn't identify, and he was covered in so many evergreen needles that it looked like he'd covered himself in sap and then tried to climb every ponderosa in the forest. His left arm had a nasty gash, but that didn't stop him from throwing a punch at Brown Feather.

Sidestepping the blow, Brown Feather grabbed Nathan by his injured arm and twisted it. The scream that followed made Raven's eardrums ache.

A second figure bolted toward the fight. Colton paused for two seconds to check on Raven, who nodded feebly that he was okay.

At least, he hoped he was okay. Raven pulled his sticky fingers away from his chest. There was a lot of blood, but he was more concerned about Creek. He crawled over to his dog, allowing the other men to deal with Brown Feather now.

"It's okay, boy," Raven whimpered, reaching out.

Creek licked his hand and tried to stand.

"Don't move," Raven said. He checked the dog for injuries. Hopefully he was just rattled and nothing was broken.

Raven glanced back at the fight. Brown Feather and Nathan were grappling in the dirt near the edge of the drop-off. Colton reached them before they could topple over the edge. He pushed the barrel of his Colt .45 against Brown Feather's head.

"Get off him, you piece of shit."

"I'll kill him," Brown Feather said, brandishing his knife. "Don't think I won't."

"Shoot him," Nathan choked.

Colton pulled the hammer back with a click. "I said get off him."

The tense silence seemed to stretch on forever. The quiet was at last shattered by Brown Feather's raspy voice. "Fine, officer." He slowly pulled the knife away from Nathan's throat, but instead of tossing it aside, he lunged for Colton in a last, desperate move.

He never made it. Raven had crept up from the side and brought his axe down in the center of Brown Feather's skull, ending things his way. The blade lodged in bone with a crack that echoed through the mountains.

A gurgling sound came from Brown Feather's mouth. It sounded like he might have been trying to laugh.

Colton lowered his pistol, and then raised it again. He fired at Brown Feather's chest until the revolver clicked empty. The impact of the rounds sent Brown Feather staggering backward. His body slumped over the side of the bluff with Raven's hatchet still wedged in his skull.

Raven and Colton leaned out to watch him splatter on the rocks below.

"That's the end of the Water Cannibals," Raven said.

Colton reached down with a hand and helped Nathan to his feet.

"You okay, Major?" Colton asked.

"Not really," Nathan grunted, massaging his ribs. "How's Sandra and her daughter?"

"They're fine," Colton said, and Raven felt the tension in his body recede.

"Estes Park is a quaint tourist town, they said," Nathan said wryly, shaking his battered head. "Stay longer, they said…"

Colton snorted, but he didn't laugh. Raven wondered how long it would be before the chief even smiled again. He reached down to check Creek. The dog sat on his haunches, tail wagging at the touch of his handler.

"I'm sorry about Captain Englewood," Nathan said, turning serious. "I didn't know him well, but I liked him."

Colton swallowed and directed his gaze to his boots. "Everybody liked Jake," he said. He swiped at his eyes and then looked up at Raven.

Raven half expected to hear Colton read him his rights for killing Brown Feather, but instead he put a hand on Raven's shoulder.

"C'mon," he said. "Let's go see Sandra and Allie."

24

By afternoon on the third day after the attack, Charlize Montgomery was walking again. She had ditched the wheelchair for a cane as soon as she could. It was painful, but she was sick of sitting down all the time.

Ahead, Albert stopped at the bottom of a ladder and put his arm out like a wing. "Lean on me," he said. When she hesitated, he added, "It's okay, no one is watching."

Charlize grabbed on with one hand. Each step was agonizing, her skin pulling and tightening. Albert helped her up the ladder and down the next narrow corridor. Sailors working below decks moved out of the way as she passed.

"Is that Senator Montgomery?" one of them asked.

Not for long, she thought.

Her next meeting was possibly the most important of her life. It would determine the fate of her son and her future with the new government. Albert helped her up a second ladder leading to the top deck. From there, they walked past the mess and the galleys. When they finally reached the Combat Direction Center, Charlize was out of breath and nearly doubled over with pain.

"You okay, ma'am?" Albert asked.

She stopped to catch her breath, palming a bulkhead with her bandaged hands.

"Yes. I'm fine," she said. "Why don't you go get something to eat?"

Albert hesitated, glancing over at the two lance corporals standing sentry outside the CDC.

"It's okay, we're safe here," Charlize said. "No one's going to try to assassinate me on this ship."

Albert stepped forward, his massive frame making her feel very small. She looked down and chuckled. He followed her gaze to his shoes. The sneakers were filthy, smeared with ash and something that looked like blood, and the shoelaces on the right one were nearly burned off.

"I loved these shoes. Don't suppose I'll be able to ever find a new pair of Jordans again," he said in a soft voice.

"You never know, Big Al."

She walked into the CDC, where Captain Dietz was waiting with his executive officer. Janet Marco's light blue eyes seemed to take everything in at once as Dietz gestured for Charlize to come inside. Behind them, the room was swarming with activity. Sailors worked at stations throughout the space, their faces basked in blue and red light.

"Follow me, Senator," Dietz said.

He led her into a small room where Diego was already

seated. He looked up from a laptop and raised a hand in greeting. His left arm was covered in a bandage.

"Ah, Charlize, welcome," Diego said.

Captain Dietz closed the hatch behind her, sealing her inside with the new President of the United States.

"How are you feeling?" he asked.

Somehow, Diego's pleasant small talk was more unsettling than if he'd yelled at her. Charlize shrugged in answer to his question and then regretted it. That *hurt*.

Diego smiled. "Probably about the same as I am, then." He scooted closer to the table and folded his hands on the table. The smiled vanished as he furrowed his eyebrows.

"Look, I'm going to be frank. I know you don't like me. I'm not the easiest man to like. We've had our differences in Congress. But those times are behind us. We have to work together now."

Charlize nodded cautiously. They were at war, and sometimes war required enemies to work together for the greater good.

"I appreciate what you did for me in that bunker. I won't forget that. You're a warrior, Charlize, and I need someone like you on my side—and in my cabinet."

"Sir," she began.

He held up a hand. "Please, let me finish."

She nodded and relaxed in her chair.

"I can't think of a better person to take on the role of Secretary of Defense. You understand the world. The war we're fighting now requires a person with your experience."

"The war—"

"Is not over, as you know," Diego said, interrupting her

again. "Our anti-submarine warfare officers have caught more of the passive sonar hits that could be enemy subs."

"Yes," Charlize said. "And I'm sure there is someone very capable to serve as your Secretary of Defense to combat this threat. I'm honored, sir. Really. But I have to be honest. I've put my country first for my entire career. As you know, I have a son. He's stranded in Colorado, at a camp for kids with special needs."

Diego grabbed a glass of water from the table and took a sip, nodding while she spoke.

"I know we're short on resources, but I have to go get him. I need my boy here with me."

"Okay, done," Diego said. He put the glass down and offered his hand across the table.

Charlize didn't trust anyone that made deals so quickly, but this was especially suspicious. Diego rarely made deals at all.

"I don't think you understand," Charlize said.

Diego withdrew his hand and frowned.

"I want to find my son myself. All I need is a Black Hawk, extra fuel, and a few good Marines."

Diego rubbed his nose. "See, that's where you're wrong, Senator. I do understand. I knew you would ask that after I spoke with Captain Dietz. Thing is, I can't risk losing you out there. That's why I've already deployed a fire team of Marines to find your son. They left an hour ago."

Charlize slowly uncrossed her arms, unable to hide her shock. Her burned cheeks warmed, but she wasn't sure if she felt angry at Diego for routing her plan or embarrassed that she'd been so easy to outmaneuver.

"Don't worry," Diego said. "I sent one of our best teams."

She shook his hand with her good hand. What else could she do?

"Thank you, sir. I'm more than grateful for what you have done and I would be honored to serve as Secretary of Defense."

A knock on the hatch sounded, and Lieutenant Marco stepped inside.

"You really like to interrupt meetings, don't you?" Diego asked.

"I'm sorry, sir, but I have an urgent message for Senator Montgomery."

Charlize felt her heart stutter. Did she have news about Ty?

"Go ahead," Charlize said, bracing herself for the worst.

"Senator, we just received a transmission over the shortwave from Cheyenne Mountain. A senior airman named Jeff Main has been trying to reach you. It's about your brother."

Charlize was shaking now, but she didn't care anymore if President Diego thought she was weak. "For the love of God, just tell me," she said.

"Major Sardetti is alive, ma'am," Marco said with a smile. "He's on the comms right now, asking to speak to you."

———

"I can't believe it!" cracked a voice from the speakers of the shortwave radio. Colton turned away from Jake's body to listen.

Nathan smiled and pushed the receiver to his lips. "It's so

good to hear your voice, Charlize! I feared the worst when I heard about D.C."

A cross between a whimper and a laugh flowed from the speakers. "Me too. I'm glad we were both wrong."

"Sardettis are hard to kill," Nathan said.

Colton left Nathan to his joyful reunion and tucked his jacket over Jake's body. He couldn't bear the thought of telling Jake's wife and daughters about this. They would be devastated.

"I'm sorry, brother. I'll look after your family."

Colton pushed himself up and joined Sandra, Allie, and Raven against the fence on the lookout. They were huddled together, wrapped in Raven's coat and listening to Nathan's conversation with amused looks on their faces. Creek was sitting beside them, tail wagging like nothing had happened.

Colton patted the dog on the head. "Everybody okay?"

Raven nodded. "Thank you for helping me find them."

Colton felt like he should say something in return, but he couldn't find the right words. His heart was all torn up. Estes Park had lost a legend and one of the kindest souls Colton had ever known. He turned back to Nathan. He and his sister had turned serious over the radio.

"Empire is right in the radiation zone," Charlize was saying. "President Diego has deployed a team of Marines to find Ty."

Nathan held the receiver for a moment before responding. "I was going to head out there in a few hours. I've got a CBRN suit and a VW van."

"No," Charlize said firmly. "Stay put for now. I'll send someone to get you. Things are bad out there. The radiation isn't the only threat. There are reports of gangs forming on the highways all over the country."

"When should I expect evac?" Nathan asked.

"I'll have the Marines pick you up after they find Ty. Check this frequency again this time tomorrow."

Nathan lowered the receiver and looked at Colton before bringing it back to his lips.

"Can you tell me where you are right now?"

"I can't say, but it's a safe place. The entire grid wasn't knocked out by the EMP attack after all. The military is going to start setting up survival centers across the country for refugees."

The news was reassuring. Maybe Estes Park would get help eventually, but Colton knew it was a long way off. Florida might as well have been the moon without a way to get there safely.

"Okay, I'll check back with you this time tomorrow, Nathan."

"Roger that, Senator."

"Madam Secretary, actually."

Nathan spluttered in shock. "Come again? I didn't catch your last."

"I've been promoted to Secretary of Defense."

Nathan smiled. "I'm proud of you. Our country has never needed you more."

"The country needs you, too, Major."

"I'll talk to you tomorrow. I love you, Charlize."

"I love you, too, Nathan."

He turned off the shortwave and walked over to Colton and Raven's family.

"Well there's some good news, but sounds like things are bad out there," Nathan said.

Colton nodded grimly. "Don't know what I'm going to do without Jake."

"He was a good man," Raven said. "A better man than me."

"Better than me, too," Colton said. He jerked his chin at Raven and Nathan, signaling them to meet him at the guardrail away from Sandra and Allie. All three men walked over and stood at the barrier. Creek limped over and sat next to Raven's feet, looking out over the valley.

It was the first time Colton really had a chance to see the beauty of Rocky Mountain National Park that day. An armada of clouds drifted across the horizon, coasting just above a fortress of rocks and an ocean of pine trees. Fall River snaked through the lush landscape.

He gazed out at the vista, wishing for a moment that he could just stay here and never move again. It seemed so peaceful, but below, in his town, he knew things were going to get much worse. The acts of violence they had witnessed over the past several days were just the beginning.

"I wish you were staying, Nathan," Colton said. "Your sister was right; the country needs good men like you, but so do we. I just lost one of the best."

"I'm sorry, Chief, but I have to go."

"I know," Colton said. "I don't blame you for wanting to be with your family. That's the most important thing at the end of the day."

Raven nodded. "I don't know how to thank you for saving mine," he said.

"Just stay out of trouble for a while," Colton said. "I'm going to have my hands full just keeping this town from boiling over."

"Hey, Chief," Raven said, his voice uncharacteristically hesitant. "I could maybe lend a hand. I owe you one."

Colton studied his face for any sign of a joke, but Raven looked more serious than he had ever seen him. "Why would you want to work with me again? I arrested you."

"Twice," Sandra said.

Colton almost smiled. He looked back at Sandra and Allie. They were watching the three men, looking to them for reassurance and guidance. Just like Kelly and Risa and everyone else would be when Colton returned to town.

Raven squared his shoulders. "There's something I want to tell you all. Then maybe you can decide if you want my help or if you'd rather put a bullet in my skull."

Sandra gave him a sharp look. "That's not funny, Raven."

"I'm not joking. I never told anyone this because technically it's treason to talk about the mission, but I guess that all doesn't matter much anymore," he said, looking out over the valley.

For a moment he seemed lost in the view, then he turned and said, "Eighteen months ago I was sent on a mission with my recon team into North Korean territory to rescue two American girls. One of them was the granddaughter of Senator Mack Sarcone. We got them out, but at a cost. I lost my best friend in the Corps, and the Gunny shot the defector who'd been our guide—executed him right in front of me. What I saw happen there had me questioning a lot of things."

Raven took a deep breath, his eyes glistening, "I think maybe this—all of this—is because of me. If we hadn't gone on that raid, maybe the North Koreans wouldn't have bombed us to hell. I'm so, so sorry."

Sandra wrapped her arms around his shoulders. "It wasn't your fault," she said.

"Your sister is right," Nathan added. "What happened has nothing to do with what you did over there, Raven."

Colton had never asked Raven about his service abroad, but now his actions back at home made more sense. The man wasn't a troublemaker; he was just very troubled from things he had seen and done. War could break men, even the best.

Everyone had their own demons, even Colton.

"I've always made my own path," Raven continued, finding Colton's gaze again. His eyes were bright but steady. "But that hasn't really worked out so well for me. It made me a damn fine hunter and tracker—hell, it made me a good Marine in some ways—but I screwed everything else up along the way. I think that I might have a chance to do some good now."

Colton had spent eighteen months learning to distrust Raven, but maybe he should have spent that time getting to know him instead. Maybe he should have simply asked him why he did the things he did. It was time to work together and bury the past.

"Brown Feather and his brother may be dead, but we've got a lot to do to protect our town from other threats in the coming months and years, Raven."

"I know," Raven replied, shaking Colton's hand. "Something tells me the battle to save Estes Park has just begun."

END OF BOOK 1

Grab your copy of *Trackers 2: The Hunted* from Amazon today, and look for *Trackers 3: The Storm* in the fall of 2017.

ABOUT THE AUTHOR

Nicholas Sansbury Smith is the USA Today bestselling author of the Hell Divers trilogy, the Orbs trilogy, and the Extinction Cycle series. He worked for Iowa Homeland Security and Emergency Management in disaster mitigation before switching careers to focus on his one true passion—writing. When he isn't writing or daydreaming about the apocalypse, he enjoys running, biking, spending time with his family, and traveling the world. He is an Ironman triathlete and lives in Iowa with his fiancée, their dogs, and a house full of books.